Round Tree
The Secrets Series Book Two

Sherry Derr-Wille

Dedication

To my readers who enjoy losing themselves in my books.

Chapter One

2009

Jocelyn Grant hurried across the campus of Havelin College, a flyer announcing Dr. Evan Clark's lecture clutched in her hand. A gust of cold wind whipped under her mid-calf length skirt, but even the chill of the afternoon couldn't cool her anger.

After taking the steps to the administration building two at a time, she embraced the warmth of its interior. While she waited for the elevator, she again read the words on the paper she held in her hand.

Dr. Evan Clark Will Be Lecturing On
The Round Tree Excavations
The Clay Auditorium
Monday At 7:30 P.M.

"Damn," she said aloud.

When the elevator doors opened, she stepped into the small cubicle and pressed the button for the fifth floor. Leaning back against the wall, she waited for the doors to again open.

Henry Bennett's office sat across the hall from the elevator. She eyed her objective and noticed the door stood ajar. Without knocking, she marched into the outer office.

The girl at the desk looked up to make eye contact and said, "Dr. Grant? I didn't know you had an appointment."

The girl irritated Jocelyn. "I don't need an appointment. I'm going in to see Henry."

"I'm sorry, but…"

Jocelyn didn't listen to what the girl had to say. Instead, she pushed her way into the inner office.

Henry sat at his desk with George Shelby, the chairman of the board of directors at the college, seated across from him. The two men were engaged in conversation and she wondered if they even knew she entered the room.

"Just what is the meaning of this?" she demanded, shaking the paper.

Henry looked up at her interruption. "What has you so upset, Jocelyn?"

She took the few steps needed to stand directly in front of him and thrust the handbill in his face. "This. Why didn't I know about Dr. Clark coming here to speak?"

"Calm down, Jocelyn. Let's talk about it."

"Talk about it," Jocelyn replied, her voice several decibels higher than usual. "We should have talked about it before you printed this flyer."

George got to his feet and put his hand on her shoulder, while Henry took the paper from her. "How did you get this? These weren't supposed to be distributed until tomorrow," George said, his tone held no sound of being apologetic.

"One of my students brought it to me. She asked what I knew about Dr. Clark's lecture. It seems I know next to nothing."

"Next to nothing?" George repeated, making her statement into a question. "How long have you been pestering the board to get someone of Clark's caliber to speak here?"

"You know it's been several years. Now you've gone behind my back. I would have thought you'd at least consult me. What good is this lecture going to do my students?"

"What are you talking about?" Henry inquired, a puzzled look on his face.

"Look at the time you have this thing scheduled. It's for next Monday, right at the beginning of the winter break. How many students do you think will be willing to stay on campus to attend it?"

"I'm sorry, it's the only date he could give us," George said.

"Besides," Henry continued, not allowing Jocelyn to speak. "We didn't call him. Why don't you sit down so we can talk about this rationally?"

Jocelyn seated herself in the chair George held out for her, not saying anything until the men also seated themselves. "What do you mean you didn't contact him?"

"His people called us. A man by the name of Robert Matelin got in touch with me. It's costing a pretty penny for him to come, especially considering they're calling it a fund-raising tour."

Henry's statement softened Jocelyn's mood a bit. "Fund raising? His project has always been supported by the state."

"Not anymore. You know how things are in the state house these days. Everything is being cut to try and balance the budget. Unnecessary, that's what the government thinks."

Jocelyn could hardly comprehend what George just said. "Unnecessary? He's unearthing one of the first settlements in this state and they call it unnecessary. It certainly doesn't make sense. I can't believe it."

"Neither could we. We even went so far as to call the capitol and inquire about it. They confirmed everything Matelin told me. When I talked to him again, he implied they're hopeful about getting enough private funding to keep the project going for a couple of more years at least."

Jocelyn could feel her temper again begin to build. "Why does the fact that Clark's project requires funding exclude me from the decision to bring him here?"

"Under normal circumstances, we would have spoken to you first, but it all happened in a span of less than an hour over the phone. We didn't have time to consult with anyone."

"Why didn't you call me before these handbills were printed?"

Henry shook his head. "I have no answer for you, Jocelyn. I'm sorry. Once the ball got rolling, we had to move fast just to get the publicity out."

"So, you left out the head of the Anthropology Department. Why is it you always seem to conveniently leave me out of things? It certainly was different when Dr. Furgeson ran this department. He was in on everything. Of course, he was a man. Believe me, I'm just as knowledgeable as he was."

George got to his feet, his face beet red. "Calm down, Jocelyn, no one here considers you any less knowledgeable than anyone else on staff. It was an oversight, plain and simple."

"Sure, like everything else around here is an oversight. Whose department is the last to get any funding? Who is the last to get extra help when you have grad students available? I know the games you play and I'm getting tired of being dumped on by you."

"Listen to yourself, Jocelyn. There are no games being played and believe me, no one would ever consider dumping on you as you so aptly put it. We were planning to tell you before the flyers were distributed, but someone jumped the gun. They must have gotten their wires crossed," Henry explained.

George sat back down and took her hand in his. "We planned to have you on stage with Dr. Clark. We want you to introduce him."

Jocelyn wanted to contain her temper, but was fighting a losing battle. "How magnanimous of you. What did you plan to do? Smooth my ruffled feathers, give me a chance to show you I know what I'm talking about? Well, with or without your approval, I will be on that stage. When I am, I do intend to introduce the man. It may just be the last thing I do around here. Maybe you ought to start looking for a new head for your precious Anthropology Department."

Her statement prompted Henry to get to his feet. Watching the two of them bob up and down like jack in the boxes was almost comical.

"You can't mean what you just said. I've never heard you talk this way before."

"I've never been this mad before. Besides, up until a few months ago, I needed this position. It gave me the opportunity to take care of my mother."

"How are you doing?" George asked, condescendingly.

His tone upset her, brought back unpleasant memories.

She couldn't help the sarcasm she knew would drip from her words. "I'm doing just great. I took care of my mother for five years while she had Alzheimer's. I didn't allow her to be put in a home, because I thought it too inhumane. After she died, my sisters finally made their appearances. She hardly breathed her last when the vultures showed up. They each wanted a third of her estate. It's left me living in faculty housing until I find something I want to buy."

Why did I even mention the thoughts that are so foremost on my mind? She knew the answer even before the question had been formulated in her thoughts. In the past, Henry acted as her mentor, especially after her father died. He and George were the first ones at the house to offer their condolences. She remembered the longtime friendship her father and Henry shared. It was probably the reason she was accepted for the graduate program in the first place.

"You'll feel differently once Clark's lecture is over and we get back to normal," Henry said. "We were going to talk to you in the morning, before the flyers were distributed. If things went as planned, we wouldn't even be having this discussion."

"Well, things didn't go as planned," Jocelyn accused.

She didn't know why she even tried to reason with these men. They made up their minds without even consulting her. One fit of anger, one outburst from her, would not change things. *Just give in. Go along with what they have set up, but make them squirm a little.* "The flyers went out today and you didn't talk to me. So where do we go from here?"

"We need to have you do some background work on Dr. Clark. Once you do it, you need to write an introduction."

"I see how this is going. Now that I've had my say, I'm useful to you. At least I shouldn't have a problem finding material on him. I already have an extensive file about both Dr. Clark and Round Tree."

Henry's smile said he thought he'd won a minor victory. "Good. When you get your rough draft done, my secretary will type it for you."

"I'll type my own speech, thank you. I don't need you making editorial comments or changing what I intend to say."

"We need to have some idea of the content of your introduction." Henry's smile quickly turned to a frown.

"Why? So you can shoot it down? I don't think so. You'll just have to trust my judgment on this. Do I make myself clear?"

George and Henry each gave her a look of exasperation. "You've made yourself perfectly clear," George assured her.

Jocelyn nodded, irritated by the tone she detected in George's voice. "If you gentlemen will excuse me, I'm going home. It's been a long and trying day, in addition to that, I still have a speech to write on *my* computer, by *myself*."

"Whatever you say, Jocelyn. Just let me assure you, we didn't intentionally leave you out of anything. You know how much we value you here. We always have. With everything going on in your life lately, it's no wonder you're overreacting to this situation."

The two men stood as she turned to leave the office. When she knew they couldn't see her face, she began to smile. *One small victory for me, a few well-chosen words and I've made them squirm.*

She continued to think about the threat to tender her resignation. She considered it for the past several months. She wondered what prompted her to say something today. Usually, she went along with everything, even accepted the chauvinistic attitudes of her superiors Why now? She knew there was no way she could ever change them.

Entering the outer office, she noticed the look of distress on the face of the girl at the desk. "Don't worry, you won't lose your job for letting me into Henry's office."

After leaving the administration building, she walked the few short blocks to her apartment. She found it sterile and completely without a personality. After spending her entire life in the old Victorian house on Maple, she could, in no way call the four small rooms home. The new furnishings carried none of the personality of her mother's antiques, even though she picked them out herself.

Once inside, she put the teakettle on the back burner of the stove. While she waited for it to boil, she rummaged through the freezer compartment of her refrigerator for a frozen dinner. She knew she needed the tea more than the plastic food she would thaw out in the microwave, but she selected one anyway.

She hung her coat in the hall closet. In doing so, her hand brushed against the paper in her pocket. Pulling it out, she again fumed over the situation with George and Henry. She knew she shouldn't let them upset her so, but days like today tried her patience to the limit. Why couldn't they see her for what she was, a damn good professor and an asset to her department? She knew why, they both remembered her as a student who surpassed Dr. Furgeson's expectations and continued to work under him until she was able to take his place.

She should have put out resumes years ago, should have gone elsewhere, but the situation with her mother made doing so impossible.

Was it impossible? Were you just comfortable here? You could have moved Mom to another town with you. Even if you didn't sell the house, you would have been comfortable. You know that now.

For some reason, she felt she had to answer the irritating voice of reason in her head aloud. "Yes, I know that now, but I didn't know it then. Besides…"

The whistling of the teakettle turned her attention back to the kitchen, leaving her thoughts unvoiced. Before going to the stove, she put the paper on the table. The aroma of the herbal tea soothed her nerves. It finished steeping when the bell rang, signaling her dinner needed to be taken from the microwave.

Looking at the nondescript food, she wondered why she chose to defrost it in the first place. She didn't want to eat it. Pushing it aside, she took a sip of tea and opened the folded paper. Carefully, she pressed out the creases. Evan Clark's face stared up at her. Although the picture was in black and white, she knew his hair was red. She wondered if his temper matched it. His strong features excited her. Having admired him ever since he started the Round Tree Project, she wondered how she would react when she met him in person.

You sound like a lovesick schoolgirl.

She shook her head in an attempt to clear her thoughts. How would she react made no difference whatsoever. She knew he would politely acknowledge her, but dismiss any memory of her from his mind once he left town the day after the presentation. Unless she could find some way to make herself unforgettable, he would probably never know she was his biggest supporter at Havelin College, perhaps even in the state.

Before she could dwell on her thoughts further, the phone rang. Picking it up, she greeted the caller. "Jocelyn, it's Henry. About this afternoon…"

"You don't have to say anything, Henry," she interrupted. "What do you say we play forgive and forget?"

"I say it won't work. I know you too well. You never forget and you're not in the mood to be forgiving. We don't want to lose you on staff."

Henry's backhanded apology irritated her further. Unable to think of a tart answer, she decided to give in. "You probably won't. What I said came in the heat of the moment. It still irks me to know you don't seem to think I count for anything around here, though. I do have tenure, you know."

"I know you have tenure. I also know you are one of the best professors we have on staff. Furgeson trained you and he did one hell of a job of it. George and I had a long talk after you left. He thought I talked to you about Clark and I thought he did."

"I didn't believe either of you were planning to rush over to my office in the morning."

"It was a misunderstanding. I hope you can accept it."

"Of course, I'll accept it. What other choice do I have?"

"As long as we've cleared the air."

"If that's what you call it, we've cleared the air."

She hung up the phone, her anger over Henry's statements threatening to consume her. The picture of Evan Clark, smiling up at her from the table, caught her attention and caused her to smile in return. In less than a week, she would meet the man she idolized. She didn't care if she acted like a lovesick schoolgirl. She only prayed she could find a way of making herself unforgettable without making a fool of herself.

The phone rang again. Hesitantly, she answered it, expecting to find George on the other end of the line, blaming Henry for this afternoon's blow up.

"Hi, Jaycee," her best friend since grade school, Ellen Dresden, greeted her.

"Ellie, it's good to hear from you. What's up?"

"When is winter break for you?"

"Next week. What do you have on your mind?"

"Vern came home tonight and told me he has to go to Germany for a week. He's leaving on Sunday. He thought you might want to come up and keep me company. If you can pull yourself away, that is."

Jocelyn sank down into the easy chair beside the phone. She wondered if Ellie could sense the smile filling her face.

"I can get away, but not until Tuesday."

"Any particular reason?"

"Dr. Clark is giving a lecture here on Monday night. I have to introduce him."

"Your Dr. Clark? Evan Clark? Congratulations on finally getting the board to engage him."

"Don't congratulate me. I had nothing to do with it. Henry made all the arrangements. If one of my students hadn't brought in a flyer about it, I'd still be in the dark."

"Why in the world would he do something like that?"

"Because then it became his idea and not mine. Of course, Henry and George tried to smooth things over by asking me to introduce Clark."

"I'm glad Vern suggested you come here. I think you need to get away for a while."

Jocelyn silently applauded her friend's suggestion. Just talking to Ellie, and having her use Jocelyn's childhood nickname of Jaycee, relaxed her. Here, no one called her Jaycee. Here, she was Jocelyn or Dr. Grant. Only the directory listed her as Dr. J.C. Grant. It certainly didn't look or sound like Jaycee the way Ellie used it.

"I guess I do. I was so angry this afternoon, I threatened to quit."

"Quit? Do you have anything else lined up?"

"Not a thing. It was only a threat, but it's one I've been considering for months."

"Can you afford to quit with nowhere to go?"

"As a matter of fact, I can. You surely remember how I scrimped and saved to be able to afford the best day care for Mom. After her death, I found her estate was in excess of three million dollars. I don't know why I never looked into her assets before. I guess I figured she only had the house and the furnishings, along with her social security. You know how she and Dad were always crying hard times. With the estate settled, I invested seven hundred and fifty thousand of it and by summer, I should be receiving some interest every month. It might not be what I'm used to, but I could change my spending habits to match my income until I can find something else. If I don't need it, I won't touch it. I kept the rest of the money liquid to do a few things I want to do."

"Do those few things include pampering yourself a little?"

"What are you getting at?"

"While you're here, let me make you over. I help people revamp themselves all the time at the shop. We can go shopping, get you a new hairstyle and throw out those horrible glasses you wear."

Jocelyn giggled at the thought of letting Ellie assist her in a transformation. Over the past several months, she often considered changing her image, but always dismissed the idea as foolish. Who would notice, or even care, if she did anything different with her appearance?

"I don't know, Ellie. The thought of becoming someone other than Jocelyn Grant frightens me."

"That's what I mean, Jaycee. I remember when we were in school and you weren't half as serious as you are now. With your mother's illness, I didn't think the timing was right before. Now there's nothing standing in your way. Do something crazy for a change, like when we were kids."

"Okay, something crazy, but I'm only doing it for you. It might be fun at that. I can't imagine getting rid of my glasses, though. How do you expect me to see anything?"

"Contact lenses, silly."

"I could never wear those things. Glasses are so much easier."

"Nonsense. Get into the twenty-first century, Jaycee. Leave all the plans to me. Call me as soon as you get your flight information. I can hardly wait to see how you turn out."

When Jocelyn hung up the phone, she picked up the now cold dinner and tossed it in the trash.

After turning out the lights in the kitchen, she started down the hall and caught a glimpse of her reflection in the mirror.

For years she wore her hair pinned haphazardly to the top of her head, a style that made getting ready for work easy. She called it her wash and go look. For the first time, it shouted old maid schoolteacher.

"Ellie's right, I am dowdy. For the time being, this will have to do. I just wonder what Ellie will come up with when I get to New York next week."

She removed the pins from her hair and allowed the golden-brown strands to fall past her shoulders. She always hated looking into the mirror. Now she knew why. She was an old maid school teacher, hanging on to a look that would never attract the one man she held above everyone else, Evan Clark.

"What is Ellie thinking of? Does she expect to make me into a glamorous person overnight? I'm definitely not glamorous or adventurous. I gave all that up when I made the decision to put my life on hold for Mom's sake. Anyway, it will be fun to pretend I'm Jaycee again, at least for a few days."

Of course, it will. Take a good look at yourself for a change. Jaycee is still in here. It's time you let her out.

Chapter Two

Evan Clark stared out the car window. After being on the road for two weeks he realized everything looked the same along this stretch of Interstate as it did along the last three thousand miles they'd traveled. "Do you remember where I have to beg for money tonight?"

Bob laughed. "You make it sound like the Chinese water torture."

"It is, but I guess it's worth it. Without the state funding, there's no way you and I can keep Round Tree going alone. Now, how about giving me an answer?"

"Havelin College."

"Havelin College? Do they even have an Anthropology Department?"

"Trust me, they do. You remember Dr. Furgeson, don't you?"

Evan nodded. "Of course, I remember him. He was old when he came out to lecture while I was still teaching in Utah. He must be a hundred and ten by now."

"Not quite. He started the department at Havelin in the early sixties. From what I hear, he retired about ten years ago. He's living in Phoenix."

"So, who's running the show there now?"

"According to the information I dug up, the department is run by Dr. J. C. Grant."

"Grant? Where did he work before this?"

"The information I could find said he got his Bachelors, Masters and Doctorate at Havelin, even did his post grad work under Furgeson."

"It's funny we haven't heard of him before. He sounds young. I don't suppose a small college like Havelin can afford anyone with more experience. He probably doesn't have so much as a clue as to what he's teaching. Give me an old duffer any day of the week."

"You're a fine one to talk. How old were you when you took the post in Utah?"

"Things were different. I got my Bachelor's when I was fourteen. By the time I turned seventeen I had my Doctorate. Most people are a lot older, physically if not mentally. I never had time for any of the things regular people do in college. I was too young. When I got to Utah, I was more than ready to settle down. I guess you could say I was born old."

Evan reflected on his words. Not only was he born old, he even felt old, if anyone in this day and age considered forty-six old.

Bob laughed at Evan's comment, as he turned off the Interstate at the exit for Havelin. They rode in comfortable silence until they pulled into the parking lot of the motel the college booked for them for the night.

As soon as they entered the room, Bob looked longingly at the bed. "It's only four. You could catch a little more sleep before we have to eat and get to the auditorium."

"I don't think so. You go ahead, though. I'm going to take a shower and go over these notes."

Evan left Bob lying on one of the two double beds in the room. The hot water cascaded over Evan's body, easing the tension of the last two weeks.

He was against this in the first place. A month on the road begging for money wasn't his conception of his work. Even when he taught, he didn't enjoy lecturing. Getting out of the shower, he heard Bob snoring loudly in the next room. If he had to make this trip, why couldn't his companion have been a woman? He laughed at the thought. He hadn't enjoyed a serious relationship with a woman, or a casual one for that matter, since Kathryn left when he launched the Round Tree Project five years ago.

Thinking of Kathryn brought memories of last summer when his kids, Brandon and Sandy, came out from California to work on the dig. Somehow, in the years since the divorce, they grew up without him. Brandon was now in his junior year at UCLA and Sandy was studying at Loyola Marymount. After their summer on the dig, they both promised to return.

The phone rang and interrupted his musings. He listened as Bob answered it, his voice heavy with sleep.

"Who was on the phone?" Evan asked, coming out of the bathroom.

Bob swung his legs off the bed and got to his feet. "It was Henry Bennett. He wanted to be sure we got in okay and could find the auditorium tonight."

"You mean he's not sending over a car to get us?"

"Hardly. We're here at our request, not his. We'll be doing good to get a minimal donation."

Evan agreed. The first several college campuses they visited allowed them to come to appease the heads of the Anthropology Departments. Although donations came from the colleges, they were nothing compared to those from the private sector.

~ * ~

The Clay Auditorium was ablaze with lights, the parking lot about half-full when Bob parked the car and popped open the trunk. Evan got out and retrieved the tray of slides and his briefcase.

He hurried inside to get out of the bitter cold.

Why can't we do something like this when it's not so cold? He knew the answer. In the warm weather, he wouldn't be able to give lectures. He would be at the dig sifting through eons of dirt to find the beginnings of native civilizations in this area.

Evan looked up to see two older men approaching them. "Dr. Clark? I'm George Shelby and this is Henry Bennett."

"It's a pleasure," Evan said, knowing he didn't mean it.

George's voice grated on his nerves and reminded him of every other member of a college board he met on this trip. They merely tolerated him. Especially considering Round Tree and not the college would benefit from tonight's lecture.

"This is Bob Matelin. I think you spoke on the phone regarding tonight."

"Of course," Henry said, extending his hand, first to Evan and then to Bob.

"Is Dr. Grant here yet?" Bob asked.

14

Evan couldn't help but notice a look of disapproval on Shelby's face.

"Jocelyn called and said she's running later than she expected."

The icy tone in the man's voice irritated Evan.

"J.C. Grant is a woman?"

It was more than a little unsettling to learn Bob's research didn't uncover the gender of the head of Havelin's Anthropology Department.

"She studied under Dr. Furgeson for several years," Bennett informed them. "He recommended her highly. Jocelyn Grant is the most talented student ever to graduate from Havelin College."

Bennett's opposite reaction to Dr. Grant surprised Evan. The two men certainly weren't in agreement about her.

"Did I hear my name?"

Evan turned at the sound of a woman's voice to see Dr. Grant for the first time. She wasn't at all what he expected. Nothing about her was easy to distinguish. She wore her hair secured to the top of her head. Depending on whether or not she colored it, she could be anywhere from twenty-five to fifty. Heavy framed glasses with tinted lenses, which successfully hid her eyes, sat perched on her nose.

He found himself wondering what kind of a figure the tweed suit, with its mid-calf length skirt, hid. *Am I desperate, or what? How can I be fantasizing about a woman professor?*

"Jocelyn," George said, his tone sarcastic. "I'm glad you finally decided to show up. This is Dr. Clark."

Evan watched the woman's face. Despite her plain features, the smile she flashed made him see an inner beauty. "I've been looking forward to this evening, Dr. Clark," she replied, her voice soft and sensual. "I meant to be here when you arrived, but I ran into a bit of a problem with one of my colleagues, Norm Petersen."

"Is something wrong with Norm?" George asked, annoyance dripping from his words.

"He called me several hours ago. He was in extreme pain and asked me if I could drive him to the hospital. It seems his wife is out of town visiting her family. When we got to the hospital, they diagnosed him with appendicitis. I stayed long enough to contact his wife and be assured she was on her way back here."

Evan nodded. He knew he would be the first one there if a friend was in the same situation. It wouldn't matter if he was late for some lecture that would probably be dry as yesterday's toast. "Sounds like a good excuse to me. This is Bob Matelin."

Evan watched as Jocelyn turned her attention to Bob. He gave her credit for her calm exterior in light of Shelby's accusing tone.

"It's time we got started," Bennett interjected. "Are you ready Jocelyn?"

"I will be as soon as I hang up my coat. I see Dr. Clark has a tray of slides. I do hope you have the projector and screen in place for him."

Evan smiled at the flurry of activity her comment instigated.

Once she seemed assured that the proper arrangements were finally going to be made, Dr. Grant turned her attention to him. "I'm sorry about the confusion, Dr. Clark. I planned to be here earlier and check everything out. I do hope you don't mind if the Media Department tapes your lecture for my students. You must realize this is coming at the beginning of winter break. Most of them won't be able to be here tonight."

"It doesn't bother me at all. Unfortunately, you won't be able to successfully tape the slide program. I'd be glad to send you a duplicate set of the slides if you'd like."

Jocelyn's features softened and her smile became more genuine than polite. "I'd appreciate it. Let me know what your processing and shipping costs are. Once I have them, I'll see that you're reimbursed."

Bob replied before Evan had a chance to answer. "Thanks for the offer. It isn't necessary, though. It's the least we can do for being allowed to be here tonight."

Evan smiled at Bob's diplomacy. The university, who contributed heavily to the project, would absorb the photo processing as well as the shipping costs, since their students helped with the lab work that needed to be done when the dig was closed for the winter.

The expression on Dr. Grant's face told him she was sincere in her offer. After hanging up her coat, along with Evan's and Bob's, she took a chair beside Evan on the stage. Bennett immediately took his place at the podium. He tapped the microphone to make certain it was live before he began his welcome.

"I thank you for coming out tonight, especially considering the weather. We are pleased to have someone of Dr. Evan Clark's prominence here this evening. Of course, I'm not the one to introduce this man. I give you Dr. Jocelyn Grant." The comment was met with polite applause.

Evan watched as she got up from her seat to cross the stage. Her grace and confidence overrode his original impression of her appearance.

"Good evening. Tonight, we will hear of Dr. Evan Clark's work on the Round Tree project."

Evan smiled to see how nonchalantly she had placed a prepared speech on the podium. He listened as she listed several of his accomplishments. Her extensive knowledge made him wonder how much she actually knew about his life.

"As several of you already know, the state has withdrawn their funding for this project. I would like to be the first, tonight, to lend my support, both financially as well as offering my help as a volunteer on his project this summer. I hope many of you will join me in my backing of Dr. Clark."

Evan got to his feet and accepted the delicate pink envelope she held out to him. He certainly didn't expect Dr. Grant to offer to volunteer this summer. As for the donation, he would withhold his judgment about it. It wouldn't be the first time a professor primed the pump, so to say, with a donation, which at a later time would be withdrawn. He knew what small colleges could afford to pay their professors. Even if her donation were honest, it would be very small. Of course, no one else in the room would ever know what happened after the lecture. Such things were a good ploy to get people to open their checkbooks and wallets.

~ * ~

Jocelyn again took her seat and listened as Dr. Clark began his lecture. She hoped he didn't notice how her hands shook when she offered him the envelope with her personal check for ten thousand dollars in it. She knew, as soon as she heard about Clark's financial problems, she would donate to the project. At the same time, she decided not to tell anyone of the size of her donation. If it became common knowledge, people would think she gave it as a bribe for a good position once she arrived at Round Tree, rather than something she wanted to do to support Dr. Clark's ongoing research.

She realized she hardly listened to the lecture when the lights dimmed and Bob took over the presentation through the slide show. Jocelyn looked up, a bit startled, when Evan took his seat beside her. She chided herself for not paying more attention to the man she came especially to hear. For some unknown reason, the smell of his cologne had a strange effect on her.

Pull yourself together. Evan Clark doesn't even know you exist. Come summer he'll be your boss. Don't let your emotions get in the way of a professional relationship.

She focused her attention on the slide program, trying not to think about the man who sat next to her. She barely listened to Bob's narrative, knowing the media department would catch it all on the tapes she would use in her classes. At last, the program ended and Dr. Clark moved to the table where he would meet with the most prominent people associated with the college as well as the city. Jocelyn knew most of them well enough to know they would be generous in their donations.

"Can I talk to you, Jocelyn?" Henry asked.

She forced her attention from Dr. Clark to Henry. "Of course, you can."

"I want to know what in the hell you were thinking of when you offered to volunteer on Clark's project this summer. What about the summer school program? Do you realize you're jeopardizing your position here?"

"Do you realize I haven't done any hands-on work in the past ten years? Most people in my position work on a dig every couple of years. As for the summer program, I've already spoken to Norm about taking it over."

"Well, you didn't speak to me. You're treading on thin ice. I want you in my office at eight tomorrow morning."

"Sorry, Henry. We'll have to table this discussion until Monday.

I'm catching the early flight for New York tomorrow morning. I should be landing at about the time you're expecting me in your office. I won't be back until late Sunday evening."

Henry snorted his reply then turned away from her. As though he experienced a second thought, he turned back. "You'll have to lock up tonight, Jocelyn. George and I have to leave."

She nodded, not at all surprised by Henry's 'punishment'. Turning back toward where Dr. Clark sat, she almost bumped into Bob.

"Trouble with your boss?"

"Nothing new."

"Evan and I are going out for dessert and coffee. Would you care to join us?"

She could feel her heart beat a little faster at the prospect of spending more time with Dr. Clark than she originally anticipated. "Thank you, Mr. Matelin. I'd be pleased to join you. There's a nice little coffee shop within walking distance you might enjoy."

Bob smiled. "If you're going to have coffee with us, you'd better start calling me Bob."

"All right, Bob, but only if you call me Jaycee."

"Jaycee? Why not Jocelyn?"

"Because only my colleagues call me Jocelyn. My friends call me Jaycee. If we're going to be working together this summer, I plan to be more informal."

She liked Bob, but couldn't take her eyes from Dr. Clark. "It looks like almost everyone is gone. I'll meet you out front as soon as I turn off the lights."

~ * ~

Evan accepted the last donation. He looked up to see Bob standing in front of him. "Jaycee said she'd join us for coffee after she locks up."

"Who?" Evan asked, aware of the lights going out around him.

"Jaycee, Dr. Grant. I asked her to come with us. She suggested a coffee shop within walking distance."

"Is she crazy? Walking in this weather? She has to be out of her

19

mind. I don't understand why you asked her to have coffee with us in the first place."

"I certainly didn't think you were chauvinistic. We usually take out the resident professor after the lecture. What do you have against Jaycee?"

"Something about her bothers me. Didn't it seem strange she made such a production out of giving us this?"

He pulled the pink envelope from his pocket and held it out to Bob.

"It's no stranger than any other donation we've received in the past two weeks. It seems to me, Janson made just as big a production out of his donation last week."

"He did, but after you left, he asked for his fifty dollars back. He said the school administration made him present it to encourage some of the other people to give more. Besides, he didn't volunteer to work with us next summer. What's she trying to do, buy a better position on the team? If that's not her idea, I'm willing to bet you a steak dinner she asks for this back before we finish our coffee."

Evan returned the envelope to his pocket and watched Bob shake his head. Together they put the checks and cash in the briefcase. Once they put on their coats, they went out to the car to lock the briefcase and slide tray in the trunk.

"Are you ready for some coffee and dessert?" Jaycee asked, approaching the car.

"Lead the way, Jaycee," Bob said.

Jaycee turned the corner and Evan followed. He shoved his hands deep in his coat pockets in an attempt to warm them. He wondered if once Jaycee Grant took back the envelope, she would withdraw her offer to volunteer this coming summer. It didn't matter if she came or not. He'd have plenty of college students to do the work. He certainly didn't need a know-it-all, female, anthropology professor to complicate his life. *She doesn't come across that way. I can't put my finger on it, but she makes me nervous.*

Neon lights spelled out Campus Coffee Shop and Evan hurried inside to get out of the cold.

A young woman met them at the door. "Dr. Grant, it's good to see you. Your usual table is available."

"Thank you, Sharlene."

Evan followed Bob and Jaycee to the table the girl indicated. Once seated, he picked up the menu to decide on dessert.

"What's good here?" Bob asked.

"Everything. I usually have French silk pie and cappuccino," she said, a mischievous smile on her face.

Evan stared at her, wondering why this woman affected him in this way. Sitting this close, he noticed how the tinted lenses now accented her blue eyes. Her lashes were long and he wondered how they would look coated with mascara, the way Kathryn used to apply her make-up.

After placing their order, Evan contemplated the woman who sat across from him. She certainly looked the part of an old maid schoolteacher. She just didn't act it. Instead of being introverted, afraid of crossing her boss, she was, if he could believe Bob, someone to be reckoned with.

"Why are you staring at me, Dr. Clark?" Jaycee asked, once the waitress took their order.

Evan looked away abruptly. He hadn't meant to stare at her, but he couldn't help it. "If you call Bob by his first name, call me Evan."

"All right, Evan. Now, why are you staring at me?"

Bob winked slyly. He certainly wasn't one to miss out on a chance to tease Evan about something like this. "She's got you there, old man. Why are you staring at her?"

Evan sighed deeply and put his hands in the air in a gesture of surrender. "I know when I'm outnumbered. I didn't mean to stare. I guess I was trying to figure you out."

"There's nothing to figure out. I'm a freak of nature. I talk back to Henry and George whenever I get the chance. In addition to that, my work is my passion, not just my vocation."

Her statement took Evan by surprise. It was as if she read his mind about her position with her superiors. As for the second part of her statement, he voiced the same opinion about his work dozens of times. He laughed at his naïve attitude. He must be tired not to consider everyone he knew, in this field, harbored the same opinion about their chosen profession.

The waitress brought the dessert before Evan could say anything more. He watched as Jaycee took a fork full of pie. She put it in her mouth, withdrawing the fork slowly, sensuously, as though savoring the rich sweetness.

When they finished eating and engaging in small talk, he reached into his pocket and took out the envelope. He watched Jaycee's expression, surprised to see bewilderment in her eyes. "Is something wrong with my donation?"

"I'm just wondering if you plan to ask for it back."

Evan knew his words sounded harsh, but he had to know where she stood

"I beg your pardon," Jaycee's voice carried the steel edge of anger that replaced her bewilderment.

"I know how these things work. Bennett tells you to make a token donation, with the stipulation you can ask for it back. It's happened before. It's a ploy to get the invited guests to open their wallets."

Jaycee's voice now turned low and intense. "Look, I don't know what kind of games you're used to playing, *Dr. Clark,* but I happen to have a keen interest in the work you're doing at Round Tree. My donation, like my offer to volunteer, is genuine. If you gentlemen will excuse me, I have to pack and be ready to be on a plane tomorrow morning. I'm certain I'll see you this summer. You can believe I'll do my best to stay out of *your* way."

She pushed back her chair and Evan wished he could take back his words.

"Please sit down, Jaycee. Evan hasn't had to use finesse in a long time. I'm afraid he's a bit rusty. This has been a trying two weeks. The last school we were at played this game with us. You know how it is when you get burned, you have a tendency to back away before it happens again."

"I certainly didn't mean to offend you," Evan said, when she again sat down. "This trip isn't the sort of thing I do well and, after our last stop, I'm skeptical of everyone. A lot of people think they can buy their way into the project, or like our friend at the last school, aren't committed enough to stand behind their pledges."

Evan watched as the muscles in Jaycee's face relaxed. Looking at her now, he realized if she fixed herself up, she could be very attractive.

"I don't understand how anyone could go back on a promise or ask for their donation back. I assure you, I put a lot of thought into my decisions, be they about my financial obligations or how to spend my time."

Evan tried to smile at her statement. In light of her pledge to volunteer, he made an almost fatal mistake.

"I did overhear your conversation with Bennett, but of course you knew that," Bob assured her, tactfully changing the subject. "You told me your problems with him are nothing new. Would you care to expand on your answer?"

Jaycee's brows knotted as she contemplated her reply. "I don't think so. This is not the time for shoptalk. Besides, you have enough problems of your own. You certainly don't need to hear about mine."

Evan marveled at her tactfulness. Every other professor who joined them for coffee insisted on detailing the work in their department, complain about their superiors, and bombarding them with questions.

Evan watched as Jaycee glanced down at her watch. "Oh, dear, look at the time. I really do have to be going. I am leaving for New York in the morning and I still have to pack."

"Let us take you home," Evan suggested.

"It's not necessary. By the time we walk to your car, I can be there. I am looking forward to this summer."

Evan and Bob both got to their feet. To Evan's surprise, she held out her hand to him. As he shook it, he began to see her in a different light. For a fleeting moment, he wanted more than to shake her hand. Knowing the thought was ridiculous he watched her walk away. She carried herself well. He couldn't ever remember meeting a more professional person, but her attitude wasn't what bothered him. He still couldn't put his finger on it, but it didn't matter. Once summer came, she would be another volunteer and he'd have far too much work to do to worry about such things.

~ * ~

Jaycee turned back and glanced at Evan and Bob before addressing Sharlene. Evan infuriated and excited her. Working with him and seeing him for an entire summer would be a challenge. "Was everything all right?" Sharlene asked.

"Perfect as usual," Jaycee replied, reaching into her purse. "How much do I owe you?"

"Nothing. Dr. Clark said he would take care of it."

Jaycee pulled a five from her wallet and pressed it into Sharlene's hand. She smiled when the girl didn't argue about taking the tip.

Stepping into the cold night, she began the walk to her apartment. Evan Clark filled her mind. She expected him to have an effect on her, she just didn't expect the feeling his very touch awakened.

Her building came into view and she hurried into the foyer. Inside her apartment, she ignored the blinking answering machine in the darkened room. Instead, she closed and locked the door, turned on the lights and put her coat on a chair with her purse.

Kicking off her shoes, she unpinned her hair and started toward the bedroom. After changing into sweats, she dragged her suitcase from the closet.

The ringing of the phone startled her. "Hello," she answered, sitting down on the bed.

Henry's irritating voice greeted her. "Where have you been? The lecture has been over for an hour. I've been calling every five minutes for the last forty-five minutes."

"Why would you be calling me?"

"You know why. We have to talk before Monday."

"Sorry Henry, I'm on vacation."

"Get off it, Jocelyn, I know you never go anywhere. I will be waiting for you, in my office at eight tomorrow morning."

"You'll have a long wait. I told you earlier, I'm going to New York."

"In that case, we're coming over to your place tonight."

"If by *we*, you mean you and George, you can save yourselves the trip. I don't want to discuss this further. Why don't you tell George, no on second thought, I'm certain you have me on speakerphone so he can listen in. Furgeson left me in charge of the summer program more than once. I know he didn't okay it with you first, because he told me as much."

She didn't give either man a chance to answer before slamming down the receiver.

~ * ~

Evan fingered the pink envelope, still trying to figure Jaycee out.

"I think we're in for an interesting summer," Bob said, causing Evan to look away from the envelope.

"I do, too."

"You know, I can almost taste that steak dinner now. We'll have to find the perfect restaurant."

Evan again looked at the envelope in his hand. Tapping it on the table, he thought about the woman who gave it to him.

"How much do you think her check is for?" Bob asked.

"Fifty, a hundred at the most."

"Would you like a chance to get out of taking me to dinner?"

"What are you talking about?"

"I'll bet it's more than you think. I'm willing to go double or nothing. Anything under five hundred, you don't owe me a thing."

"At least I'm betting on a sure thing this time."

He remembered pinching pennies when he taught at a small college.

He picked up a knife from the silverware on the table and slit open the envelope. Inside, he found a delicate pink check with an embossed rose in the corner. When he pulled it further from the envelope, his eyes focused on the dollar amount. "This has to be a mistake."

"From the look on your face, Amanda will be joining us for dinner. Is it more than a thousand?"

Mutely, Evan handed Bob the check. As soon as he looked at it, he let out a low whistle. "Ten grand. Can this be right?"

"I don't know, but I intend to find out."

Evan turned toward the cashier's desk, where moments earlier Jaycee stood, engaged in conversation with their waitress. To his disappointment, she was gone. "You take care of the bill. I'm going to see if I can find her outside."

Not allowing Bob to say anything, Evan shoved the envelope into the breast pocket of his suit and pulled on his overcoat.

Outside the cafe, the wind seemed to have died down. Evan wondered if he imagined it or if the air actually felt warmer. Ahead of him, he saw someone turn the corner, but he couldn't tell if it was Jaycee. Taking a chance that it might be her, he hurried to catch up.

"Wait for me," Bob called, from behind him.

Evan turned to see Bob running to catch up. "I think I saw her turn the corner. I don't want to lose her."

"It's possible you did. The waitress said she lives just around the corner."

To Evan's dismay, turning the corner did not do him much good. Jaycee was nowhere in sight. The street ended in a cul-de-sac. Each side lined with apartment buildings. Evan assumed them to be faculty and student housing units. To his dismay, three units lined each side of the street with one at the end, making seven of them in all.

"Does it seem a little strange to you for Jaycee to be living in one of these apartments?" Bob asked.

"In light of a ten-thousand-dollar donation, it certainly does. The only problem is, which of these places is hers. I guess we'll just have to check them all out and hope she has her name listed somewhere."

"It would be easier to go back to the cafe and call her on the phone," Bob commented.

Evan knew the look he shot Bob said going back now was out of the question.

The look on Bob's face could only be described as a Cheshire cat grin. "All right, I'll take the places on the right, you check out the ones on the left. I'll meet you at the end. This ought to be interesting. What do you plan to say? Excuse me, Jaycee, but couldn't you use this check for a down payment on a nicer place to live?"

"You think you're pretty smart, don't you?"

"Well, I'm not the one stuck paying for two steak dinners because I chose the wrong side of a bet."

Evan laughed at Bob's comment. When would he learn? In the two weeks he and Bob were on the road together, Evan lost every bet they made. Without giving the matter further thought, he entered the first building and scanned the mailboxes in the foyer. None of them contained the name he was looking for. He continued on until he met Bob at the last building.

"Why is it, no matter where I start, I always end up finding what I want in the last place I look for it?" Evan asked, as he stopped at the last mailbox. On it he read *J. C. Grant Apartment Eight.*

At the end of the upstairs corridor, he saw the door with the number eight on it. "This must be the place."

He pressed the button, alerting not only Jaycee, but also her next-door neighbor she had a visitor. For a moment he heard nothing, then detected footsteps from inside.

"I thought I told you not to waste your time," Jaycee said, before she recognized Evan and Bob. "I'm sorry, I thought you were someone else."

"Someone else?" Evan questioned.

Jaycee nodded. "Henry. He called a few minutes ago. I don't think he's too happy with me at the moment. I'm sorry. Where are my manners? Please come in. So, what brings you two here? I didn't expect to see you until summer."

Evan pulled the envelope with her check in it from his pocket. "This."

"Now what? Did I forget to sign it?"

"No."

"Didn't I make it clear about not wanting it back?"

"Good god, Jaycee, why not?" Bob asked. "This check is for ten thousand dollars."

"I know how much it's for. I should, I wrote it, didn't I? Is it against the law to donate to worthy causes?"

Her eyes spoke volumes.

Evan stepped closer to her, close enough to smell her perfume. "Of course, it isn't. It's just, well, I know what small colleges like this pay their professors."

Jaycee began to smile and he wondered if this could be the same woman, he shared coffee with earlier. With her hair loose around her shoulders, she looked much younger. The sweat suit she wore accented curves that the tweed suit camouflaged.

"Oh, I get it. I'm a professor, at a small college, living in facility housing, so you think I'm destitute. You shouldn't jump to conclusions, Evan. Until recently, I lived with my mother. After her death, everything was sold. I took this apartment until I find a place to suit my needs. The way things have been going the last few days, it's a good thing I haven't found it yet."

"So, that explains why you're living here. What about the check? Is it meant as a bribe to assure you'll be assigned a better position this summer?"

The look on Jaycee's face told him he pushed too much.

"It's a bribe all right, a bribe to Uncle Sam. Since I got my inheritance, I need a write off. If you don't want it, I'm certain I can find someone who will appreciate it."

"I don't think that will be necessary," Bob said, coming to Evan's rescue. "You'll have to admit, most professors don't have ten thousand dollars to give to worthy causes."

"I guess they don't. I kept a good amount for myself, to do as I pleased. When I heard your funding got axed, I decided to do something to help out. Believe it or not, I'm one of your biggest supporters. I can't stand to see such a worthy project go under."

Evan sat down on the couch, amazed by her sincerity. "No more questions, Jaycee. No more accusations. So far, you've cost me two steak dinners. I don't plan to make good on them until summer. Can we persuade you to join us?"

"I don't understand."

"What my friend is trying to say is, he misunderstood your intentions. He's also not anyone I would take to Las Vegas."

Jaycee began to laugh. "Well, Evan, as long as you're buying, I'll accept your invitation. It's been a long time since a red-haired man, with a quick temper, asked me out to dinner."

Chapter Three

Jaycee stared into the bathroom mirror. As it had for the past several months, the reflection looked alien to her. Ellie's promised transformation still left her speechless. With her long hair cut into a fashionable style and glasses no longer perched on her nose, she hardly knew the woman in the mirror. Even her clothes belonged to a stranger. She smiled as she remembered Ellie coming home with her for a few days and giving away the wardrobe that once hung in the closet.

She continued to stare at the image in the mirror. "Well, Jaycee, this is going to be an interesting summer. Perhaps an interesting rest of my life, considering my run in with Henry before I left." For this summer, Dr. Jocelyn Grant would not exist. She'd made it quite clear to Evan and Bob, no one was to know her by anything other than Jaycee.

After applying a moisturizing make-up, to guard against the June heat of the dig, she went back into the bedroom of the motel to repack her overnight bag.

The man behind the desk looked up from his morning newspaper. "Are you checking out, Ms. Grant?"

"Yes. I just need to settle up my bill."

The man ran Jaycee's credit card and handed her the slip to sign. Looking down at the imprint on the bill, Jaycee signed her name, as it appeared, *Dr. Jocelyn C. Grant.*

Will you ever be Dr. Jocelyn C. Grant again?

Her parting argument with Henry rang in her ears, causing her to cringe. "You'll regret this, Jocelyn. If you go through with the crazy idea of taking a year off, don't expect any kind of a recommendation from me. I'll expect to see you, at your desk, on the first day of school." Jaycee shook her head to silence Henry's aggravating voice.

Once finished in the motel office, she picked up Bob's map and made her way toward the dig. For the next three months, she refused to think about Henry Bennett, Havelin College or the once bright future she may have extinguished.

~ * ~

"It's a beautiful day," Bob said as he entered the office.

Evan looked up from the notes regarding this year's progress to date on the dig. The clock read seven-thirty and the calendar was turned to the proper day. Under the date, he read the words he wrote when he first arrived in late March: *volunteers and Jaycee due today.*

"It will be if all the volunteers show up. Did they all make it?"

"All but two, Patti Kelly and Jaycee Grant."

"I should have known," Evan said, silently cursing himself for counting on Jaycee Grant, for looking forward to seeing her again. "I'm willing to bet..."

Bob's laughter cut Evan short. "I thought you learned not to bet with me. You always lose. I talked with her just last week. Believe me, she'll be here."

Outside the open window, Evan heard a car pull up and stop in the gravel.

"Sounds like at least one of them is here," he said, getting up to look out the window. In front of the building which housed his office, he saw a teal blue Nissan. The car door opened and the shapely leg of a woman gave the first clue to her identity.

Going out to greet her, Evan's gaze wandered past her work boots, up the woman's perfect calf, to the hem of her khaki shorts, to her waist, breasts and face. To his dismay, wire rimmed sun glasses hid her eyes from his view.

Pull yourself together. You could be Patti Kelly's father. Don't go getting all heated up over a student volunteer.

"Bob, Evan, it's good to finally be here."

"Jaycee, is that you?"

She took off the sunglasses and he looked into incredibly blue eyes. A touch of mascara lengthened already lush lashes. A hint of color in her cheeks made him smile at the transformation in her appearance.

31

"It's me, in the flesh. I'm sorry if I'm late. I zigged when I should have zagged. I should have told you; I never could read a road map."

Her infectious laughter made Evan smile. She certainly didn't resemble the woman who sat across the table from him at Havelin, the woman who seemed poised to pounce on his every word.

"I hope you're ready to get to work," Bob said, handing Jaycee a manila envelope.

"What's this?" she asked.

Evan was quick to take over the conversation from Bob. "Your work and housing assignments. You didn't want any special treatment, so Bob fed your information into the computer like everyone else. We work on a three-week rotation. Three weeks in the sorting shed, three weeks in the catalog department, three weeks in the research lab and three weeks at the site. You'll get to work under all of the supervisors."

"So, where do I report today?"

"Only the computer knows," Evan said. "Guess you'll just have to open the envelope to find out."

Jaycee slipped her finger under the flap of the envelope to open it. He enjoyed watching her pull out the sheets and read the computer printout.

"Let's see, it looks like I start this morning in the sorting shed. Let me guess, I won't be working with either of you for the first three weeks."

"Good guess. Since we're only waiting for one more person to arrive, I'll take you to the sorting shed myself."

Another car pulled down the gravel driveway as Evan went around to the passenger side of Jaycee's car. "It looks like our last lost sheep has arrived. You can take care of Patti, can't you, Bob?"

He saw Bob nod, before he got into Jaycee's car and closed the door.

"Do you always take such a personal interest in your volunteers?"

"Not always. I thought I might be able to talk you out of this nonsense about remaining anonymous. I know, I promised I wouldn't give you any special treatment, but..."

"...but nothing. I've looked forward to being just another volunteer ever since your lecture. Don't spoil it for me."

"All right, you win. Let's change the subject. I received a rather interesting call from Henry Bennett last week. It sounded like he didn't believe you would actually be spending your summer here. Is there something going on between the two of you? Something I should know about?"

"Nothing I can't handle. He gave me an ultimatum before I left Havelin. I have a feeling he'll carry through with his threat."

"What kind of threat?"

"It's not anything I want to go into right now. Henry will just have to stew in his own juices for a while. I don't intend to think about it while I'm here."

Evan wondered about her statement, but from past experience didn't press her further. "Just pull into the lot across the street. We can walk to the sorting shed from there."

~ * ~

Jaycee cringed at the mention of a call from Henry. *Why can't he just stay out of my life? No matter how many summers I devoted to my mother and Havelin, it never seemed to be enough for Henry.* She switched off the ignition, unable to look into Evan's eyes, afraid he might guess how adversely her argument with Henry affected her.

"The sorting shed, right?"

She pointed to the metal building in front of them.

"Good guess. Let's go in and get you started. This isn't glamorous work, Jaycee. I could easily arrange for you to work at the site for the entire twelve weeks. Are you sure...?"

"Of course, I am. I told you when we first met, I gave this careful thought."

She got out of the car and walked toward the metal shed. Stepping inside the door, she heard the good-natured teasing of young voices. Upon closer inspection, she noticed about twenty college age students engaged in their work. A man came over to them.

"Chris, this is Jaycee. Jaycee, this is your boss for the next three weeks. He's been with me ever since his junior year in college. Now he's teaching high school in Missouri. We're lucky he still likes to come back here in the summer."

"It's a pleasure, Chris." Jaycee shook the young man's extended hand.

"Tell me what a pleasure it is tonight," Evan said, turning to leave.

Jaycee watched him walk toward the door, then turned her attention to Chris.

"I'm ready to start. Where do you want me?"

"There's a place for you over here with Brandon. I hope you like doing puzzles. They bring us all the pieces of pottery from the dig, so we can put them together and see what they once looked like."

At the long table, Chris introduced her to Brandon, a young man of perhaps twenty-one or twenty-two, from UCLA, with reddish brown hair and blue eyes.

"So, is this your first dig?" Brandon asked without looking up from his work.

Jaycee contemplated her answer. She hadn't been on a dig in over ten years. She'd forgotten the exhilaration of touching the shards of antiquity she knew no one gazed upon in centuries.

"It seems like it. I did work on a dig, but that was a long time ago. I'm very excited about being here."

"Where do you go to school?"

Jaycee smiled. She knew her new look made her appear younger than her thirty-five years, but she never expected the people here to take her for a student. "Havelin."

"Good school. I hear they have a tough professor of Anthropology there. I met a student from Havelin on Christmas break. He said he has to work his tail off just to maintain a B average."

"Who is he? Maybe I know him."

"Cliff Norris. Is the name familiar?"

"I've seen him around campus. I think he was in one of my classes. It's strange I wouldn't call Dr. Grant tough. I actually enjoyed the class."

"So did Cliff. I think he meant the statement as a compliment. He said Grant made things more interesting than any of his other professors."

Jaycee fell silent. Before her were the pieces of a bowl with a beautiful design. To her amazement, each piece she picked up seemed to match perfectly with the last one. Using a small brush, she coated each clean surface with quick drying glue, then held them together with enough pressure to assure they would stick.

She put the last piece into place, when she saw the image of an old woman, bent with age, working over the bowl, then heard a voice. *The secret is in the writings.*

She turned quickly to Brandon. "Did you say something?"

Brandon put down the piece he was working on and looked at her. "No, why, did you hear something?" The question barely escaped his lips when a whistle blew.

"What was that?"

The unexpected shrillness of the sound caught her off guard.

Brandon began to smile. "Lunch. I think you need a break. It sounds like you're hallucinating." He glanced down at the bowl she put together. "It's a beautiful piece."

"Yes, it is. I hate to send it to the research lab."

"Don't get too attached to it. You'll get another set of pieces this afternoon. In this department, it's a never-ending flow of work."

Jaycee looked at the beginning of what looked like a water pitcher Brandon was working on. A flash of light assailed her and the vision of a young girl filling the pitcher from a stream appeared before her eyes. *The secret is in the writings.* As quickly as she saw the girl, the vision dissolved, leaving Jaycee a bit disoriented.

To her surprise, she felt Brandon's hand on her shoulder. "Is something wrong?"

She shook her head to rid herself of the remnants of what she just experienced. "No. I guess I do need to eat lunch. Does everyone eat at the same time?"

"Usually, unless Dad doesn't make it up."

"Does your father work on the dig?"

"My dad is the dig."

"Evan is your father?"

"Has been ever since Round Tree opened."

The realization Brandon was Evan's son, coupled with the recent visions of the old woman and young girl, added to her confusion.

As soon as Jaycee entered the dining hall, Bob approached her. "I see we haven't scared you off."

"On the contrary, I'm very excited about what I've been doing today."

Brandon put his hand on her shoulder before addressing Bob. "You should see the bowl she put together this morning. She's giving the rest of us an inferiority complex. I can't remember seeing anyone put a piece together so quickly."

"I got an easy one," Jaycee explained.

Bob began to laugh. "If you did, you're the first one on record. There have never been any easy ones before."

"See, I told you," Brandon said. Turning his attention back to Bob, he continued. "She even knows the tough professor I told you and Dad about, the one at Havelin."

"Oh, she does. Funny, Dr. Grant didn't strike me as being tough. Do you get that impression, Jaycee?"

Bob's statement sent up warning flags in Jaycee's mind, prompting her to shoot him a glance she hoped said, 'don't blow my cover'.

"Excuse us, Brandon, I have someone I want Jaycee to meet."

"No special treatment?" she questioned, as they moved away from Brandon.

"He already knows you're from Havelin. He must assume we met there. How could you stand there and lie about knowing the tough professor they have?"

"It wasn't hard. I do know Jocelyn Grant, perhaps better than anyone else. As for the tough part, I always considered her a pussy cat."

"Pussy cat or lion, I think it's wrong to keep your true identity from these kids. They could learn just as much from you this summer as they could working the dig."

"Look, Bob, for more years than I care to count, I've been Dr. Grant. Is it so wrong to want to be Jaycee for a little while?"

"I guess not. I just don't understand why. Believe me, no one knows who you are. We gave you our word on it. Unless you want people to know, they won't hear it from me."

"What about Evan?"

"He's promised not to tell anyone either, even though he doesn't approve of your keeping it a secret. Just don't let him bet on anything."

Jaycee laughed. "I still can't believe the two of you were betting on whether I would take the money back."

"I'm glad you didn't get mad enough to change your mind about working here this summer. As for the donation, it certainly helped. With what we raised this past winter, we can keep the project afloat for another two or maybe even three years."

"How much did you raise?"

"Well over a million dollars. Of course, with inflation, we'll have to watch every penny to make it last."

Jaycee looked up and noticed a woman approaching them. Bob put his arm around the woman's shoulder and kissed her cheek.

"Jaycee, this is my wife, Amanda."

Amanda extended her hand to Jaycee. "I'm pleased to finally meet you. Bob tells me we're all going out to eat at Evan's expense."

"I don't know if I'll be up to going out anytime soon. This morning was exhausting to say the least."

Amanda began to smile. "It grows on you."

"I hope so."

"Where does the mastermind computer have you working?"

"In the sorting shed."

"When in the rotation do you get to cataloging, in my department?"

"Not until the last three weeks."

"It's a shame, although I have a feeling you will be happier in the lab or out at the site."

"Oh, I don't know. I'm enjoying the sorting shed. I put together the most exquisite bowl this morning. As I did, I could see the people who used it."

"Keep getting those images. We need all the help we can get. It's a shame these people didn't leave a written language."

The words she'd heard earlier echoed in her mind. "You're kidding. They must have left a written record of some kind."

"No. Evan says it's not uncommon in these cultures. I can't believe he didn't mention it in his lecture."

Jaycee searched her memory of the lecture Evan gave at Havelin. She remembered him saying something about no written language. "I guess he did. It just doesn't make any sense, considering…"

"Considering what?" Evan asked, joining the group.

"Nothing." Jaycee wished she never mentioned anything about being able to see the people who used the bowl. The last thing she wanted was to draw unnecessary attention to herself.

"It must be something or you wouldn't have mentioned it in the first place," Evan pressed.

"Jaycee thinks she had a vision of the people who once lived here, while she was working this morning," Amanda said, her voice filled with excitement.

Evan's eyebrows shot up and his eyes sparkled. "What did you see?"

"I don't know if I saw anything. Maybe I was hallucinating."

She could see excitement turn to irritation in Evan's green eyes.

"Quit beating around the bush, Jaycee. If it didn't seem important to you, you wouldn't have mentioned it to Amanda. I need to know what you think you saw. On a project like this one, everything is important. You, of all people, should know that."

Jaycee sighed. She knew she'd dug herself into this hole and now she couldn't talk her way out of it. "When I finished putting together a piece of pottery this morning, I saw an old woman working with it, mixing something. Later, I saw a young girl getting water from the stream."

She watched Evan's brows knot, as he absorbed what she said.

Inside, a small voice of conscience admonished her for not mentioning the voice she heard earlier. *What good would it do? These people had no written language. All of this is just my imagination working overtime.*

"Very interesting." Evan's words silenced the voice of reason. "Interesting and exciting."

"Exciting? I think it's more frightening than exciting."

She noticed Bob and Amanda left them alone during their conversation.

"Don't let it frighten you. I wish I could see the people who used these utensils. One morning and you already see old women and young girls. Who knows what you'll be seeing by the end of the summer?"

"I don't consider it anything to envy. I'm certain it's only my mind playing tricks on me. I've always had a vivid imagination."

"Time will tell. Keep me advised if you see anything further."

Jaycee relaxed, as Evan's tone became more teasing than intense. He led the way to the long table filled with the makings for salads and sandwiches.

"Whom did you work with this morning?" he asked, as they sat down at a table.

"Your son."

"Damn, I forgot he's working the sorting shed. These first few days are hectic. I tend to conveniently forget things I should readily remember. He didn't..."

"He thinks I'm a student at Havelin. He wanted to know if I studied under the tough Anthropology Professor they have there. I told him I didn't think Dr. Grant was so tough."

Evan laughed. "He told me about meeting a young man from Havelin, when we talked last night. The kid must have made quite an impression for him to have mentioned it to me. He even said he wanted to do his post-grad work at Havelin so he could work with Dr. Grant. It seemed good to be able to talk to him on an adult level."

"What do you mean, on an adult level?"

"Up until last year, Brandon and I didn't communicate much. My ex-wife, Kathryn, took the kids and moved to California before the divorce was final. She wanted to put as many miles as possible between the kids and me. She didn't want me influencing them. She always thought I was crazy to give up a good teaching position to come out here and dig in the dirt. Since then, I usually see them at Christmas and a couple of times through the winter. Last summer was the first time she let them anywhere near Round Tree."

"Your ex-wife doesn't approve of any of this?" Jaycee asked, unable to fathom anyone being married to an archaeologist and not being excited about this dig.

"Good heavens, no," Evan replied. "She enjoyed her position as the wife of the head of the Anthropology Department, even though she didn't know how little money I actually made. I did my best to keep her comfortable."

"How?"

"By tutoring. In addition to my duties, I also worked with five or six students a semester. It paid for the luxuries."

"How unselfish of you," Jaycee commented, between bites of sandwich.

When she looked up, she noticed Evan looking at her intently.

"I meant to tell you this morning, you look very different from what I remembered."

"You can thank my friend, Ellie, for it. She insisted I have a complete make over."

"I can understand the make over, but what happened to your glasses?"

"I don't know how Ellie did it, but she talked me into contact lenses. She also insisted I get my hair cut. I didn't think anyone could ever convince me to cut it."

"I'm glad she did. I like the look. It makes you appear much younger."

"It must if Brandon mistook me for a college student."

"Am I going to have competition from my son?"

"Competition? Competition for what?" Jaycee asked, secretly pleased by the ease with which they talked.

"Don't you know?"

"No, I don't. If I didn't know better, I'd say you were jealous. Judging by our first meeting, you don't have any reason to be. We haven't gotten off on the proper foot. As I remember, we only seem to irritate each other."

Jaycee continued to eat, pleased to see this side of Evan. From what she saw during their first encounter, she assumed he wasn't at all interested in her as a person, only as a benefactor and volunteer.

"The next three months should remedy the situation. Having you at Round Tree will give us a chance to get to know each other."

Someone called Evan's name and he excused himself, leaving Jaycee alone to think over their conversation. Ever since the night of the lecture, she'd been daydreaming about him. Could he be harboring the same feeling about her?

"Looks like you and Dad found a lot to talk about," Brandon said, as he sat down at her table.

"He was being nice," she replied, quickly finishing her sandwich.

"Believe me, I know my dad. He isn't nice to just anyone, especially during the first days on the dig."

Jaycee smiled. She wanted to be somebody special to Evan Clark. Perhaps she got off to a good start this time.

Jaycee worked through the afternoon without a repeat of the morning's visions. The bowl she held carried a different design from the first one, different, but still beautiful. The clay that shaped the deep center of the bowl was stained a brilliant red.

She stared at the finished product, pleased with her work.

Human sacrifice, the voice she heard earlier said. To her horror, the bowl filled with blood before her eyes. *The secret is in the writings*, the voice continued.

Her hands began to shake and her head started to spin. Afraid she might accidentally break the bowl, she carefully set it down on the table in front of her. With her hands free, she braced herself by putting her hands on the edge of the table. *Please stop this, you're scaring me,* she silently implored, trying to communicate with the disembodied voice.

She hardly knew Brandon came to her side until she heard his voice. "Are you all right, Jaycee? You're shaking. You look like you've seen a ghost."

"I think I'm just tired," Jaycee replied, unable to take her eyes from the blood-filled bowl.

"Look at me, Jaycee," Brandon ordered, turning her face away from the scene before her by putting his hand under her chin.

"You're white as a sheet and trembling. Did you see something?"

"See something?" she repeated his words as a question.

She couldn't remember going into detail about what she saw earlier.

"Bob told me about your vision. He wanted me to keep an eye on you. Did you see something?"

She nodded.

"You'd better tell Dad about it."

"I'm not sure I can tell anyone about it. I just want to forget it. Promise you won't say anything to Evan."

"I'm sorry, Jaycee. I can't make a promise I know I won't keep. It's quitting time. You'd better go back to the dorm and lie down for a while."

"I guess you're right."

She took one last look at the now empty bowl. When she returned in the morning it would already be in the lab and another set of pieces would take its place. She wouldn't have to think about the horror it represented. From what she could remember, Evan had not mentioned anything about human sacrifice in his lecture. All of this had to be a product of her imagination running amok.

Next to it, sat the still unfinished pitcher. Again, the vision of the young girl assailed her. *The secret is in the writings.*

Why me? These people left no writings.

You will soon find that of which I speak and everything will be made clear.

She waited for another message, but the only voice she heard belonged to Brandon. "Come on, Jaycee, it's time to call it a day."

Jaycee agreed and followed Brandon to the parking lot, away from the visions, away from the voice.

Once at the dorm, she checked her rooming assignment. Her room would be at the end on a long hall of the one story building and her roommate's name was Sandra Clark.

Is this a conspiracy, or what? First, I spend the day working with Evan's son and now I'm rooming with his daughter. The only thing to do now is to make the best of it and not let my crazy feelings for Evan show.

Chapter Four

Evan found Brandon waiting for him at the apartment. "I didn't expect to find you here. Can I get you a beer or a soda?"

"A beer sounds good."

Evan led the way into the stuffy apartment and flipped on the air conditioner. From the refrigerator, he pulled two beers and popped the tops. He didn't question the reason for Brandon's unexpected visit until they were seated in the living room. "I can't believe this is a social visit when there are so many cute volunteers out there to be conquered."

"You're right, it's not. I'm worried about Jaycee."

Evan took a drink of his beer. "Did something more happen?"

The look on Brandon's face answered Evan's question. "She put together another bowl, in record time, this afternoon. When she finished it, she stared at it as though she could see something I couldn't. The color drained from her face and she was shaking. When I asked her about it, she insisted I shouldn't tell you. Whatever it is she saw, scared her half to death."

"I don't blame her for being frightened. I talked to Chris at lunch and he says she works on her projects like she's obsessed. It's as though she's being guided by something or someone."

"That's another thing. I was talking to her and it seemed as though she was listening to someone else. Maybe she shouldn't even be here."

"Oh, she should be here. There's no question about that. God knows she bought the right to be here."

"What are you talking about?"

"Nothing, nothing at all. I shouldn't have mentioned it."

"It is something. Did you meet her at Havelin? It certainly looked like you were old friends at lunch today."

"Yes, I met her at Havelin. I don't know about the old friends bit, though."

"I think you're falling for her and I'm pretty sure I know why. This morning I thought she was a student. Now I'm not so sure. What is her last name?"

Evan cringed. Earlier he promised not to tell anyone about Jaycee's true identity. Now, faced with his son's direct question, he couldn't lie. "It's Grant."

"I knew it. She's Dr. Grant. Boy, did I make a fool out of myself."

"On the contrary. You flattered her with your assumption. This business about her identity has to stay between the two of us. She wants no special treatment while she's here. She gave us a large donation when we were at Havelin, large enough to abide by her wishes."

~ * ~

Jaycee finished putting the clothes from her suitcase into the drawers and closet, when she heard a key in the door.

"Hi," a girl she judged to be about eighteen, said, as she entered the room. "You must be Jaycee. I'm Sandy Clark."

"I'm pleased to finally meet you."

"Are you getting settled?"

Jaycee nodded.

"Do you mind if I grab a quick shower? I think I've got half the dirt from the dig on me."

"Not at all."

Inwardly, Jaycee smiled at how comfortable she felt with Evan's daughter.

"We're going out for pizza. Do you want to join us?"

Jaycee contemplated the invitation. "Can I take a rain check? I need to soak in a hot tub. It's been a long day."

"Yeah, Brandon told me. I can't imagine having visions."

Sandy closed the bathroom door, leaving Jaycee to think about the events of the day. Things she thought she could forget until Sandy mentioned them. Sandy's knowledge of her situation made her feel ill at ease. She certainly didn't blame Brandon for sharing the strange goings on with his sister.

By the time Sandy emerged from the bathroom, Jaycee was back to her unpacking. Sandy's short red hair needed to be dried, but of course a lot of girls didn't go in for the blow dry look. Perhaps she was one of those girls who preferred air-drying their hair. Dressed in white shorts and a colorful top, she looked ready for an evening on the town.

"Did I upset you by mentioning your visions?" Sandy asked, while she put on a pair of white sandals.

"Not really," she lied. "I think Brandon was right. I was probably hallucinating."

"I saw you talking to Dad at noon," Sandy continued, seemingly oblivious to Jaycee's comment.

"He was being nice."

"My dad isn't particularly nice to volunteers. Don't get me wrong, but he does have a job to do here. The volunteers are a means to an end. People just have to learn to understand him. He gets moody sometimes, especially at the beginning of the summer when he doesn't know anybody. He sure took to you, though."

Sandy returned to the bathroom to put on her make up before she said anything more. "The papers I got said you're from Havelin. Did you meet him there?"

Jaycee felt her stomach begin to do flip-flops. She wished Bob hadn't included the information about Havelin in the packet he gave to Sandy. First Brandon questioned her about going to Havelin and now Sandy. Sooner or later the truth about her identity was bound to slip out. "Well, sort of..."

"What do you mean, sort of?"

Jaycee weighed her words carefully so as not to be caught in a lie. "He spoke there during winter break, so the Media Department taped it."

Sandy nodded. "I guess he did say something about winter break and not many students being there. I think it disappointed him. It's a good way to recruit volunteers."

Jaycee agreed, then returned to her unpacking as Sandy went back into the bathroom to curl her hair. When Jaycee finished, she stored her suitcases under the bed. Trying to remember where she put things, she quickly found her inflatable bath pillow and one of the romance novels

Ellie insisted she bring.

"I don't want you reading journals and text books this summer," Jaycee could hear Ellie saying when they talked on the phone after the books arrived. "It's bad enough you read those things all year long. Lighten up and have a little fun this summer."

Jaycee looked at the book in her hand and turned it over to read the blurb on the back cover. "Gerald laced Megan's silky strands through his fingers, as he contemplated making love to this fiery vixen," she read aloud.

She shook her head. *Is this love thing really so easy? You certainly couldn't prove it by me. Over the past few years, I couldn't find time to contemplate a relationship for pleasure. Maybe if I read these books, I might learn something.*

"Are you sure you won't join us?" Sandy asked, when she came out of the bathroom.

"Positive."

Once Sandy left the room, Jaycee began to prepare for her bath. Closing the drain, she turned on the tap and poured a cap of expensive bubble bath under the stream of water. With the tub full, she eased herself into the steaming water, adjusted the bath pillow and began to read the book. She hardly realized the water went cold while she read the first half of the story. Hurrying to finish her bath, with the now cold water, she opened the drain and turned on the shower to wash her hair. After blowing it dry and using her curling iron, she decided she should find some place to eat. As she entered the bedroom, the phone began to ring. Assuming it would be for Sandy, Jaycee answered prepared to take a message.

"Jocelyn? Is that you?" Henry's annoying voice greeted her.

"Henry? What are you doing calling me here? I thought I made it clear I don't want you tracking me down this summer."

"You did, but I want to talk to you one last time about next fall."

"I told you two months ago. I'm taking a year's sabbatical. I'm committed here for the summer and I've been accepted on a dig in Peru this winter. I'm very comfortable with my decision, thank you."

"Listen to yourself, Jocelyn. Think of your position. How can you jeopardize your future?"

"I can't see where I'm jeopardizing anything. You didn't tell Jinx Kramdon he was jeopardizing his future when he went to England to study Elizabethan literature."

"That was different."

"Just tell me how. Jinx did his research at Oxford. I'm doing mine on a dig."

"Jinx is..."

"Jinx is a man and I'm not. Get into the twenty-first century, Henry. Gender makes no difference when we both hold the same position."

She paused to be certain she chose the correct words before continuing. "Let me phrase this so even you can understand it. If you, or the board terminates me, I'll file a lawsuit charging sexual discrimination. I won't be deprived of this opportunity."

Without saying more, she slammed down the receiver.

~ * ~

Evan watched Brandon shove his hands into his pockets and walk down the sidewalk. He knew his confirmation of Brandon's assumptions could endanger the relationship Evan planned to cultivate with Jaycee. He would have to find a way to tell her Brandon knew about her. He also wanted to question her about what happened this afternoon. Brandon didn't usually get unduly upset about the happenings on the dig.

Picking up the directory of rooming assignments, Evan ran his finger down the list of names until he found the name of Jaycee. To his surprise, he saw Sandy's name above Jaycee's.

This is great, she works with my son during the day and rooms with my daughter at night. It's not going to be easy getting to know her.

Evan shook his head with the realization of where his thoughts took him. He wanted to get to know her, to feel her in his arms. He couldn't remember ever wanting a volunteer before. Hell, he hadn't wanted to make love to a woman since Kathryn left. His feelings for Jaycee certainly confused him.

Picking up the receiver, he entered the number for Jaycee's room.

The phone on the other end rang only once before Jaycee answered.

"Look here, Henry," she greeted him.

"Henry?"

"Oh, Evan, I'm sorry."

"You know, I'm getting tired of being taken for Henry. Is something going on between the two of you?"

"Nothing worth talking about."

"Have you had dinner?"

"Not yet. As a matter of fact, I just got out of the tub. I've been trying to decide where to go."

Evan allowed his mind to wander so he could envision her draped in a towel, talking on the phone.

"I'd like to take you out. I'll pick you up in about twenty minutes."

She hesitated for a moment, as if uncertain of how to answer. "I'd like that."

He hung up the phone, cursing himself for not mentioning Brandon's visit or the true reason he asked her out. He wondered if her hesitation came from her conversation with Henry or the experience Brandon told him about earlier.

After a quick shower, Evan used his electric razor on his face. When he finished, he ran his hand over the smooth skin, before applying aftershave. Dressed in Khaki pants and a knit summer shirt, he slipped his feet into boat shoes without socks. He certainly didn't have time to worry about putting on clean socks, to say nothing of trying to find them.

Evan got into his Jeep and turned toward the dorms. When he pulled up in front of the building, Jaycee came out onto the steps, wearing a sundress with a shawl over her shoulders. The way the material fell against her body, he realized she didn't wear a bra. He wondered if it were by plan or something she did without thought.

He got out of the Jeep and went to meet her. As he got closer, he could smell her perfume. The touch of her hand coupled with the taut nipples of her breasts pressing against the cotton of her dress made him involuntarily harden. He couldn't help thinking of how long ago anything like this happened. He enjoyed the sensation and wondered if she had any idea how she affected him.

"Not much of a chariot," he said, holding open the passenger door of the Jeep.

He steadied her as she climbed up into the seat. As he did, he noticed the way her skirt hiked up over her knee, showing him as much leg as he saw when she wore her shorts this morning. Much to his regret, she followed his gaze and quickly pulled down her skirt. He wondered what she tried to cover up, considering the length of the shorts she wore earlier. He saw more of her leg then than he could now.

"How did the rest of your day go?"

He didn't have to ask. He knew the answer. He did it so he could hear her describe the happenings of the afternoon.

"It went well. I put together another bowl."

"Chris tells me you work very fast."

"I wouldn't say that. Things just fell into place for me."

"Don't be disappointed when they stop falling in place. One of these times you'll get a piece that will take longer than you think."

"I'm sure I will. How was your day?"

"Hectic. I only had two experienced people at the site. I spent most of the day babysitting and teaching instead of working. Thank goodness for Sandy. She learned quite a bit last summer. She gave me a lot of help today. Speaking of Sandy, how do you like her as a roommate?"

"Ask me in a few days. I haven't gotten to know her yet. She does seem very nice."

"She's a good kid no thanks to me."

Jaycee's silence at his comment surprised him. He expected her to insist he'd been a good father. It would have been a good way for her to gain his approval.

"I hope you like Italian," he said, changing the subject.

"Yes, I do."

"Good. I have a favorite Italian restaurant just outside of town, called Montanelli's. They do some of the best pasta I've ever tasted. I thought you might like it as well."

"To be truthful, I enjoy anything that doesn't resemble my own cooking." She paused for a moment, then continued. "I just turned Sandy down for pizza. I'll have to come up with a good reason for going out with you."

Evan chuckled at her comment. "I don't blame you for not wanting to go out with the kids. I've done it, on occasion, and find it hard to keep up. What excuse did you use?"

"I told her I wanted to soak in a hot tub, which I did. I asked her for a rain check."

"If you plan to continue this charade, you'll have to mingle with them eventually."

From the other side of the vehicle, he heard Jaycee sigh deeply. "I don't know if I want to go on with the charade."

"Why not?"

"I don't have the energy to keep up with these kids. They're all so much younger than I am. I feel like the old woman who lived in the shoe when I'm around them. Why didn't you recruit some more older people, like me?"

"The more mature people usually can't take the time. As far as the kids are concerned, you have one less to worry about."

"What do you mean?"

"Brandon."

"Brandon?"

"He came over to my place tonight. He knows who you are."

"You told him?"

"No, he guessed. It answered a lot of questions for him. He's worried about you."

"I don't see why," Jaycee said, her tone less than confident.

"He told me about your vision this afternoon."

"What vision?"

The tone of her question was definitely defensive.

"I think you know what I'm talking about. Since we're at the restaurant, I won't press you until later."

Once inside, Jaycee seated herself across the booth from him. After reading the menu, they made their selections and Evan ordered a bottle of house wine.

"Do you come here often?"

He realized she was making polite conversation in an attempt to skirt the question he asked her moments earlier.

"It's a good place to take visiting professors and prospective investors. I doubt if Bob plans to let me off with anything this reasonable when I have to make good on the bet."

Jaycee rolled her eyes but said nothing, since the waitress returned with the wine and two glasses.

Evan tasted his wine and smiled at the look of pleasure on Jaycee's face when she tried hers.

"How about telling me what's going on?"

"Going on?"

"For starters, what about Henry?"

"Henry is in a snit about me taking a year's sabbatical."

"A year? Where will you be this winter? The dig closes down by November."

"I've been accepted on a dig in Peru after the first of the year."

"Montoya's?"

"Yes. How did you know?"

"I made a good guess. I ran into him at a conference this spring and he asked me to come down for a few weeks. It sounds like we'll be getting better acquainted than we originally planned."

"It looks that way."

A hint of a smile crossed her lips. With that bit of encouragement, he decided to probe further.

"So, what does Henry have against you doing a year of research? Other than the fact he won't have the best professor he's ever had on his staff."

"I doubt you felt the same way when you first learned I was a woman, but I do thank you for the compliment. Henry's trying to tell me he plans to terminate me for taking a year off."

Evan could hardly believe anyone would try something so ridiculous. "Terminate you? Can he do that?"

"He seems to think he can. I figured he'd stick to his guns, so I threatened him with a lawsuit. He'll have to think long and hard before he carries through."

"I'm sure he will. What kind of a suit are you planning?"

"Sexual discrimination."

Evan smiled at her statement. He liked her spunk. He wondered if he were in the same position if he would be able to carry through on such a threat. "Remind me not to get you mad at me."

He enjoyed watching her expression turn from anger over her situation to amusement at his statement. He liked the way her features softened when she smiled, the way her eyes twinkled at his comment.

Jaycee's anger at Henry seemed to have drained from her mind as Evan's statement made her smile. "Enough about Henry. I'm sure you didn't ask me out to dinner to discuss my problems at Havelin."

Evan's smile faded. "No, I didn't. Brandon says you had another incident this afternoon. Do you want to tell me about it?"

~ * ~

"I don't know if I can talk about it just yet."

She certainly didn't want to tell Evan about the frightening vision and have him laugh at her. At the same time, she knew she needed to tell someone, to share the horror and hopefully make it go away.

"I think you'd better talk about it."

Jaycee trembled, not only frightened by the memory but also intimidated by the sound of Evan's voice. He no longer asked, but demanded to know what happened. Resigned to the fact she could no longer keep her visions to herself, she took a deep breath before beginning. "I told you about the visions I experienced this morning. What I didn't tell you was I heard a voice both times."

"A voice? What did it say?"

"Please don't laugh at me when I tell you. It said the secret is in the writings."

"That's hard to believe since there are no writings, Jaycee."

The look in his eyes told her he didn't believe a word of what she just said.

"I know. Amanda told me. It's the reason I didn't say anything before this. I decided I must have been hallucinating, until this afternoon."

"When you had the vision Brandon told me about?"

Jaycee nodded. "I put together a second bowl. This one had different markings on it. I assumed it must be a ceremonial bowl. The inside of it was stained a very bright red. When I finished, I heard the voice again. This time it said human sacrifice and before my eyes the bowl filled with blood. I put it down immediately and the voice again said the secret is in the writings. I don't know if this is actually happening or if I'm a victim of my overactive imagination. It's very frightening."

"I told you this noon, I find it exciting. I want you at the site with me tomorrow morning."

Evan's statement took her by surprise. "What about no special treatment? I'm not due to work the site for another six weeks in the rotation."

"Don't worry about it. If you're seeing these things from fragments of pottery, I want to know what you see when you're actually at the site."

"Whatever you say, but I doubt if I'll see anything."

After agreeing to go to the site with him, Jaycee relaxed. Telling Evan wasn't as hard as she thought it would be. She questioned what her reaction on the site would be then laughed at her worries. She'd have to chalk all of this up to the first day jitters. Tomorrow, nothing out of the ordinary would happen and she'd be just one of the volunteers. As the thought crossed her mind, she wondered if becoming one of many would jeopardize the relationship between her and Evan. She enjoyed being with him, being close enough to smell his Old Spice aftershave. It was a scent that was, once again, becoming popular. It reminded her of her father.

His gaze wandered down from her face and focused on her breasts, causing her to cringe. She knew she should have worn something different. When she realized she forgot her strapless bra, it was too late to do anything about it. The other two dresses she brought both needed to have the wrinkles pressed out of them. At the time she decided it was better to wear this than to go looking like she just slept in her clothes, now she wasn't so certain. The way Evan looked at her made her more than a little self-conscious.

Evan glanced at his watch. "Look at the time. It's past ten. You should be in bed."

In whose bed? she thought, immediately admonishing herself for such crazy ideas.

Pull yourself together. You don't want to be in Evan's bed, or do you?

She watched Evan pick up the check and allow her to lead the way out of the restaurant.

"That was an excellent meal," Jaycee said, knowing she didn't mean it.

If anyone asked her what she'd eaten, she didn't know if she could answer. Her mind remained too full of Evan to remember something as mundane as food. The man she idolized spent the evening sitting across from her, more exciting than she ever imagined him, more at ease in casual clothes than in the suit and tie he wore at Havelin.

~ * ~

Evan held open the door to the Jeep, unable to get past the feelings Jaycee evoked in him. *She must be a witch, a good witch. No one else has made me feel this way. I decided such emotions died when Kathryn left.*

They talked about inconsequential things as they drove back to the dorm. "I usually insist the volunteers are in bed by ten," he commented, once they were parked in the lot.

"Do I have a penalty to pay for breaking curfew?"

Evan noticed a note of amusement in her voice.

"If so, I do too. I'm right along with you. I'd like to take you out again, Jaycee."

She turned and he could see the smile on her lips by the bright parking lot lights. "Even if I don't have any more visions?"

"With or without visions. I want to get to know you. Maybe I'll be able to figure out what makes Jaycee Grant tick."

"I'd like to get to know you better, too. Unfortunately, I'm afraid you'll find the subject of Jaycee Grant to be a rather dull one."

Evan switched off the ignition before going around to open Jaycee's door. He focused his gaze on her shapely leg, trying not to stare at the outline of her breasts pressed against the material of her dress.

On an impulse, Evan pulled her into his arms and entrapped her lips with his. Surprisingly, she opened her mouth slightly, inviting his tongue to do battle with hers.

Evan didn't want to leave her there. He wanted to take her back to his apartment and make love to her. The idea struck him as ridiculous. Jaycee Grant was a volunteer. Evan's mind told him to back off, but his body pressed on.

"Way to go, Dad," Brandon's voice shattered the silence, causing Evan to break the embrace.

Turning around he saw both Brandon and Sandy standing behind them.

"What are you two doing here?"

"Waiting for you," Sandy replied. "Brandon joined us for pizza and mentioned Jaycee's visions. I got worried, especially when she wasn't here when I came back."

"We called your apartment, Dad," Brandon said. "Since you weren't home, we figured the two of you might be together. We decided to wait out here for you. You know, curfew and all."

At Evan's side, Jaycee began to giggle. "It looks like we got caught, Dr. Clark."

"Since when are you calling me Doctor?" Evan asked, snaking his arm around her waist.

"Since now," she replied, making no move to free herself.

"Speaking of calling people things, what should I call you, Jaycee?" Brandon asked.

Evan felt Jaycee cringe.

"No one knows but Sandy and me. I thought she should know the truth about her roommate."

"Jaycee will do just fine, Brandon. I left Dr. Grant back at Havelin. Here, I'm just another volunteer."

Evan pulled Jaycee just a bit closer. "You won't be calling her anything tomorrow, Brandon. She'll be working out at the site with me."

"In that case, I'll miss you."

"You won't get too lonely. Once your dad realizes today was a fluke, he'll send me back to the sorting shed. I'm looking forward to putting together more pieces."

Evan wondered if she meant it or if she only said something about seeing no more visions to calm her own nerves. He hoped she did have more supernatural encounters. If he came up with dramatic new finds about this culture, the state might reinstate his funding. With Sandy and Brandon looking on, Evan kissed Jaycee lightly on the cheek.

Pulling out of the parking lot, he tuned to see Jaycee and Sandy engaged in conversation. He harbored mixed emotions about Jaycee. As a woman, she excited him. As a professor of anthropology, the visions she had today could renew interest in Round Tree Dig. He wondered if he could separate his feelings for the woman from his need for her visions to enhance his work.

Chapter Five

The alarm clock rang and Jaycee got out of bed. On the other side of the room, Sandy stirred and cursed mildly about it being morning already.

Jaycee harbored no such aversion to getting up. Her dreams were filled with ancient people and bowls of blood, along with the ever-present voice. She tossed and turned for hours. In an attempt to block the disturbing dreams, she tried to concentrate on Evan's kisses. Although it worked while she lay awake, as soon as she slipped into slumber, the voice and images returned.

Sandy rose up on one elbow. "What time is it? It's still dark out."

"I'll reset the alarm for you. It's only four. I have to meet your dad for breakfast at five."

Sandy groaned and pulled the pillow over her head.

In the bathroom, Jaycee scrubbed her face and applied moisturizing make-up. With the dust of the dig, she would certainly need it today. She made a mental note to call Ellie and thank her for suggesting it. As she came back into the bedroom, she noticed Sandy sleeping peacefully. The alarm would go off in another hour and forty-five minutes and Jaycee wondered if Sandy would be as upset about getting up when it rang, as she was earlier.

~ * ~

Evan arrived at the dining hall just prior to five and watched Bob and Amanda pull in behind him. He called them last night after he got home. He knew they'd been in bed. "Sorry about last night," he greeted them.

"No problem," Amanda replied.

"So, what's up with Jaycee?" Bob asked.

Evan hardly knew where to begin. "A lot. She had another vision yesterday afternoon. I'm taking her to the site this morning. If there is anything to these visions, it could be a big boost to the project."

"A boost to the project?" Amanda echoed. "Is that the reason you took her out to dinner last night? After seeing the two of you together yesterday at noon, I thought…well you know."

"Don't confuse the issue. I can only deal with one thing at a time. Right now, it's her visions."

"Just like it was her money at Havelin?" Bob accused. "If you ask me, you'd better check out the issue of how you feel about her. No matter what you say, you've been attracted to her since you first met, even if you won't admit it."

Evan shook his head. He never considered himself transparent where his feelings were concerned. Now, in less than twelve hours, both his kids and his best friends questioned his intentions toward Jaycee.

"There will be time for private feelings later. For now, I want to take her to the site before the volunteers get there, I want to see how she reacts."

"What if nothing happens?" Bob asked,

"If it doesn't, we'll see about the other. *We* both want to get to know each other better, but who knows what will happen."

Amanda began to smile broadly. "I knew it. There is a spark of something. I think she's exactly what you need in your life. I guess I'm just an incurable romantic. Isn't that right, Bob?"

Evan saw her wink broadly. Bob nodded. "Especially in the summer when the kids are visiting their grandparents and we're working out here. It's a wonder I have any energy left to do my job."

"Okay, you two love birds, I get the picture. Sooner or later, I'll have to decide what to do about my feelings for Jaycee."

"Why do anything about them, rather than expand on what you have? At least she wants to be with you. After the way you acted when you first met, it's a good sign."

Bob's question brought back the memory of Kathryn's cruel words when he told her about the opportunity he had to invest in Round Tree and take on the position of head archaeologist for the project. You would have thought he asked her to pack up and move to the ends of the earth rather than to the West Virginia countryside. In the future, would Jaycee come to feel the same way?

"I'm sorry, Evan, I forgot about Kathryn."

"I wish I could forget about her. Let's go in and get some breakfast. Jaycee should be here soon. I want to be ready to get out to the site as soon as possible."

Inside the dining hall several early risers were already eating. From the opposite side of the room, Chris waved, and Evan went over to talk to him about Jaycee before going to the buffet table.

After filling his plate, he sat down at the table Bob and Amanda chose. From his chair, facing the door, he saw Jaycee enter. He smiled to see her dressed in shorts, shirt and work boots.

"Good morning, I hope I'm not late."

"No," Amanda said. "You're not late. Evan is early. He's always early. Bob and I keep trying to get places earlier and earlier, but we never beat him."

Evan noticed the questions in Jaycee's eyes. "I thought you might be more comfortable with another woman along. Of course, I couldn't ask Amanda without including Bob. Go grab something to eat. I want to get started as soon as possible."

Jaycee nodded and Evan watched as she made her way to the table laden with food. When she returned, he took inventory of the items on her tray. It contained a piece of fruit, a carton of yogurt and a cup of coffee.

Evan couldn't hide his annoyance with her selection. "That will never do."

Before she could set the tray on the table, he took it from her hands.

"Where are you going?"

He could hear her footsteps following closely behind him. "I intend to get you some breakfast. I watched the way you ate at lunch and dinner yesterday. The first thing we have to do is change your eating habits."

"What is the goal here? Do you want me to look like Two Ton Tilly by the end of the summer?"

"I suppose the next thing you plan to throw at me is you don't eat breakfast."

"I don't," she declared, defiantly.

Without giving her any choice, he filled her plate with bacon, eggs, hash browns and toast, lastly, he added a glass of juice to the tray. "Well, you do now. I want you to go and sit down."

"I don't know how you expect me to eat all of this," she said, when he sat the tray in front of her.

"The same way we eat ours, one fork full at a time. It won't kill you, Jaycee. This isn't easy work. It takes a lot of energy."

"I thought Henry was a slave driver. He can't hold a candle to you."

"At least I'm not discriminating against you. I insist everyone eat good meals."

Jaycee picked at a slice of bacon, irritated with Evan for the way he tried to dictate her lifestyle. She knew she should voice her opinion to him, but realized it would probably be fruitless.

"Consider yourself welcomed to Round Tree," Bob said. "You have now received the official 'You Have To Eat Good Meals' lecture."

"What I don't understand, is why they put out the yogurt if certain people won't allow you to eat it."

"Some of the volunteers prefer yogurt to milk. Speaking of which, where is your milk?"

"I don't drink milk."

"In that case, you eat the yogurt, it's your choice."

Jaycee looked down at the amount of food on her plate. By no stretch of the imagination could she manage to eat a carton of yogurt on top of the food already staring her in the face. "I'll drink the milk," she finally said.

She started to get up, but Evan stopped her. "I'll get your milk, while you work on finishing your breakfast."

When he returned, she reluctantly thanked him. "Is this some kind of punishment, or what? Are you stuffing me with food for breaking curfew?"

Evan shook his head. "Give it a couple of days and you'll understand why I insist you eat right. I refuse to have you passing out because of a poor diet."

~ * ~

Jaycee finished her breakfast about the same time as everyone else. Together with Amanda, she took her tray to the kitchen. She waited until Bob and Evan left the area before she said anything. "Is he always this bossy?"

"You'll get used to it. Evan likes things done his way and I agree. Eating a proper breakfast is part of it. You can always go light on lunch. Just remember you haven't had anything since last night. Your body needs to be refueled."

Jaycee allowed her mind to wander back to her evening with Evan. She wondered how the man who sat across from her then could be the same man who bullied her into eating breakfast this morning.

"Where did Evan take you to dinner last night?"

Jaycee looked up, surprised to realize Amanda knew about Evan taking her out. "To Montanelli's. How did you know?"

"He told us. At least he picked a good place. They have great food."

"I wouldn't know."

"What do you mean?"

"It was a strange evening. I couldn't even tell you what I had other than a glass of wine."

"I diagnose your condition as a bad case of Evanitis. Thank goodness things are different this time."

"This time?" Jaycee repeated.

"Every year at least one of the volunteers comes down with it. Until now, Evan didn't even know they existed. I think he's very taken with you. He's especially interested in your visions."

"I wish everyone would stop making such a fuss over my visions. I should have never mentioned them."

Amanda turned to face Jaycee. "Why do you insist on downplaying them?"

"Because they have no meaning. I hear a voice that tells me the secret is in the writings, when this culture had no written language. It doesn't make any sense at all."

"Maybe not, but it's happened to you more than once, if we can believe Evan. Why don't you reserve judgment until after we go out to the site?"

"What do you think will happen when I don't see or hear anything? I wanted to spend the summer being just plain Jaycee Grant, no special treatment, no one knowing who I am. Now I don't know what I want. If something happens at the site, I'll never know if Evan wants to get to know me for me or for the visions. If nothing happens, he may lose interest all together."

"Don't let it bother you," Amanda assured her. "Either way, you'll have a tough time getting rid of Evan. For the first time since the divorce, I've actually seen him smile at the mention of a woman."

"Have you known him long?"

"Bob studied under him in Utah. When we first met, we couldn't believe how young he was. Several years after Bob graduated, Evan got a chance to be one of the backers for this dig. He called us right away to ask us if we'd be interested in investing some of our money and joining him. We've worked together ever since. Kathryn came out here with him for the first month. After that, she packed the kids off to California. He's never gotten over the divorce. Not until he met you, that is. Since he was at Havelin, your name seems to come up a lot."

Butterflies crowded Jaycee's stomach. She saw the way Evan reacted to her at Havelin, when all she wanted was his acceptance. Since then, she changed her entire persona in the hopes of attracting his attention this summer. Evan Clark was her idol, and once she met him, he became the object of her fantasies. Hearing Amanda say Evan brought up her name in conversation pleased her.

"Are you girls ready to go?" Bob asked.

"Just about," Amanda replied.

Jaycee followed them out to the parking lot. Seeing Evan standing beside the Jeep confused Jaycee's emotions even further. As soon as he saw her, he held open the door. "You'll ride with me."

Jaycee looked to Amanda for an invitation to join them, but she was already in the truck. When the invitation didn't come, Evan took her arm.

"I don't bite, Jaycee."

"You couldn't prove it by me. I'm not used to people trying to control my life."

"Aren't you? What about Henry?"

Jaycee laughed at Evan's comparison. "I can blow Henry off."

"I'll warn you right now, I'm not someone you can blow off. I know I came on a little strong this morning, but I come on strong with all of the volunteers. Can you accept my terms?"

Jaycee turned to face him. "If I intend to work the dig this summer, I guess I have to. I owe you an apology. Breakfast was surprisingly good. I realize I'm not at Havelin now. I expected things to be different here. I never considered seeing visions and hearing voices as part of the difference. With luck, nothing more will happen."

Evan started the jeep, then turned to her with a sly wink. "Apology accepted."

They rode in silence until Evan pulled off the highway and onto a dirt road. Jaycee could feel her heart pound wildly in her chest as the sign reading *Round Tree Archaeological Dig* came into view.

As though Evan could feel her excitement, he smiled broadly. "What you saw yesterday is only part of it. This is the heart of the project."

"It's impressive."

They drove a little further until they stopped at the edge of a grassy field. Several yards away sat the site, a deep cut in the lush grass.

After Bob and Amanda arrived, the four of them walked toward the excavation. The hole in the ground beckoned and frightened Jaycee.

"Are you ready to go down?" Evan asked.

A vision of many people and dwellings filling the field assailed her eyes. Forcing her mind to make it go away, she nodded.

Evan went down the ladder ahead of her then held out his hand.

Once at the base of the steps, in the belly of the dig, Jaycee gasped, pleased at the sight which greeted her. Ancient timbers framed the outline of a building. She ran her hand over the now petrified wood, trying to imagine the people she saw in her visions living here.

"It's magnificent," she finally said, her voice hardly more than a whisper.

"Is it what you expected?"

"Everything and more. The slides don't do it justice."

Again, she touched the wood. As she did, a warm feeling

encompassed her body and a sudden sadness filled her mind. Unbidden tears spilled from her eyes, bathing her cheeks. Evan's hand rested on her shoulders, causing her to wince at his touch.

This is a place of sadness. You must sense that.

I sense it deeply.

This is a place of sadness. This is not a place for you. This is not what you seek.

How do you know what we seek?

Not we, you. You seek your destiny. You must learn what happened in this village to finally be at peace with yourself.

What happened? When? Where? I don't understand.

You will. The secret is in the writings.

What writings? These people had no written language. Explain it to me.

Not here.

If not here, where? I need to know where.

To Jaycee's disappointment, the voice remained silent. As though from far away, she heard another voice.

"Jaycee, Jaycee, what's going on?" Evan asked.

Completely exhausted and unable to speak, she began to tremble. Unexpectedly, her knees buckled and a warm darkness encompassed her.

~ * ~

Evan watched as Jaycee went into the trance like state. Seeing her move away from him, mentally, frightened him. She even took on a different appearance, a faraway look in her eyes. He knew she couldn't hear him. Even though he placed his hands on her shoulders and repeatedly said her name, she remained oblivious to him. He wondered if it was his imagination or if she was crying. He wished he knew why.

As suddenly as the phenomenon began, it ended. Evan saw her start to tremble them crumble toward the ground. On instinct, he scooped her into his arms and held her protectively.

At the ladder, he called up to Bob. "Jaycee's unconscious. Take her while I climb up." He carefully handed Jaycee's limp body up to Bob's waiting arms.

"What happened down there?" Bob asked, once Evan emerged from the pit.

"I don't know. It was as though she went into a trance. When she came out of it, she was crying, then she collapsed."

A few feet away, Amanda knelt next to Jaycee. To Evan's relief, he saw her begin to stir.

Evan hurried to her side. "Can you hear me? Are you alright?"

He sighed deeply when she opened her eyes. "Evan? What happened?"

"That's what I want to know. What did you see?"

"Nothing other than the excavation, once we went down the ladder. I only felt an overwhelming sense of sadness and I heard the voice."

"What did it say?"

"Something about this being a place of sadness and it wasn't what I was looking for. It said I needed to know what happened. I didn't understand it at all. When I asked more questions all he would say was the secret is in the writings, whatever that means. It's as though he knows me personally."

"Do you believe in past lives?" Amanda asked.

Evan snapped to attention. "Past lives? Are you crazy?"

Amanda glared at him. "I didn't ask you, Evan. Do you believe in reincarnation, Jaycee?"

"I've never given it much thought. It goes against everything I've ever been taught."

"Well, I do," Amanda declared. "I think you lived here, in another life. I think it's the reason you're so drawn to this dig."

"I think it's the most asinine thing I've ever heard," Evan exploded. "Why fill Jaycee's head with this nonsense?"

"It's not nonsense," Amanda countered. "I have a friend in town. She's a psychiatrist who's done several regressions. She knows what she's doing."

"A psychiatrist," Evan exclaimed, angry with Amanda for suggesting something so ridiculous. "Do you have any idea what something like that would cost? We can't afford it."

"This isn't your decision, Evan," Amanda said, her eyes pleading for understanding.

"Since when? Everything concerning Round Tree has been my decision ever since we first came here."

"This doesn't concern Round Tree. Jaycee needs to find out what is going on here for her own peace of mind."

Turning back to Jaycee, Amanda continued. "Would you consider it? I think you need to find out."

"I don't know. I agree with Evan. I don't believe in any of this. I'd have to give it some thought."

Evan breathed easier. He'd known Amanda for several years and never once guessed she might believe in anything so ridiculous.

"Don't give me your answer now. Just promise me you'll think about it. You too, Evan."

Jaycee allowed Evan to help her to her feet. She wished he would take her in his arms, but he didn't.

"I think you'd better get back to the sorting shed," he declared.

"No. I'd rather stay here."

"Even with your not so friendly voice?"

Jaycee nodded, then turned to face Amanda. "I know you mean well by your offer. I'm just not convinced it would do any good. I promise to give it some thought, though."

Once Bob and Amanda left, Evan took Jaycee's hand in his. "I think you ought to go back to the dorm. You need to rest."

"I'd rather stay here," Jaycee repeated, this time adding more emphasis to the words.

"If you insist on staying, why don't you walk around and get the lay of the land. Keep an eye on the sky, though. It looks like we could get a storm. If it starts raining, come on in. We can't work out here in the rain."

~ * ~

Jaycee agreed and started walking away from the site. To her surprise, she realized she had an idea of where she wanted to go. Over the next rise, she knew she would find a stream.

When she reached the crest of the hill, she experienced disappointment when all she saw was a grassy ravine. She sank down on top of the ridge and wrapped her arms around her knees, tucking them under her chin. She wished she could see the lifestyle that went on here centuries earlier.

I always loved you, the now familiar voice sounded in her mind.

Who are you?

You will know, soon enough. No matter what you remember, I did love you. I knew you would come back here.

Come back? I've never been here before. I only came for the summer to work the dig.

I realize you have never been here in this life. It is not this life, which concerns me. Your other life must not be a concern to you.

I don't understand you at all. Of course, I'm concerned, as well as frightened.

Do not be frightened. I will not harm you again.

Again? Have you hurt me before?

Yes, but only because it could not be prevented. When the time is right, I will show you where to look. The secret is in the writings.

"Jaycee," she heard Evan shout from behind her. "I've been looking all over for you. What are you doing out here in this storm? I told you to come in if it started to rain."

"Rain?" she questioned, for the first time suddenly aware of the water dripping from her hair. "I didn't notice."

He helped her to her feet. "Did you have another incident?"

"Yes. Did there used to be a stream here?" she asked, pointing to the bottom of the ravine.

Evan nodded. "We figure it used to run right down this wash. Why?"

"I just feel this is where there used to be a stream."

"Let's get back to the Jeep. We can discuss this once you get some dry clothes and something to eat."

Jaycee agreed and hurried to keep up with Evan. At the Jeep, she tried to decipher her feelings concerning the words the voice spoke. Earlier, he said the site was a place of sadness. Only moments ago, he seemed to confirm her past life and that he loved her. If that were the case, why did he say he hurt her?

"Do you think Amanda could be right?" she asked, when Evan stopped at the dorm.

"Do you mean about you having lived a past life? I don't know. There is no scientific proof of reincarnation. It's usually something you read about in the tabloids. You know the kind of kooks who dream this stuff up."

His comment hurt. All morning she tried to tell herself this wasn't happening, to no avail. Now to have Evan make fun of her decision upset her. "You'd better start lumping me in with those kooks. I've read the Christian religion is one of the few in the world who doesn't believe in it. I'm beginning to wonder if there isn't something to it."

"What did you see out there?"

"Nothing. I only heard the voice. It's as though he knows, or knew, me. He said he loved me."

"I don't want you going out to the site again. I see it as dangerous."

"It is not dangerous. He said he would never hurt me again."

"Again?"

"Never mind, you wouldn't understand."

"What do you mean I wouldn't understand? What did you hear?"

Jaycee shook her head and got out of the Jeep to hurry into the dorm. Evan's tone bothered her.

"Why did you run from me like that?" Evan demanded, as Jaycee fumbled for her room key, in her fanny pack.

She ignored Evan and fit the key into the lock.

"Answer me, Jaycee," he said, following her into the room.

"Why, so I could look like a fool or worse yet, a kook? I can't help what happened to me. Damn it, Evan, I'm scared."

She started to turn away, but Evan's hand on her arm stopped her. "I'm sorry about the comment concerning kooks. I thought it would lighten the situation."

Jaycee nodded and allowed him to pull her into his arms. Wet plastic touched the bare skin of her arms and for the first time, she realized he wore a rain slicker.

Evan's eyes pleaded with her. In them she noticed fear. "I guess I'm just as frightened as you are. I've worked out here for the past several years and I've never had anything like this happen before. You get on some dry clothes and I'll call Amanda. With the weather the way it is, no one will be going back out to the site today. Maybe her friend can see you this afternoon."

Jaycee smiled at his suggestion. Although the thought of exploring the possibility of a past life frightened her, she wanted answers. His comment about calling Amanda put her at ease.

~ * ~

Evan pulled off his rain slicker and threw it in a corner, while Jaycee went into the bathroom. Alone in the room, he assessed the small living space. The bed by the bathroom door was unmade, as though its occupant left for work with no time to make it. In direct contrast, the bed by the window was neatly made. On it laid a notebook. He couldn't resist picking it up.

> Round Tree Dig
> Day 1: Arrived at 7:30 AM - Somehow, I think it annoyed Evan I didn't get here last night. Worked in the sorting shed with Evan's son, Brandon. Put together one bowl this AM and...

"What are you doing?" Jaycee asked, before he could read more.

"Sorry. I shouldn't have picked it up. I just thought..."

Jaycee waved her hand. "I don't mind if you read it. If I considered it private, I would have put it away. It's only a journal for my research. Did you reach Amanda?"

Evan shook his head, embarrassed to be caught snooping. "I'll call her now."

~ * ~

Jaycee pulled her clear plastic raincoat from the drawer and put it on over her shorts and blouse. She didn't bother to dry her hair. It would only get wet again once she went out. Behind her, she could hear Evan talking to Amanda, but paid little attention. She knew he only placed the call to pacify her and to ease his guilt about her catching him reading her diary.

"Are you going to answer my question, Jaycee?" Evan asked once they were in the Jeep.

"What question?"

Evan turned to look at her, exasperation showing in his eyes. "You know very well what question. What did you hear when we were at the site?"

"Oh, that. I think I need to digest it before I can talk about it."

She prayed he wouldn't press her further. To her relief, he merely grasped the steering wheel more firmly and pulled out of the parking lot.

When they arrived at the dining hall, they saw people arriving from various directions, all hurrying to get out of the rain.

Inside, Jaycee spotted Bob and Amanda seated at a table. "You go and join them," Evan said. "I'll get us something to eat."

The thought of Evan filling her plate with more food than she wanted caused Jaycee to shake her head. "I'll get my own lunch, thank you. I seem to remember you filling my plate at breakfast."

Evan's hearty laughter irritated her. Under his watchful eyes, she chose a chef's salad and a bowl of melon. "Good choice," Evan said, his voice low.

"You mean you approve? I thought you'd insist on a seven-course meal," she commented, hoping her voice sounded tart.

"Come on, Jaycee, I'm not a monster. I only want you to understand the need for a balanced diet. You aren't sitting in a classroom. You're doing physical labor. Your body needs more fuel to keep going."

Jaycee couldn't help but smile. Even though she was irritated with Evan, she wanted his approval and enjoyed his attention. If only this crazy voice and the visions it prompted would leave her alone, perhaps she could pursue a relationship with the man she'd idolized for the past several years.

"Did you call your friend?" Evan asked, when they sat down at the table.

Amanda nodded. "She said she can see Jaycee this afternoon at two. What made you change your minds?"

"Jaycee experienced another episode this morning. Unfortunately, she doesn't think she can tell me about it."

"Why not?" Bob asked.

Jaycee swallowed a mouthful of salad before answering. "I think it's best if I see what Amanda's friend has to say first. If there is nothing to this, I can dismiss it and get on with what I came here to do. If there is, I'll have to learn to deal with it. We'll have plenty of time for me to go into it after I meet with the doctor."

Jaycee continued to listen to the conversation going on around her as she ate. "You hold the purse strings, Bob," Evan said. "Can we afford this?"

"What do you mean *'We'*?" Jaycee asked, not giving Bob the opportunity to answer.

Evan turned toward her. "The project of course."

"Why? My decision has nothing to do with the project."

"Doesn't it?" Bob asked. "I think your voices and visions have everything to do with it. Think about it, Jaycee. Your visions could be very helpful to us. Now, to get back to your question, Evan, we can't afford not to look into this."

Jaycee continued to eat. She wondered if Evan would be quite so attentive if she hadn't lived through the terrifying experience of the past two days.

Chapter Six

Evan pulled into a parking space at the building where Amanda's friend kept an office.

"Do you believe in this?" he asked, when they stood in the elevator.

"Not really, but I have to try something. Will you go in with me?"

Evan thought for a moment. He realized how this must frighten her. It scared the daylights out of him. The feeling she generated within him every time he got close, made him want to protect her, to shield her from the reality of the visions. "Do you want me there?"

"Of course, I do. I'm afraid of what might happen. I don't want to do this alone."

"In that case, I won't leave your side. Just remember, I'm a dyed in the wool skeptic. I honestly want this to be a bust. The only thing is, I agree with you, we have to find out what's going on in your life."

The elevator stopped at the seventh floor and Evan held open the door to the office with the name Dr. Sharon Tess on it. He assessed the office. It looked like any number of doctor's waiting rooms he'd visited over the years, right down to the outdated magazines on the table.

He estimated the woman who greeted them to be in her early forties. "I'm Sharon Tess. Amanda told me you're both very skeptical about this."

"We most certainly are, but I need some answers," Jaycee replied.

"The important thing is, you've taken the first step. I must assume you're doing this willingly."

Evan watched Jaycee's expression as she laughed nervously.

"No one forced me to come here, if that's what you mean."

"Good, then if you excuse us, Dr. Clark, we'll get started."

"Please, can Evan be with me?" Jaycee asked, putting her hand on Dr. Tess' arm.

"I don't see why not, if both of you are willing."

She opened the door to an inner office and motioned toward a space-aged recliner.

"What?" Evan questioned. "No couch?"

"Although I am a psychiatrist and a hypnotist, I don't fit the stereotype people have stuck on us over the years. I don't use a couch, nor do I do party tricks. I am a firm believer in hypnotherapy."

"I'm certain Evan didn't mean anything derogative. We're both nervous."

"You have every right to be. Let's see what we can do to put you both more at ease."

Evan watched Jaycee position herself in the recliner as he settled into an overstuffed chair on the other side of the room. Vowing to keep unobtrusively out of the way, he listened to both the soothing tape, which played in the background, and Dr. Tess' reassuring voice. It amazed him how receptive Jaycee was, how easily Dr. Tess put her under. "Is she asleep?" he asked.

"Completely. Now it's time for the work to begin. How far do you want to go back?"

"To the time of the dig outside of town."

"I thought as much, but I wanted to be sure. Amanda told me what's been going on. Since she is having these experiences, this life will be close to the surface and ready to be revealed."

Dr. Tess turned on the recorder. "Can you tell me where you are?" Dr. Tess said, after coaxing Jaycee's subconscious to go back into time.

"I am at the stream," Jaycee said, in a voice Evan didn't recognize. "I am getting water."

"Who are you?"

"My name is Noya."

"How old are you?"

"I do not understand your question."

"Are you a child?"

"No. I became a woman early in the season of warmth. If my family were alive, I would be married by now."

"How long have you lived?"

"Dostra says it has been twelve turnings of the seasons. She is very

73

powerful. She knows of these things."

"Who is Dostra?"

"She is my mistress, the high priestess. I am her slave. Sayo says it is not right. If he had been able to save me, he would have done it, but he had no power then."

"Who is Sayo?"

"He is her son, the high priest."

"How did you become a slave?"

"When my parents sinned and became very sick, I was but a small child. After their deaths, the council gave me to Dostra, since I had no one to care for me. She took me into her household to work with The Old One."

"The Old One?"

"She is also a slave. Her husband was killed while hunting, many turnings of the seasons ago. If she had not agreed to enslavement, the council would have killed her. No woman can exist without a man to provide for her."

"Is Dostra a good mistress?"

Evan noticed a catch in Jaycee's voice and saw tears in her eyes. "She beats us, especially The Old One. She uses a willow switch cut from the stand of trees by the stream."

"Does Sayo beat you?"

Jaycee began to smile. "No. Sayo never even beat The Old One when he lived in Dostra's dwelling. He no longer is there, for he lives in the sanctuary. He loves me. During this journey of the sun, I will tell him I carry his child. Even though it will mean he must give up his priesthood, I know he will insist we live together as man and wife. He will not allow Dostra to send me to the house of pleasures."

"The house of pleasures? What is that?"

"It is a dwelling, set apart from the others, where the men go when their wives are either carrying a child or are confined to the house of the women. They can couple with the women who have been sent to live there for that purpose."

"She's talking about a whore house," Evan gasped. "Why would anyone send a twelve-year-old child to a whore house?"

"You must remember she was not a child, but a woman. As an archaeologist, you must know about these practices."

"I do. I just don't always understand them. Ask her about the writings."

"Can you tell us about the writings, Noya?"

"It is forbidden. No one must know about them."

"Someone knows. They told you."

"Sayo told me, but he warned me the knowledge must remain secret."

"Why?"

"Because it is against the laws of the people. They would kill both Sayo and me if they learn of them."

"The people are not here. No one will harm you. Please tell me about the writings."

"They are secret. Sayo keeps them hidden. The man god, who is his father, taught Sayo the new language, but the people have decreed any such thing to be taboo. There must be no written record. The storytellers must tell all such things. Sayo disagrees. He is the only one who can read them."

"Did Sayo tell you where they are or what they say?"

"He has told me many things regarding them, but I do not want to know where he keeps them. If anyone were to find out about their existence, his life, as well as his immortality, would be in danger." Jaycee paused; a sob caught in her throat.

"What is the next thing you remember, Noya?" Dr. Tess asked.

"Sayo does not believe me about the child. I have run away from him, but Tarros brought me back. Dostra has told me I will be sacrificed for the feast of the harvest. It is more than I can stand. I don't know how anyone can be so cruel. My life does not matter, but my child will never have a chance to live. I am at the sanctuary. Dostra and Sayo are arguing about her choice for the sacrifice. He says he will not do it. They are fighting and now he is lying motionless on the floor. I fear she has killed him. She has removed my mantle and now is preparing me for the sacrifice. My heart will be cut from my body. I will no longer exist. I can only pray I will be rewarded by a better life in my next reincarnation. I am going to die."

"I need to bring her out of the trance," Dr. Tess said to Evan. "She's seeing the end of Noya's life. To go further might do more harm than good."

Evan nodded, still reeling from what he just heard. "I'm glad you taped this. She'd never believe it otherwise."

"Most people don't. I'm going to bring her out of it very slowly. She'll be exhausted. I recommend you take her home and insist she rest."

"I will. How much do we owe you?"

"I usually charge a very high fee for this, but in light of what we've uncovered today, call it a donation. I've been meaning to contribute ever since Amanda told me about the state funding being taken away."

"Thank you," Evan said, surprised by Dr. Tess' generous offer.

"I'd like to regress her again."

"Why? We've uncovered what we want to know."

"You amaze me. We've only scratched the surface. She is a well of information and we've only taken a small taste of what she has to tell us."

"How much more can there be? She was only twelve, hardly more than a child."

"As I said before, in a society, such as this, they considered her a woman. She's already told us she was pregnant when she died. She should have been married, not sacrificed."

Evan knew Dr. Tess made sense. The knowledge Jaycee possessed was worth more than all the research he'd done over the past five years. He watched as Dr. Tess slowly brought Jaycee back through the centuries, to the present.

"Did anything happen?" she asked, as soon as she opened her eyes.

"Yes," Dr, Tess replied. "We have it on tape. Did your voice give you a name?"

Jaycee shook her head no. "All he said was no matter what I remembered, he loved me and wouldn't hurt me again. He said when the time was right, he would tell me where to find the writings."

"Why didn't you tell me this before?" Evan questioned.

"The voice frightened me so much, I hesitated to say anything. Considering we were planning to come here, I wanted to see what we found out first."

"Perhaps it's best you didn't say too much," Dr. Tess said.

"I want you to rest before you listen to the tape. I can tell you your name was Noya and you were a slave. In the end, your mistress, Dostra, the high priestess, ordered your sacrifice."

Jaycee began to shake. "Oh, Evan, the bowl, the blood in the bowl was mine…hers. No wonder it affected me so adversely."

"I told Dr. Clark; I want to regress you again."

Evan could see the concern in Jaycee's eyes. "What do you think, Evan?"

"I agree with Dr. Tess. You will too, once you hear the tape."

"I don't think your visions will be quite so frightening once you understand Noya better," Dr. Tess continued. "My receptionist will set another appointment for you in a week."

~ * ~

Jaycee seated herself on the passenger's side of the Jeep, the tape clutched in her hand. *Do I want to know what this says? Do I want to learn about Noya?"*

"A penny for your thoughts," Evan said.

"I'm sure you know them. I'm worried about what I might hear."

"Don't be. It will answer a lot of questions.

"If that's so, why can't I listen to it now?"

"For one thing, I don't have a tape deck in here. For another, Dr. Tess wants you to rest first. It's always wise to follow the orders of your doctor."

"Rest," Jaycee echoed. "I don't want to rest. I want to go back out to the site and see if I have any more contact with Sayo."

"Not today. Not until it comes up in your rotation. Tomorrow you'll be going back to the sorting shed."

"Why?"

"No special treatment, remember. I saw how it affected you today. I don't want you to go out there until you're stronger."

"You're talking nonsense."

"Am I?"

Jaycee didn't answer. Was Evan concerned about her well-being or worried about what she might see? She knew there would be no answers until she heard the tape.

"Where are we going?" she asked, when Evan turned down a street she didn't recognize.

"To my apartment."

"Your apartment? Why not the dorm?"

"Because Dr. Tess wants you to rest. At the dorm, no one would insist you do it."

"Don't be ridiculous, Evan."

"Are you contradicting your boss? No wonder Henry comes down on you so hard."

Jaycee sobered at the mention of Henry's name. "I'm not contradicting you, but..."

"...but nothing. I told you earlier, I'm not Henry. You can't blow me off. I expect you to do what I say."

Jaycee didn't argue. She planned to make notes on the day's happenings when she returned to the dorm. Unfortunately, going against Evan would do her no good. She wanted him to see her as a woman rather than a willful child. "Even though I'm not tired?" she finally asked.

"You're tired. You just don't know it."

"Since when do you know my body better than I do?"

"Since I listened to you in Dr. Tess's office."

"I guess I don't have any choice but to do as you say. I could rest at the dorm, though."

"Look Jaycee, it's not like I don't trust you, but I don't trust you," Evan said, a teasing tone to his voice.

"Men," she said, pretending to pout.

She enjoyed his concern. It seemed like forever since someone worried about her. She immediately chided herself. *Ellie cares, but it isn't the same.*

Jaycee remembered Stan Jackson. He swept her off her feet during her junior year at Havelin. After several nights together, she believed his words of love. When he graduated and left the campus, his letters went from two a week to one a month, until she heard he was planning to marry someone else at Christmastime.

Devastated, she threw herself into her studies, living at home and shunning a social life. Caring for her mother, combined with her work at Havelin, occupied her mind and kept her from sharing her life with another person.

~ * ~

Evan unlocked the door to his apartment. Inside, the window air conditioner hummed. Leaving her standing at the threshold to his apartment, he hurried across the room to turn it off. "It's freezing in here. Let me open some windows and warm things up."

"It's still raining. Do you think it's a smart move?"

Evan smiled at her question. "The windows I plan to open, crank out. It rarely rains in. The bedroom is at the end of the hall. You can go back and lie down, while I get things squared away here."

This is dangerous. Do you think it's wise to put Jaycee in your bed, even if it is just for a nap?

"It's not what I expected," Jaycee's voice broke into his thoughts.

He turned to see her leaning against the door jam. "So, what did you expect?"

"Oh, I don't know. Maybe a waterbed, satin sheets, mirrors on the ceiling. You know, a real bachelor pad."

"Something like that doesn't fit me. What about you? I didn't get to see your bedroom at Havelin. When you're at home, do you have a waterbed with satin sheets and mirrors on the ceiling?"

"No, just a single with a bad mattress. At least you have a king and from what I can tell the mattress isn't bad either."

Evan smiled at her comment. *If she has no need for anything larger than a single bed, she must not have a man in her life.*

"Make yourself comfortable and I'll see what I can rustle up for supper."

"You don't have to feed me."

"I do, if I want to keep you healthy."

Jaycee shrugged her shoulders. "When am I going back to the site?"

"I told you. Not for six weeks."

"I thought you were joking. How can you keep me away for six weeks?"

"No special treatment, remember?"

"Yes, I remember. I should, you've reminded me of it twice in the past hour."

"Good. Now you go and lie down. I'll be back to check on you after I finish up a few things in the other room."

Evan turned from the bedroom when the phone rang. "Dr. Clark?" the caller greeted him. "This is Joe Campion, of the Gazette. We got a lead. Something about one of your volunteers having visions. Would you care to comment? Can you confirm it?"

"What are you getting at?"

"I want to know if this is a publicity stunt. It's common knowledge you lost your state funding. Some of the staff, down here at the paper, has questioned the validity of such a rumor."

"It's not a publicity stunt. Now why don't you leave me alone? I don't want to comment about anything."

"You sound a bit too defensive, Doc. Maybe I should come out there and start asking questions. I'm sure someone will be willing to talk to me about this."

"Look, Campion, I'm only going to tell you this once. You step one foot on Round Tree and I'll kick your ass off. When the time is right, I'll make a statement, and not before."

"Whatever you say."

The man's tone irritated Evan. "I'll hold you personally responsible. If I see one word in that rag of yours or the tabloids, you'll have a lawsuit on your hands. When and if this becomes something that the public should know about, I'll call you, unless, of course, it leaks out first. If that happens, I'll see you in court."

"Fair enough, Doc. By the way, that was one cute little volunteer you took to dinner last night."

"How did you know?"

"My wife and I went to Montanelli's for dinner. I saw the two of you together. She's a real looker. I never pegged you for someone who went for college students, though."

"She's not a student, just a volunteer," Evan said, wondering why he felt compelled to defend himself to this man.

"You could have fooled me. I'll be looking forward to hearing from you. If I don't hear from you in the next two weeks, I'll call you back."

Evan hung up the phone and silently cursed whoever leaked the information about Jaycee to the press. Before going back to the bedroom, he took two chicken breasts from the freezer.

He stopped at the bedroom door and smiled to see Jaycee sleeping peacefully. For the first time since they met, he realized she looked completely relaxed. He knew the past two days were tiring for her and wondered if the past months at Havelin were equally exhausting.

No sense in playing guessing games, he told himself, as he went back to the living room to go through the mail he took from the box when they came in. The first letter in the stack was from the state.

> Dear Dr. Clark:
>   We have received your request for a grant for the coming year to fund Round Tree Dig. We are taking the matter under consideration.

Evan crumpled the paper. They were taking it under consideration, whatever the hell that meant. He didn't want their damn consideration, just their support. If this business with Jaycee proved correct, the state would be falling all over itself to give him what they needed.

Evan pushed back the recliner and closed his eyes. Sleep overtook him almost immediately.

The image of a young, brown skinned girl, her breasts exposed, a modesty apron tied around her waist, entered his dreams. She turned and Evan could see the scars from old beatings laced across her back. When she again turned around, she became Jaycee. Her perfect white breasts made him stare uncontrollably. Behind her appeared Henry Bennett, a willow switch in his hand, obscenities spilling from his lips.

A light rap at the door shattered the image from his subconscious. His body ached from sleeping in an unnatural position, his mind spun from the memory of the dream.

"Hi, Dad," Brandon said, when Evan opened the door. "How's Jaycee?"

"She's exhausted. The regression took a lot out of her. She's sleeping."

"I figured she'd be here. I ran into Amanda, and she told me you were taking Jaycee to Dr. Tess' office. Surprisingly, I missed her today."

"You won't be missing her for long. She'll be back at the sorting shed tomorrow morning."

Brandon seated himself on the couch. "Do you mean to tell me she's not going out to the site with you?"

"I thought you talked to Amanda. Didn't she tell you what happened out there this morning?"

"Of course, she did. I figured the way she reacted; you'd want her out there with you."

Evan swallowed hard. Of course, he wanted Jaycee with him, but he couldn't risk upsetting her further. He saw how she reacted to Sayo's voice, how she collapsed. He didn't want to see it happen again.

"I told her she won't be back out there for six weeks, when it comes up in her rotation. Going out there too soon could destroy her. It might be different if she saw something but she only heard the voice. I think it's best if she returns to the sorting shed."

"So, you believe in her visions."

"I didn't until Dr. Tess regressed her today."

"You still can't convince me the two of you believe in that reincarnation crap."

Evan smiled at hearing Brandon echo his sentiments of less than six hours earlier. "I don't know what I believe anymore. After hearing Jaycee talking about her past life, it's hard to remain skeptical."

"What do you mean?"

Evan paused for a moment, before he put into words all he'd learned during Jaycee's regression.

"Now I know you've lost it," Brandon said, when Evan finished his narrative. "How can you believe in this stuff?"

"I don't think she could make it up. We'll know more when and if we find the writings she keeps talking about."

"You told me, there are no writings."

"I know, but I'm beginning to believe I'm wrong. Just because we haven't found them doesn't mean they don't exist. It could take years, especially with our funding gone. We may run out of time."

~ * ~

Jaycee fought her way back from sleep to full awareness. It took several seconds for her to remember where she fell asleep. From the fringes of her mind, she heard voices coming from the other room.

Swinging her legs over the side of the bed, she looked at her reflection in the mirror over the bureau. Strangely, she didn't look any different than she did hours earlier.

"I thought I heard voices out here," she said, coming into the living room seeing Evan and Brandon engaged in conversation.

Evan got to his feet and put his arm around her shoulder. "Well, if it isn't Sleeping Beauty. I thought you weren't tired."

"Guess I was wrong. How long did I sleep?"

"About three hours," Evan replied, before turning to Brandon. "I was just getting ready to fix dinner. Would you care to join us?"

"Not tonight. You see I met this great girl at lunch. She's working over in Amanda's area."

Evan began to laugh. "This sounds like the same story you told me yesterday, about Jaycee."

"Come on, Dad," Brandon began, evidently embarrassed. "This time it's real. We're going out tonight. Montanelli's worked for you, I thought it might work for me as well. I came over to borrow some money."

Jaycee watched as Evan reached for his wallet. "Sure. How much do you need?"

"Enough for a good meal and a bottle of the house wine."

Evan pulled three twenties from his wallet and handed them to Brandon.

"How about you, Jaycee?" Evan asked, once Brandon left. "Are you ready for dinner?"

"Sounds like a good idea to me. Is there anything I can do to help?"

"How are you with baked potatoes a la microwave and tossing a couple of salads?"

"I think I can handle that much. I'm not much of a cook, but I do great things with potatoes and a microwave."

Once Evan picked up the chicken and went out to the patio to start the grill, Jaycee began to open cupboards in search of potatoes, onions, cooking utensils and a casserole dish. Finding a package of bacon in the refrigerator, she began to prepare a potato casserole. With it in the microwave she made the salads, then set the table.

"Something sure smells good," Evan commented, when he put Jaycee's chicken on her plate.

"It's the one thing my mother would eat. She usually complained loud and long about the quality of my cooking."

"You told us about your mother's illness. Why didn't you hire some help?"

"I foolishly didn't look into her assets. It took her Social Security, along with most of my salary to pay the bills and keep her in an Alzheimer's day care program. There just wasn't enough left to hire someone to cook and clean."

Unbidden tears sprung to her eyes and rolled down her cheeks before she could stop them.

"I'm sorry. I'm afraid I've dredged up some rather painful memories."

"It's all right. As time goes on, I know I'll be able to handle this better. We were almost constant companions for more years than I care to count. Without her, there's a very deep void in my life."

After dinner, Jaycee began to clear the table. As she did, Evan put his hand on top of hers. "Leave it, I think it's time you listened to the tape."

"Let's get this done first. I don't know if I'll feel much like cleaning up once I've heard it."

She knew she was stalling, putting off the inevitable.

Evan got up from the table and helped her rinse the dishes before putting them into the dishwasher. "What excuse are you going to use now?"

"None. I honestly do want to hear the tape. I'm just a bit apprehensive is all."

Evan indicated she should seat herself on the couch while he put the cassette in the tape deck. Dr. Tess' voice began, as Evan seated himself beside Jaycee. She hardly realized he put his arm around her shoulder, as she listened to the strange voice of Noya.

By the time the tape finished, Jaycee couldn't control the tears cascading down her cheeks. "How could a society enslave widows and children?"

"Who else would care for them? Remember it wasn't like today. Without a man to provide for them they would have died. At least as slaves, they were fed and given a place to live."

Jaycee nodded, trying to see things from Evan's point of view. "It does explain the visions. The old woman is The Old One, the young girl is Noya and the blood in the bowl was her final sacrifice. I have to believe the voice belongs to Sayo."

Evan pulled Jaycee into his arms. His tender kisses silenced her fears and took her mind to more pleasurable pursuits. She hardly realized he laid her back on the couch, until he unbuttoned her blouse and undid the front closure of her bra.

A small voice, in the back of her mind, cautioned her about giving herself to a virtual stranger. The pleasure of his touch on her breasts, his fingers manipulating her nipple, combined with his probing kisses pushed the voice aside.

He continued to knead her breast with one hand while the other slipped to her shorts. Once the button and zipper were undone, he moved to the soft tuft of hair hidden by her panties.

Before he pulled them aside, the phone rang, breaking the magic of the moment. They tried to ignore it, but the original passion could not be regained.

"Hello." Evan greeted the caller, leaving Jaycee to compose herself and straighten her clothing.

She hurried into the bathroom to splash cold water on her face.

"Who are you?" She asked the reflection in the mirror. "How could you so easily allow yourself to get carried away?"

"That was Bob. He and Amanda are coming over."

Jaycee turned to see him standing next to her. "In that case, I should go back to the dorm," she said, unable to keep the disappointment from her voice.

"They're coming to see you and hear the tape. I don't want you to go just yet."

"I don't suppose you do," she replied, surprised by her reaction to his exploring hands.

"We didn't do anything wrong, Jaycee. We aren't teenagers, we're consenting adults, for god's sake."

"What would have happened if the phone hadn't rung?"

"We would have made love."

"How can you be so casual? You don't even know me. Is this how it is every summer?"

"Hardly. It's been a long time since I've wanted a woman the way I want you. It hasn't happened since my ex-wife left."

"Are you asking me to believe with all the young women at the dig, you haven't, well you know, since your divorce?"

"Believe what you want, but I haven't. There hasn't been anyone I've wanted to make love with until now."

"What are you trying to tell me, Evan? Do you love me?"

"I don't know. I guess I'm telling you I want to make love with you. What about you? You certainly weren't very hesitant. You didn't say no."

"It's been a long time. I got carried away by the sensation."

"What do you mean a long time?"

"My one and only love affair happened in my junior year of college. I allowed someone to get very close to me. I let him make me feel loved. When he left, I got hurt. I can't allow it to happen again."

"What about your feelings for me?" Evan asked.

Jaycee felt her heart threaten to take precedence over her mind. "You're not playing fair."

For the first time since the beginning of the exchange, Evan took a step toward Jaycee. "Why?" he questioned, when he put his hand on her arm.

"Whether you know it or not, I've kept you on a high pedestal for longer than I care to admit. You're doing what I've always wanted to do. I've been a supporter of this dig, verbally if not financially, since it began. What you're doing is a worthwhile project."

"Is that the reason you don't want me to make love to you?" Evan accused.

"That's where you're wrong. I want it more than anything else in the world. I just don't want to be a notch on your belt or a conquest. It has to be right."

The ringing of the doorbell stopped any further discussion. Evan stared into her eyes for a moment before going to answer it.

Alone in the bathroom, Jaycee finger combed her hair and tried to calm the emotions churning within her. Taking a deep breath, she went back into the living room. Amanda immediately embraced her.

"I talked to Sharon. She told me she couldn't disclose anything you said under hypnosis."

"Do you want to hear the tape?" Jaycee asked.

"Only if it won't upset you."

"I've heard it and cried over it. I should be all right hearing it again."

"What do you mean you've cried over it?" Bob inquired.

"You'll understand, once you hear it."

She noticed the look Evan flashed her.

"Did we interrupt something?"

"No, we'd just finished listening to the tape when you called," Evan lied, as the tape rewound.

She watched the expression on Bob and Amanda's faces. As Jaycee predicted, Amanda cried, while Bob shook his head.

"This is so bizarre. I don't know what else to call it."

Jaycee managed a weak smile. "Call it what I do, Bob, unbelievable. I wonder whose voice is on that tape. If it's mine, how much did you and Evan pay Dr. Tess to get me to say those things?"

The look on Evan's face was one of shock. "I was there, Jaycee. No one paid Dr. Tess anything. What you hear is exactly what you said."

Amanda nodded in agreement. "Evan's right, Sharon told me she never encountered a more receptive subject. Noya must be very close to the surface for you right now."

"I know. She wants to regress me again. I'm frightened about doing it again. I agreed to it before I heard the tape, so I guess I can't back out now."

Bob turned to look at Evan. "How do you feel about this, Evan? You were off the wall over it earlier."

"I'm excited. Jaycee is giving us insights we never thought possible. Now all we have to do is find the writings. If we can believe Sayo..."

"Sayo?" Bob interrupted. "What does he have to do with anything?"

"I'm convinced his is the voice Jaycee has been hearing. As I said, if we can believe him, he'll show Jaycee where the writings are. This could be the biggest breakthrough the project has encountered."

Jaycee ceased listening. The only thing she meant to Evan was his damn breakthrough. He only wanted to make love to her because of Sayo's voice and her connection to Noya. She shouldn't have fooled herself. Evan Clark didn't love her. He loved the dig. It represented his wife, family and lover. Even his own kids admitted he wasn't very nice. She could only come to the same conclusion about his feelings for her. His attentions were because of what she could do for him. They had nothing to do with her as a woman, only what she could bring to the love of his life.

"Morning comes pretty early," Bob reminded them. "Amanda and I better get going."

"You wouldn't be heading toward the dorm, would you?" Jaycee inquired.

"Do you need a lift?"

"I'll take Jaycee home," Evan said.

His tone surprised Jaycee. It sounded as though he was angry with her for asking Bob and Amanda for a ride.

"There's no sense in you going out. Since Bob and Amanda don't mind, I'd just as soon ride with them."

She didn't miss the look of disappointment in Evan's eyes.

"Are you sure you don't want me to take you home?" he asked, as he reached out to touch her hand.

She pulled away, as though burned by a hot poker. "I'm positive."

"In that case, I'll see you tomorrow."

"Maybe."

"I will see you tomorrow."

More than anything else, she wanted to believe Evan, but she couldn't. "It depends on how things go."

The touch of his hand reminded her of the feelings he generated in her earlier. "Thank you for going with me today. I'm sure it won't be necessary next week. I know where the office is and like we said earlier, I'm not a teenager. I'm a big girl now."

Jaycee turned and hurried out to where Bob was parked.

"We did interrupt something, didn't we?" Amanda asked, when they got in the truck.

"Not really."

"Don't give us that," Bob began. "I saw the look on Evan's face when you asked us to take you home. Were you two...?"

"Let's put it this way," Jaycee interrupted. "I was foolish enough to think I could compete with Round Tree. He caught me in a weak moment. It won't happen again."

"Well, it should. Evan needs someone like you."

"Evan has everything he needs all wrapped up in Round tree. He needs it to prosper. As for me, it's been a very long and tiring day. I need to get home and go to bed."

"What about Noya?" Amanda asked.

"Noya has been dead for hundreds of years, so has her child and her lover. She'll wait a few more days to be uncovered."

At the dorm, Jaycee thanked Bob and Amanda then hurried to her room. As she did, she remembered the tape she left in Evan's tape deck. She should have taken it, but she realized she didn't want it. Like Evan, it belonged to Round Tree.

"How is everything going?" Sandy asked, when Jaycee entered the room.

"Fine," Jaycee replied, unenthusiastically.

"Did you and Dad, well, you know?"

"Your father and I are good friends," Jaycee said, wishing she could confirm Sandy's suspicions, yet ashamed at what almost happened.

She wanted Evan to imprison her in his arms and impale himself within her, to make love to her forever. Now she realized it would never happen. Evan would never completely give himself to her and she could accept him on no other terms.

~ * ~

Evan watched Jaycee get into the cab of Bob's truck. He continued to stare after her until they turned the corner and disappeared from his sight. If only Bob hadn't called, they would have made love.

Forty-eight hours ago, Evan would have laughed at the thought of himself and Jaycee in any kind of a relationship, to say nothing of love. Now, he realized how much he wanted her. He couldn't get the picture of her out of his mind. What made her eyes, her expression and her tone turn so cold? Why didn't she want him to take her home? He gave Jaycee enough time to get back to the dorm, then called her room.

"It's your nickel, have at it," Sandy greeted him.

Her flip answer annoyed Evan. "Sandy, it's Dad. Is Jaycee there?"

"What happened tonight?" Sandy countered, without answering his question.

"Nothing. Why?"

"For some reason I don't believe you. I think something did happen. Jaycee's very upset. She's been in the bathroom ever since she got home. I'll tell her you're on the line, but I won't make any promises about her talking to you."

Evan heard Sandy call to Jaycee, but he couldn't hear her reply.

"Sorry, Jaycee is in the tub. She said she doesn't want to talk to you. For god's sake, Dad, what did you do to her?"

"I didn't *do* anything."

"You must have. So, help me, if you pulled one of your moods on her..."

"One of my moods. What are you talking about?"

"Come on, I know you well enough after last summer. I know how you get when the program first starts and you're faced with people you don't know. You were in one of those moods yesterday. I saw a little of it this morning. Jaycee deserves better."

"My moods have nothing to do with it."

"Think about it, Dad. Jaycee is a real sweetheart. She isn't like some of the airheads you get out here. She knows what she's talking about. I think the two of you would make the perfect pair."

"Funny, so do I."

"Really? I mean, you aren't just saying that. Brandon and I would like nothing better than for you to find someone. You always seem to be such a loner. "

"Guess I am, but I hope to change my image."

"Good, but you're the one who has to convince her. No matter what I say, she'll come to her own conclusions. Think about it. I'll see you in the morning."

Evan hung up the phone. Sandy made sense. He and Jaycee did make a perfect pair, but he didn't know where to go from here. The kids talked about his moods, but what about Jaycee's. He'd seen them change so drastically tonight, yet he had no idea what triggered it. If he did, he might be able to counteract whatever it was he did wrong. Without knowing, he remained in the dark.

Chapter Seven

The night seemed to last forever. At five, Jaycee finally got out of bed, unable to stand being there any longer. Instead of going down to the dining hall, she drove into town. She found a small cafe open for breakfast and drank three cups of strong coffee while reading a morning paper. Unable to force herself to eat anything, she remembered Evan's insistence she eat a large breakfast.

Just who the hell does he think he is, anyway? I know my body, as well as my needs. He had no right to force feed me the way he did.

Once back at the sorting shed, she threw herself into her work. The hours rolled by, very slowly, as she struggled with the piece in front of her.

"How's it going?" Brandon asked, diverting her attention from the broken pottery.

"Very slowly. Your dad said it would happen. I got something that didn't fall into place."

She picked up the next fragment and decided Noya must have had no connection with it.

"Any visions?" Brandon pressed.

Jaycee shook her head. "Maybe my ancient friend didn't use it."

"Are you disappointed?"

"I think the word is relieved."

"I shouldn't have asked the question. Dad's afraid the wrong people might get wind of it and leak something to the press."

"When did he tell you such a thing?"

"This morning, at breakfast."

"It's funny, I would think he'd want the press to know about it."

"Why?"

"Isn't it obvious? He needs state funding. My visions, even the regression would help him, give him the ammunition he needs to get it.

I'm convinced it's the reason he's been so attentive."

"Now I know you're wrong. Dad likes you because you're you. He wants to protect not only you, but Round Tree as well."

"I'd like to believe you, but I don't. You're young. You'll understand when you get older. When someone loves something as passionately as your dad loves Round Tree, personal feelings don't mean much."

"Now you're being ridiculous, Jaycee. Dad does like you. I can tell."

Jaycee couldn't stop the lump which formed in her throat. She couldn't explain Evan's love for Round Tree to his son. "I know what Evan wants and it's not me."

"What do you plan to do now?"

"I'll keep working. He doesn't want me on the site for six weeks. I can continue doing my job here. I'll handle my rotation with Evan when the time comes."

The bell rang before Brandon could say more. Jaycee put down the piece she held in her hand and started for the sink.

Her mind engaged itself in a tug of war. She wanted to get closer to Evan, but after the fiasco in college, she could see the warning signs. She did a much better job at being a dedicated professional than she did a lovesick woman.

"That's a beautiful platter you've been working on," Brandon said, as though trying to change the subject.

"Yes, it is. I can almost see it filled with fruits and vegetables."

"I thought you weren't having any more visions."

"I'm not. I'm certain I silenced them yesterday with the regression."

"Well, if that's the case, let's put the subject to rest. It's time for lunch. I'm starved. If we don't get down to the dining hall, we might not get anything to eat."

"You go on ahead. I need to run into town and do some errands."

She watched him walk away from her, before going to get into her car. By going into town, she could avoid seeing Evan. For today it would work, but what would happen tomorrow?

~ * ~

93

Evan left the site early for lunch. He could see no reason to stay out there until noon, since he hadn't been able to concentrate all morning. The day started early. At five he went down to the dining hall to wait for Jaycee to arrive for breakfast. By eight she hadn't come in and he knew he needed to get to work. By going to lunch early, Evan hoped he would get to talk to her. He needed to see her and find out what he did to so upset her.

He pushed aside his plate with its half-eaten sandwich and took another drink of coffee. He stopped counting how many cups of coffee he consumed since five this morning. Across the room he saw Brandon.

"Isn't Jaycee with you?" Evan asked when Brandon stopped at his table.

"Should she be?"

"Of course, she should. It's lunch time."

"She said she had errands she needed to run in town. There's no law about her eating here. What went on after I left you two last night?"

"Nothing to concern you," Evan replied, unable to keep the irritation from his voice.

"Fine, I was just wondering. Jaycee is very different this morning."

"What do you mean, different."

"She's very quiet and seems to be struggling with the piece she's working on."

"Has she had any more visions?" Evan questioned, hungry for information regarding Jaycee.

"She says no. The closest thing to a vision was when she said she could see the platter she's working on laden with fruits and vegetables."

Evan didn't want to seem overly interested in Jaycee's activities. "How about you? How's your pitcher coming?"

"I should have changed projects with Jaycee. She would have had it finished by now."

"I waited for her at breakfast, but she never came in," Evan said, unable to stay away from the subject of Jaycee.

"She drove over to the sorting shed. Maybe she ate in town."

"If she ate at all. I talked to your sister this morning. She said Jaycee was up and gone when she got out of bed. Did she say anything about not coming back this afternoon?"

"No. She said she'd see me after lunch."

"Good. I think I'll pay a visit to the sorting shed."

"Really? Don't you mean you're coming to see Jaycee? What did you do to her?"

"Why does everyone keep saying that? You, Bob, even your sister has brought up the subject. I didn't do anything to her."

"It must be something. You usually don't get this upset about nothing."

"What's coming next? Are you planning to tell me it's because of one of my moods? Well, if you are, don't. Your sister laid that trip on me last night after Jaycee got home. Let's just set the record straight. *I don't have moods.*"

"Since when? Face it, Dad, you do. Everyone knows about them. I'm sure Jaycee knows it by now as well. You'd better watch your step. You could lose her."

"You can't lose what you don't have."

He couldn't remember feeling so dejected about another person since Kathryn left.

Brandon shook his head and started toward the buffet table. Evan downed the last of his coffee, before dumping his uneaten lunch in the garbage. He needed to go for a walk and clear his head.

On his way to the sorting shed, Evan replayed the events of last night in his head. Everything was fine right up until Bob called. Without warning she turned into an iceberg.

After talking to Sandy last night, he called Bob. Evan couldn't get Bob's words out of his mind. "Jaycee says she can't compete with Round Tree."

What's there to compete with? Round Tree is a thing and Jaycee Grant is a person, a very important person. Why can't she see there is no competition?

At the sorting shed, Evan stopped at the workstation he knew to be Jaycee's. He ran his hand over the platter. It would take only a few more pieces to be finished.

"Is something wrong, Evan?" Chris asked, from behind him.

"Just checking things out."

"You usually don't check things out. What's bugging you?"

"Do you know where Jaycee is?"

"She said she wanted to go into town. Why do you ask?"

"No particular reason. I'll wait for her. Shouldn't you be eating lunch?"

"I already did. I like to go down early. I guess you didn't see me. As long as you're here, I want to talk to you about Jaycee."

"What about her?" Evan realized his voice sounded a little too defensive.

"There's a lot of talk going on. It all revolves around her having visions, hearing voices, and being involved with you. What's the real story?"

Evan sighed deeply. "I can vouch for the visions and the voice. As for my involvement, that's another story."

"What do you mean another story?"

"She's avoiding me like I have the plague. I need to find out why, along with the reason she didn't come to the dining hall for either breakfast or lunch."

"There's another question I want answered. Who is she? She's definitely not a college student or a frustrated housewife. If she were, you wouldn't be taking such an interest in her."

"She's a professor of Anthropology."

"I should have guessed. Professor J. C. Grant. I read a paper in one of the journals by her a few years back. I never put two and two together, never thought it might be written by a woman."

"You weren't supposed to know about her job. She just wants to be one of the volunteers."

"Only she's not. I know it and so do you. Where does that put us now?"

"Good question. She hasn't been on a dig for a long time. When I spoke at Havelin I was looking for all the help I could get, both financial and physical. Jaycee offered both, a large donation and her help this summer. The donation came with no strings attached, but the offer of help did. It's getting harder and harder to keep her secret."

"You know I won't say anything. Does Brandon know?"

Evan nodded. "Sandy, too. Brandon thought she should, considering she's rooming with Jaycee. It's an impossible situation."

"What do you mean?"

"You hit the nail on the head when you asked if we were involved. Only I'm beginning to think it's pretty one sided."

"Which side?"

"Can't you guess? It's mine. She backed off last night like a scared rabbit. I can't even get her to talk to me."

~ * ~

Jaycee waited in line at the drive through window for the burger, fries and iced tea she ordered. The air conditioner spit out cold air as the engine idled. A flash of red caught her eye when the HOT light came on. She tried to remember what her dad told her about things like this. She quickly turned off the air conditioner and shoved the lever over to heat. The sweltering hot air forced her to roll her window down until the light went off.

Coming into town was foolish. I could have picked up a strapless bra anytime, even tonight. The mall is open until nine.

The car ahead of her moved and Jaycee pulled up to the window. She handed the gum snapping high school girl her money, then took the bag of food from her. After pulling out of the parking lot, Jaycee unwrapped the burger and took a bite. The taste of it made her stomach churn, even the greasy fries didn't set well. Throwing both back in the bag, she picked up the iced tea and pulled out into traffic.

Being careful about her speed, she drove back to the dig, acutely aware of the time registered on the dashboard clock. She parked across from the sorting shed at twelve fifty, with ten minutes to spare.

As she entered the building, she noticed Evan engaged in conversation with Chris. There would be no way to avoid him any longer.

Walking toward them she could not help but hear their conversation. "She's a good worker, Evan, I'll certainly hate to lose her when the first three weeks are up."

"If I wanted to, I could pull her right now and take her out to the site with me. I realize it would be selfish. She needs to work the rotation, like everyone else," Evan replied.

"Are you saying I do get to keep her for the next three weeks? I can't say I'm disappointed."

"You get to keep who for the next three weeks?" Jaycee asked, making her presence known.

"You," Chris answered when they turned to face her.

Jaycee didn't miss either the smile on Chris' lips or the look of annoyance in Evan's eyes.

"Where have you been?" Evan demanded.

"I needed to go into town."

"So, you skipped lunch."

Jaycee thought of the bag containing the burger and fries she dropped in the dumpster on her way to the sorting shed. "I grabbed something on the way back."

"Something?" Evan said, turning the word into a question.

"I picked up a burger and fries," *which I didn't eat.* "Does it meet with your approval?"

"What about breakfast?"

Jaycee swallowed hard. She certainly didn't want to lie. On the other hand, she couldn't tell him she only drank coffee and didn't eat anything. "I went into town and stopped at the cafe."

"Why? So you could avoid me?"

Jaycee didn't answer.

"We need to talk," Evan said, taking her by the arm and moving away from Chris.

"I'm sorry Evan. I have work to do."

"I'm your boss and I say we will talk this out."

"That's funny, I thought I just heard you say Chris is my boss for the next three weeks. It's better this way."

"What way, you here and me wondering what's going on? Come out to dinner with me tonight."

"I have plans."

"What kind of plans?"

"I don't know yet, but I'll make some," she retorted, surprised at how tart the words sounded.

"Why are you shutting me out? What did I do?"

"Look, I'm only a means to an end for you. Maybe it's time we went to the press with all of this."

"This?"

"You know, the visions, Sayo, the regression. Better yet, maybe we ought to contact the state, skip the middle man altogether."

"Maybe I ought to take you over my knee and paddle some sense into you. What do you think you'd accomplish leaking any of this to people on the outside?"

"I'd be able to give you what you want, what you need. There would be no need for you to feel you had to cater to me."

"How do you know what I want or need? Right now, the only thing I want is for you to have dinner with me tonight."

"What about the dig?"

"What about it?"

"You need to get your funding back."

"If I get it, I get it. If I don't, I can go back on the road this winter. They say it gets easier and easier to beg."

"That's just what I'm getting at. Why beg when I have it in my power to give it to you?"

"The funding has nothing to do with you. I want to get to know you. Not because of the visions, Sayo or what you might be able to do for me. I want to get to know you, because for the first time in years, I've found someone who I could come to care for. What do you want?"

"I want this business with Sayo and Noya to go away. I want to be Jaycee Grant again. I want someone to want to be with me because of who and what I am, not because of what I see or hear."

Evan loosened his grip on her arm and Jaycee held her breath. She wanted him to hold her close. Instead, he held her eyes prisoner with his. "Promise me you won't go to the press."

"Why? It would be the best thing for Round Tree."

"Because, at this point, it would look like a publicity stunt. Besides, I've already told them to keep their noses out of it."

"When?"

"Yesterday when you were sleeping."

Several workers returned to their projects and Evan released Jaycee's arm. "I saw the piece you were working on this morning," he said, glancing down at both her unfinished platter and Brandon's pitcher. "Brandon says he thinks he should change projects with you."

Jaycee relaxed. Talking about the pieces of the past, sitting on the table, put them on more neutral ground.

"What do you see when you look at it?"

She again tensed. No matter what Evan said, her visions and Sayo's voice were important to him. "Nothing today. I think my session with Dr. Tess silenced Sayo."

Not silenced, I thought you needed time to digest what you learned, to come to grips with who you are.

Who am I?

Isn't it obvious? You are my beloved Noya.

Who are you?

You already know who I am. I am Sayo. Because Noya was pure her spirit has returned to this world several times. My thanks to the man gods for finally allowing her to return to me.

Why are you still here?

Because I was not pure nor was I so evil the Gods completely destroyed me, as they did Dostra. They left me here to contemplate my life until such time as I could make amends and move on.

"Jaycee, Jaycee," Evan's voice drowned out Sayo's. "What's going on?"

Jaycee shook her head. Although the room began to spin, she willed herself to remain conscious.

"What did you see?"

Jaycee shook her head. "I didn't see anything. It was Sayo. He confirmed what happened yesterday."

Evan turned her so he could look into her eyes. "What did he say?"

"I can't talk about it right now. Please understand, Evan. I'm not withholding anything from you. I just need to put it into perspective first."

Evan backed off. "I won't press you, not about this or about tonight."

"Thank you." Jaycee said, her voice hardly more than a whisper.

"Would tomorrow be too soon for you? I'll even ask Bob and Amanda to come along if you'd like."

Jaycee knew she couldn't put off the inevitable. "Tomorrow will be fine. You're right, I would like Bob and Amanda to be there."

"Good. We'll pick you up at the dorm at six."

Jaycee nodded. It would do her more harm than good to turn Evan down. She would have to remember who they were. She was Jaycee Grant, a frustrated romantic who wanted Evan in her life. He was Evan Clark, a dedicated archaeologist who would go to any lengths to protect his project.

~ * ~

Evan reluctantly left the sorting shed. He wanted to force Jaycee to tell him what Sayo said to so upset her. He couldn't forget the memory of Jaycee trembling when she went into the trancelike state. He knew better than to push. He was already in a precarious position with her, even if he didn't know why. He shoved his hands into his pockets and touched the litter he had picked up while at the site, earlier in the day. Ahead of him, he saw the dumpster and stopped to throw away the trash. As he lifted the lid, he noticed a white bag with the logo of a local fast-food restaurant printed on it. He picked up the confirmation of Jaycee's lunch, surprised by its weight. Inside, he found a burger with one bite missing and a full carton of fries. The only empty thing in the bag was a cup that had held some kind of beverage. The straw protruding from the plastic cover carried traces of her lipstick.

Evan dropped the bag back into the dumpster. His gut feeling told him to go back to the sorting shed and confront her. His heart told him to keep his distance. At least they were talking. There was no sense in upsetting her further. The memory of Jaycee going into the trance when she heard Sayo's voice permeated his mind. He wished he knew what she heard, but she closed the door on that subject. It was obvious she didn't want to talk about it.

Tomorrow night we'll talk about it after dinner, when we're alone.

Looking back at the sorting shed once more, Evan got into the Jeep and turned toward the site.

Chapter Eight

Jaycee took extra pains in dressing. She didn't want to appear provocative, yet she felt the need to look exceptionally nice for Evan. She knew it was crazy, but she couldn't stop dwelling on the look in his eyes when he told her he wanted to get to know her better.

You're out of your mind, Jaycee. Evan Clark is in love with Round Tree. How can you even think he could care for you?

She dismissed her thoughts and remembered watching Evan walk away from her yesterday. She hadn't seen him since then.

She did receive a message, through Chris, about a change in their plans. They would be leaving earlier than he originally thought.

She slipped the white sundress she purchased especially for a night with Evan, over her head and put on the lace jacket. She remembered Evan and Bob asking her to join them for dinner, when Evan made good on his bet with Bob. At the time she'd been flattered by the attention, so much so she bought the dress in New York. She'd paid far too much for it. She could only think about spending the summer working with the man she idolized. No matter what happened in the past few days, she remembered Evan's touch when things were interrupted.

This is ridiculous. I want Evan to touch me, to make love to me. It doesn't have to be a lasting relationship. I just need someone to treat me like a woman for a change.

Jaycee again looked into the mirror. When at last her appearance satisfied her, she turned away. No matter how foolish it seemed going into town yesterday, she realized the dress definitely needed her new strapless bra. She would be much more comfortable than she was the night Evan took her to Montanelli's.

"You're a real knock out," Sandy declared, when Jaycee entered the bedroom. "If that doesn't get Dad's juices flowing, nothing ever will."

"This dress is not meant to get anyone's juices flowing, as you put it," Jaycee replied, knowing she told a white lie.

"Well, it will. What is it with old people? You don't get into this spontaneous thing like we do."

"Old people? I don't consider myself old."

"Well, you're not like me. You aren't a teenager anymore. Let's face it. You have to be the oldest volunteer on the dig. Everyone here is in their late teens or early twenties. You're a professor. You have to be at least thirty."

Jaycee couldn't help but laugh. "Thirty-five," she confessed.

"See what I mean. You're thirty-five and Dad's in his forties. The two of you are almost ancient."

"Gee, thanks. I'll try not to forget my cane. Maybe I should order a rocking chair for this room and do some knitting in my spare time."

"You know what I mean," Sandy said, as though trying to make amends.

"Of course, I do. When I was your age, I thought anyone over the age of thirty had one foot on the proverbial banana peel and the other in the grave."

"Well, you do look great. I think you and my dad would be great together."

"Me, too. I'm afraid it will take more than a steak dinner and a white sundress to do it, though."

"Oh, well, it's a start."

Sandy returned to the book on her lap as Jaycee hurried out the door. Knowing Evan, he would be waiting for her in the parking lot.

She smiled when he pulled up, just as she came through the door. "So where are Bob and Amanda?" she greeted him, when she got into the Jeep.

She assessed his appearance. He wore a comfortable looking summer shirt, open at the neck, with a pair of slacks. The slacks appeared to be new, since they still carried the perfect crease put in at the factory.

"We're meeting them just outside of town. We're taking their car." Without further conversation, he pulled out of the lot and onto the street.

"Car? I thought they drove a truck."

"The truck is Bob's. The car is Amanda's. We thought it would be more comfortable than the Jeep. It doesn't make sense for both of us to drive."

She noticed an edge of nervousness in Evan's voice. "I didn't see you at lunch today," she commented, hoping to break the tension.

"I ate early. I didn't want to upset you."

She tried to read his meaning, but couldn't. "You wouldn't have upset me, Evan."

"Wouldn't I? It seems like every time I get around you, I upset you. I would like to avoid it if possible."

"So, that's why I didn't see you at breakfast."

Evan nodded. "I saw you coming in when I was leaving. You don't have to ask the question."

"What question?"

"I'm not going to grill you about what you ate today. Anything has to be more than yesterday."

"What do you mean?"

"I have no idea what you ate for breakfast, but I can vouch for lunch. Let's see, one bite of a hamburger and a carton of untouched fries. Stop me if I'm wrong."

"How did you know?"

"I had a candy wrapper in my pocket. When I threw it in the dumpster, I saw the bag and checked it out. I was curious about what you ate."

"So, why didn't you come back and chew me out?"

"I alienated you enough without confronting you about it."

"I'm usually not so defensive. I guess this whole thing has me spooked."

"I know it does. Tonight, there will be no talk of digs, visions, or voices. I want this to be a pleasurable experience. Maybe even a chance for us to start over."

"Where are we going?"

"Bob found a new place in the next county. It's supposed to be good as well as expensive. I told you he wouldn't settle for Montanelli's."

Jaycee smiled at Evan's comment. For the first time since Stan walked out of her life, she found herself relaxing with a man. She realized she'd spend the past several years competing with her counterparts and fighting with Henry. Having Evan concerned about her eating habits as well as hearing him admit he wanted to try and start over made her heart feel light.

Sandy's comment about not being spontaneous crowded Jaycee's thoughts. She wondered if she pulled away too soon. She certainly enjoyed Evan's attentions, his caresses.

"At least we don't have to wait for Bob and Amanda," Evan said, as they pulled into the wayside.

Jaycee wished they were going to be alone. It might be fun for her to practice spontaneity.

~ * ~

Evan parked the Jeep then went around, helping Jaycee out of the car. He noticed she wore a bra, unlike Monday night when she went braless. Her bustline was definitely more defined, rather than the natural look he'd enjoyed just a few days earlier. He wished she'd forgotten it.

At the restaurant, the table talk remained light, but Evan noticed a hint of tension in the air. It made him wonder if Jaycee wanted to talk about Sayo and the visions.

"Wherever did you get your dress?" Amanda asked.

"In New York, right after I met Bob and Evan."

Evan didn't like the way she put Bob's name before his. Hiding his annoyance, he continued to listen.

"That's right," Bob said. "You were getting ready to go and visit a friend."

Jaycee nodded. "We had a good time. Of course, Ellie and I always have a good time together. We've been close friends forever. We shopped. I had a makeover and decided to try contacts, and we talked for hours. Unfortunately, I needed to go back to work and her husband came back from Europe."

"Sounds like a great time," Amanda said, wistfully. "With the kids I rarely get to do such things."

"We don't have them in the summer," Bob countered.

Evan smiled. He knew what happened in the summer, they worked at Round Tree, putting in more hours than anyone other than himself.

"Sure, I don't have the kids in the summer, just you and the dig."

Bob pretended to pout, while Jaycee laughed at Amanda's good-natured teasing.

"Why don't you tell us more about yourself, Jaycee," Amanda prompted in an obvious attempt to change the subject.

Evan sat back, content to listen. He hoped he would get some insight into her character.

She told them about losing her father just prior to her graduation from Havelin. His death made it necessary to pursue her doctorate at Havelin as well, in order to stay home and care for her mother. She also described her mother's illness in great detail, along with her work.

For a moment, Evan envied Jaycee, while at the same time pitying her. He spent very little time with his parents, going away to school at such an early age. At the same time, he couldn't imagine living such a sheltered life. No wonder everything at Round Tree seemed to overwhelm her.

"It must be very rewarding to know you're so respected in your chosen field," Amanda commented when Jaycee paused.

"It's funny, I've never thought of it that way. All I see is the struggle with the day-to-day running of my department and the ongoing fight with Henry just to be recognized. Until I came here, I had no idea how anyone outside of Havelin viewed me."

"I say it's about time you saw yourself in a better light," Evan said. "I figured you were in complete control on the first night we met. Can you honestly say you were putting on a front?"

He searched her eyes for an answer to his question.

"You met me in my element. Henry and I thrive on our daily feuds. His attitude has surely rubbed off on me. Enough about Henry and me, what is it you do in the off season, Amanda?"

"I teach first grade. It's rewarding, only in a different way. I'm not considered God's great gift to the teaching profession. No one asks me to write papers, but one toothless smile from a six-year-old is worth all the laurels in the world."

"I don't know where you ever got such an idea about me,"
Jaycee said, lowering her eyes, a hint of a blush creeping into her cheeks.

"Now, where do you think?" Bob asked. "From Brandon, of course. You're all he's been talking about since he arrived. Something tells me he's been putting you on a pedestal ever since he met the young man from Havelin last winter."

"I guess I underestimate the impact I have on my students. I certainly never thought any of them would speak so highly of me."

"I can't understand why someplace other than Havelin hasn't snapped you up," Evan commented.

"It doesn't surprise me. I haven't been looking. Let's face it Havelin is fairly safe. They all know me and don't expect too much."

Although he didn't agree, Evan knew he could listen to her talk for hours. He certainly enjoyed hearing her voice as well as her naive outlook on life. She had no idea how others viewed her, or did she? Could she be putting on a front for him?

After paying the bill, Evan followed the others to the parking lot. He didn't want the evening to end, didn't want to have to say good night.

At the wayside, Evan held open the door for Jaycee. Watching Bob and Amanda drive away, he came to the realization he didn't want to drop Jaycee at the dorm. He thought about tonight throughout the day and reveled in the possibility of taking her back to his apartment. Now he wondered if Jaycee would turn away from him as she did days earlier.

"Amanda asked you about the weekend," Evan said, before he started the engine. "What are your plans?"

"Like I told Amanda, I think I'll just hibernate. It's been a long and exhausting week."

"Could I be included in your plans?"

"I honestly don't know."

She purposely turned away from him.

"Why not? Am I so terrible?"

"Of course, you're not. I just need to step back from all of this for a while."

"I won't push you. Would you like to come back to my place for a nightcap? It's still early. We have plenty of time before curfew."

He expected her to turn him down flat. Instead, she shyly nodded her head.

"Sure, it sounds good to me."

Evan felt his spirit's soar. In the hopes Jaycee would agree to come back to the apartment, he put a bottle of wine in the refrigerator to cool. In case she agreed to stop by, he purchased a box of condoms. At the time, the idea seemed foolish. He lived the past several years without buying any of those things, why start now? He knew the answer. He wanted to make love to Jaycee and he wanted everything to be right.

~ * ~

Jaycee allowed Evan to hold open the apartment door for her. She immediately saw two wine glasses sitting on the counter. "You must have been sure I'd agree to come back here with you," she said.

"Not really. I just hoped you would."

Jaycee smiled, pleased to think Evan wanted to be with her. She watched him open the bottle and pour the wine. She accepted the glass he held out to her and took a taste. "This is the house wine from Montanelli's."

"I knew you liked it, so I picked up a bottle last night after you agreed to go with us. I don't want to push you too fast, but I do want to get to know you better."

Jaycee stepped back. "Do you want to get to know me because I'm me, or because of my link to Sayo."

"Give me more credit than that. I thought we worked past this. It's you I want. As for the visions, your regression, even Sayo, they're all only an added bonus."

Jaycee wanted to believe him, but she couldn't resist asking one more question. "When are you going to go to the press?"

He took her hands in his before answering. "Not until we're both comfortable with it."

His touch prompted the memory of Sandy's comment about being spontaneous. The romance novels also alluded to it.

Am I being too old fashioned?

"Are you alright, Jaycee?" Evan questioned, before her mind could formulate an answer to her own speculations.

She nodded. "I was just thinking about something. Why did you bring me here?"

"I thought we needed to talk, alone."

"I hear an and in your voice. Were you thinking we might make love?"

Evan's look of surprise shocked her. "If it happens, I wouldn't be opposed to it, but it's not the reason I brought you here."

"I think I want to make love with you," she said, hardly aware she put voice to her thoughts.

"It isn't that easy, Jaycee. Just because you think you want to try it doesn't mean it's the right thing to do. I don't want you doing something because you think it will please me."

"You must know me better than that. I rarely do things just to please others. You have no way of knowing how much I care for you, have always cared for you. Just being on this dig is a dream come true. Having you obviously want me is more than I ever dreamed could happen. It's been a long time since I've even wanted to make love with a man."

Evan pulled her into his arms and silenced her with a kiss. His tongue pressing against her lips, begging for entry, made her forget her inhibitions and open herself to him.

She wondered if he would guide her gently to the floor and make love to her in the kitchen, the way the hero in the romance novel she finished last night took the heroine. Instead, she felt him pull away. "We aren't teenagers. We can at least do this the right way."

He led the way to the bedroom, where she napped two days earlier. Instead of the glaring ceiling light, he turned on a bedside lamp, which illuminated the room with a soft glow. He then returned to her side to slip the jacket from her shoulders, running his hands down her arms. When it fell softly to the floor, he returned his hands to the zipper and pulled it down to the bottom of the track. He slipped the thin straps from her shoulders allowing it to fall to the floor before unhooking her bra.

Jaycee stood, her breasts exposed to Evan, her emotions churning.

She chided herself for her momentary indecision. It was two days earlier when Evan gazed upon her breasts, even touched the heart of her woman's soul. She wanted him then as she did now. Relaxing, she reached to unbutton Evan's shirt and run her fingers across the soft mat of hair on his chest. The feel of him beneath her fingers excited her more than she thought possible.

Moving her hands to the buckle of his belt, she quickly undid it as well as his pants, exposing silk boxer shorts that obscured the sight of his symbol of manhood. Before she could go further, he took her hands and put them to his lips.

"Is this what you really want?" he asked, his eyes filled with desire, his voice with concern.

"Yes. Only not for the reasons you might think. I need to be loved by someone I care for."

His smile assured her he approved of her answer. He took off his slacks, the reached for his wallet and produced a small round packet.

"Are you always so prepared?" she teased, as he awkwardly took the necessary precautions.

"Damn," he said, when he had trouble putting on the condom.

"I thought men didn't have any trouble with things like this."

"Things have changed. When I was dating, twenty-five years ago, I never used a condom."

"What about recently?"

"Recently there hasn't been anyone I've wanted to be with. Until now, that is."

"You really haven't been with anyone?"

"No," he replied, again taking her in his arms.

"I'm sorry I doubted you."

"I'm sorry you thought you had reason to doubt me. I guess it's natural. I had my doubts about you as well. It's hard to believe you've only had one lover. Someone as beautiful as you..."

"You saw me at Havelin. I certainly wasn't beautiful then. As for the lovers, you can believe the number. There hasn't been time. I haven't had the desire. Now I have both time and desire."

He rested his hands on her hips, but she couldn't take her eyes from his sheathed organ, which promised such delights. He moved his fingers to the elastic of her panties then pushed them down toward the floor. After they dropped, she stood, unashamedly naked, in front of Evan, ready for any lovemaking he had in mind.

Gently he eased her down onto the bed. He moved his hands seductively across her body. He touched her taut nipples and caressed her flat belly until he reached the soft tuft of hair between her legs. Cautiously, he slipped his fingers into the moist crevice, in search of the nub of desire.

Jaycee moaned as he readied her for his entry. She felt almost guilty being the recipient of such pleasure without giving anything in return.

Evan moved to position himself over her. With his shift in weight, she parted her legs to give him easier access. The explosion of her emotions drove her to match him stroke for stroke, until at last they both climaxed. For a long moment, he lingered within her, kissing her neck and caressing her cheek.

When they parted, he rested his hand on her breast. "I'm falling in love with you, Jocelyn Grant," he said.

She looked into his green eyes and read sincerity. Although she enjoyed Evan calling her Jaycee, his use of her given name in this intimate moment excited her even further.

I have always loved you, the voice she recognized as belonging to Sayo sounded in her head.

She began to tremble, frightened, tears cascading down her cheeks.

"What's wrong, Jaycee?" Evan asked, as he pulled her back into his arms.

"Sayo," she gasped, choking back a sob. "He's here."

"Are you certain?"

"What a question for you to ask. Of course, I'm certain. I've been hearing his voice all week. I know what he sounds like."

"What did you hear?"

You heard my voice, beloved. How I envy this man who coupled with you. He can enjoy your body, while I can only be heard in your mind.

Why can't you leave me alone?

Because you must free me from this prison. I need to prepare you for your destiny.

Sayo's voice silenced and Jaycee became aware of Evan's loving embrace. "Is he gone?"

Jaycee nodded.

"Good. I worry about the effect he has on you."

"I do too."

"I hesitate to suggest this, but maybe you should get away from here for the weekend. Is there someplace you can go?"

"I could go and visit my friend, Ellie, in New York."

"I don't want you to go, you know that. I'd prefer to keep you here, but I can't protect you from Sayo. You need to rest. Going away for the weekend might be for the best."

"I don't want to go away. I don't want to leave now, but…"

"I know. Sayo is too close to the surface here. We'll have other nights. Somehow, we'll find a way to silence him. We have to, our future depends on it."

Jaycee dressed, using none of the care she did earlier. Staring at the bed, she knew she wanted to stay, to fall asleep in Evan's arms. Sayo's voice shattered the beauty of the experience she shared with Evan and left her frightened of the very place that represented such pleasures.

Jaycee watched as Evan pulled on sweat shorts and a tank top. Lastly, he took his keys from the pocket of the pants he discarded earlier.

"Are you ready to go?"

Jaycee nodded.

"Are you sure you'll be alright tonight?"

"I'm sure," she replied, not at all convinced about the statement she just made.

They drove back to the dorm in relative silence, each lost in their own thoughts and the memory of the evening spent together.

"Do you want me to walk you to the door?" Evan asked, once he parked the Jeep.

"There's no need."

Instead of listening to her, he got out of the vehicle and went around opening the car door, then walked her up to the dorm. Before leaving, he took Jaycee into his arms, kissing her long and hard. His kiss promised more nights of delightful lovemaking in their future.

Reluctantly, she left the security of his arms and went into the building alone. Turning back, she watched Even get into the Jeep and pull back out onto the street before he disappeared around the corner.

Once inside, the coolness of the air-conditioned building made her sigh with relief. Was it only her imagination or did the night seem unnaturally warm?

Standing in the lobby area, she pulled her cell phone from her bag. Sandy would, most certainly, be asleep. Rather than disturb her roommate, Jaycee decided to call Ellie before going up to bed.

The phone on the other end rang twice before a sleepy Ellie answered.

"Jaycee? I certainly didn't expect to hear from you. Aren't you at the dig?"

"Yes, I am. Ellie, can I come to New York and see you tomorrow?"

"Tomorrow?" Ellie echoed.

"Tomorrow night, actually," Jaycee corrected herself. "I want to come and spend the weekend with you."

"What's wrong, Jaycee? You sound strange."

"I can't go into it over the phone. I promise I'll tell you all about it tomorrow."

"When will you get here? I'll meet your plane."

"I don't know. I'll call you at the shop when I book a flight."

"You sound scared to death."

"Believe me, I am," Jaycee said, breaking the connection without giving Ellie a chance to ask further questions.

As she did, Sayo's voice again sounded in her head. *Are you running away from me, Little One?*

You frighten me.

You will be back.

Yes, I know I will.

Before you go. Learn more of the truth. Learn who and what you were.

Do you mean I should have another regression?

Is that what you call it?

Yes.

That is what I mean. Go to the woman who brought it forth the first time. Learn about yourself.

Jaycee swallowed the lump in her throat. *I don't know if I want to learn more about her.*

Of course, you do.

If I learn more, will you go away?

Not until I make amends. Not until the man gods say I can be free. Only you can free me.

~ * ~

Evan watched Jaycee go into the dorm in his rear-view mirror. He certainly didn't want to take her back there. He wanted her to be with him, but the spell had been broken and couldn't be repaired tonight. If only Sayo hadn't talked to her, she would have been content to stay in his bed. The memory of her horror at Sayo's words made him shudder.

There had to be some way to make Sayo go away and leave Jaycee alone. Evan knew he would have to find it so they could spend their time getting to know each other without the interference of a long dead spirit.

Chapter Nine

Jaycee's dreams were troubled. After tossing and turning for hours, she saw herself naked, bound hand and foot, lying on a stone altar. Above her stood two men, each handsome, each in direct contrast with the other.

Sayo's dark features stared down at her, a stone knife clutched in his hand. "I love you too much to sacrifice you, Noya."

Next to him, Evan's green eyes flashed angrily. "She's not Noya, she's Jaycee. She belongs to the twenty first century, not your time. I love her too much to allow you to harm her."

The alarm clock rang, shattering the remnants of the dream. Jaycee turned over in time to see Sandy reach for the clock to silence its annoying buzz.

"How did things go with Dad last night?" Sandy asked.

The question brought back the memory of Evan's lovemaking.

"Fine," Jaycee muttered, her words still thick with sleep.

"Are you two getting together over the weekend?"

"No, I'm going to New York to see my friend, Ellie."

She knew she'd been too quick to answer and her words were said a bit too emphatically.

"Why? Wouldn't you much rather spend the time alone with Dad?"

"Of course, I would, but I need to get away from Sayo for a while."

Sandy nodded and headed for the bathroom. Jaycee wished she understood as easily as Sandy. She hated the thought of leaving the dig, of going to New York, of spending the weekend without Evan, but she knew she had to put distance between herself and Sayo.

While she waited for Sandy to finish in the bathroom, Jaycee packed a bag to take to New York.

~ * ~

Evan dressed and went down to the dining hall for breakfast. The oppressive heat prompted him to leave on the air conditioner when he left the apartment.

The memory of making love to Jaycee hours earlier mingled with the terror in her eyes when she heard Sayo's voice. Evan remembered promising to silence Sayo, but how could he hope to silence a troubled spirit?

To Evan's surprise, Chris waited for him at the dining hall. "You're up early," he commented.

"I haven't been to bed," Chris replied.

"Hot date?"

"Something's hot, but it wasn't a date. I stayed late last night. It's a good thing I did. The air conditioning went out at the sorting shed about eight. I went up on the roof. The way it looks, we blew the compressor. My dad runs a refrigeration company, so I know a little about these things. I called someone out, but they have to order the part. It won't get here much before Monday, so I transferred everything down to the storeroom at the lab. It doesn't look like we'll be able to get back to work until next week."

"Why didn't you call me last night?"

"I knew you were out with Jaycee. By the time you got back, I'd already taken care of it. The only thing left to do was move the artifacts."

Evan shook his head as complete understanding made him regret his harsh words. "Sorry I barked. I trust you, otherwise you wouldn't be in the position you're in. I'm just uptight. What more can go wrong this summer? First, we lose our funding, Jaycee has to contend with Sayo and now this. I'm beginning to think we're cursed."

Jaycee entered the dining hall, along with several other volunteers, and saw Evan engaged in conversation with Brandon and Chris.

"No work for you today," Evan said, when he motioned for her to join them.

"What do you mean?"

"The air conditioner at the sorting shed took a dump. We can't get the parts until Monday. With the heat, we can't expect anyone to work in there today."

"What about the fragments? You aren't leaving them in there, are you? The effects of this humidity could be catastrophic."

"My sentiments, exactly," Chris said. "That's why I called Brandon last night. He helped me move everything down to the lab."

Chris and Brandon left them alone. "This isn't something you made up, is it?" Jaycee asked.

"Good grief, no. The cost of repairs is going to put us behind. I almost hesitate to tell Bob about it. He goes ballistic when it comes to money. All kidding aside, can I take you to breakfast?"

Jaycee worked hard to suppress a giggle. "Your offer sounds very generous, considering the dig provides a bountiful breakfast."

"Will you be leaving this morning for New York?" Evan asked, as Jaycee filled her plate.

"I will, if I can get a flight."

"I should never have suggested it."

"Don't be silly. I would have probably gone anyway."

"Wait until tonight and I'll go with you. We can get a hotel room..."

"You can't go with me, Evan. You're needed here. Brandon told me about how you mingle with the tourists on the weekends."

"I don't want to talk to tourists. I want to be with you."

"We can be together when I get back on Monday."

"Is that a promise?"

Jaycee nodded.

"Do you think Sayo will be silent if you go to New York?" Evan asked, when they seated themselves at a table.

"I hope so. He says he's a prisoner here. I don't think he can follow me."

"I don't understand."

"He says the man gods won't let him be free because of something he did."

"Do you mean the sacrifices?"

"I don't know. It could be the sacrifices or maybe falling in love with the wrong woman. What kind of gods punishes you for loving someone? He says he can't be free until he makes amends. I don't understand him."

"Maybe he wants to prepare you to find the writings, wherever they are."

"Maybe," she said, thoughtfully.

"Can I call you in New York?" he asked, taking hold of her hand.

"I wish you wouldn't."

"Why?"

"Because I need to put everything in perspective. Talking to you would only churn up my emotions further. Please don't misunderstand. I need to deal with what's going on by myself. I've always taken care of my problems alone. I can't change now."

"I understand. I don't approve of you working through things on your own, but I do understand. We're too much alike in that respect."

~ * ~

Jaycee continued to eat in silence, her emotions torn. She wanted him to make love to her, but she worried about hearing Sayo's voice again. Going to New York, getting away from everything would be for the best. She just wished the best wasn't so hard.

After breakfast, they walked out into the oppressive June heat. "How will you be able to work in this?" Jaycee asked.

"It's not so bad. All I have to do is stay out of the air conditioning and I don't mind it. I can take the heat. I just don't know if I can survive until Monday without you."

"You'll do just fine. We only had one night. I think you'll make it," Jaycee teased.

She wondered if she would survive. How could one night so quickly change her life? She tried to tell herself things were different for her. She realized she fell in love with Evan the first time she saw his picture, the first time she read one of his articles about Round Tree.

During their meeting at Havelin, she volunteered in order to spend the summer with him. She changed her appearance and jeopardized her future to work with Evan. She certainly never expected to spend an evening entwined in his arms. She only planned to keep to herself, not to wear her heart on her sleeve. Now she knew she must put distance between herself and the man who so easily turned her emotions to jelly.

Evan's arms, pulling her close, silenced her internal ramblings. She could feel a blush rise in her cheeks as he kissed her in full view of everyone in the area.

"Come back to me soon," he whispered, before they parted.

"I will," she promised.

For a long moment, she watched him walk away. Once he seated himself in his Jeep, she turned toward the dorm.

Alone in the room, she called Dr. Tess. "Can you see me this morning?"

"Yes, I have time. Have things gotten worse?"

"You could say that. I've been hearing Sayo's voice. This time he's prompting me to see you and learn more about Noya."

"It sounds as though he's desperate for you to understand him. Can you be here in an hour?"

~ * ~

Jaycee awakened from the hypnotic trance Dr. Tess induced, wondering, as she had days earlier, if anything happened. The look on Dr. Tess' face ceased her worries.

"Did it go well?" Jaycee asked.

"Yes, very well."

Jaycee held out her hand to accept the tape. "I wish I had the time to sit and listen to this with you. I don't want you to listen to it alone."

The look on Dr. Tess' face said volumes. There must be something horrifying on the tape for the therapist to insist she not listen to it alone.

Jaycee nodded her reply, as she closed her fingers around the cassette. "I'm not so certain I want to listen to it at all."

"I'm sure you will, eventually," Dr. Tess continued. "I do have some questions for you about Sayo. You said he's been coming to you again. Perhaps you can answer them for me."

"I hope so. I thought I silenced him with the first regression, but he's come back, even more determined to drive me crazy. It's not just at the dig anymore. I heard him at Evan's apartment as well as at the dorm. I have to get away from all of this. Since Sayo believes he's a prisoner here,

I pray he won't follow me to New York."

"You aren't leaving for good, are you?"

"No. Just for the weekend. I have friends there. I can stay with them He says he speaks to me now, because I'm the only one who can free him. I'm not too proud to say I'm frightened."

"You answered my questions without me even asking them. I don't blame you for being afraid. I can only hope you're right about getting away. His being a prisoner could mean he's imprisoned on an earthly plain and not confined to this area alone. If he thinks you're deserting him, he may follow you. Maybe you should listen to the tape before you leave."

"No. I'm taking it to Evan. He can listen to it. I'm too frightened of what I might hear."

"I don't blame you. I do wish I could meet Sayo face to face and ask him what he plans to do."

"I'm afraid I know what he plans to do. At this point, I'm certain he will eventually destroy me."

"I don't think so. From what I've learned about Noya, they were very much in love. She was a frightened child, who saw Sayo as a very powerful man, a priest. If we can believe her, she considered him handsome. I think he loved her too much to ever cause you any harm."

Dr. Tess' words prompted Jaycee to remember her unsettling dream. Sayo's handsome features filled her mind. "Yes, very handsome, indeed."

"You've seen him?" Dr. Tess questioned.

Jaycee wished she hadn't said anything. Feeling trapped, she related the details of the dream.

"I think your friend, Sayo, is not only desperate to be released, he's also jealous of Evan. Unfortunately, the woman he loves isn't Jaycee Grant. I hope he can accept who you are."

"So do I."

"Getting back to Noya. I think she felt very secure with Sayo. His inability to save her life came as a terrible blow to him. In the end, he couldn't protect the one person he loved, just as he couldn't overpower his mother and the man gods. Maybe it's the reason he hasn't been able to leave. I think we should pity him."

"I can't imagine pitying him. Just hearing his voice makes me agree with Noya. He is a very powerful man."

"Put aside your fears and think about how he feels. He lost his lover as well as his child, saw his mother destroyed and considers himself a prisoner. He sees you as the key to his freedom. Promise me you'll listen to the tape with Dr. Clark before you judge Sayo too harshly."

"I will, but not until I get back."

"I do wish we had longer to talk, but I have another patient."

"It's all right. I have to get to the airport and see if I can book a flight to New York. I'll talk to you when I get back."

Jaycee went down to the car and studied the cassette in her hand. Minutes earlier she promised Dr. Tess not to listen to it alone. Now she couldn't resist the urge to hear what happened under hypnosis.

She pushed it into the cassette deck of her car and listened as Dr. Tess' reassuring voice greeted her. Almost immediately, the voice she recognized as belonging to Noya, began to speak. Jaycee sat, transfixed, unable to do anything but listen.

Thirty minutes later, the tape ended and Jaycee knew why Dr. Tess insisted she not hear it alone. Noya's story, the revelations Jaycee heard, sent chills through her body.

She set the tape to rewind as she pulled out of the parking lot. Instead of going directly to the airport, she drove to Evan's apartment.

Taking a pad of sticky notes from her purse, she wrote a few words.

Evan – I went to see Dr. Tess this morning. Please listen to the tape. We'll talk about this when I get back - Jaycee.

After attaching the note, she placed the tape in Evan's mailbox.

At the airport, Jaycee purchased a ticket on the next flight to New York. With a twenty-minute wait, she called Ellie with her arrival time and flight number.

The plane soared into the bright blue of the June sky and Noya's voice, as well as the memories of Sayo's words, haunted Jaycee. She closed her eyes and imagined the site, as it must have looked at the time their village thrived, when the stress of the modern world didn't interfere.

Behind her closed eyelids, Jaycee saw Noya, bare breasted, a modesty apron tied at her waist. At her side stood Sayo, tall, with broad shoulders and handsome features.

She watched as Sayo reached up to stroke Noya's black hair, dropping his hand lower until it caressed her breast.

"I carry your child, Sayo," Noya said.

To Jaycee's surprise, Sayo turned from Noya, causing the girl to burst into tears and run from him.

"We are making the final approach to LaGuardia. The temperature in New York is seventy-six degrees." The voice of the pilot, on the plane's intercom, shattered the vision Jaycee experienced.

As soon as she entered the waiting area, Ellie ran to meet her. "Oh, Jaycee, you look terrible. What's going on?" Ellie asked, holding Jaycee at arm's length.

"I'm so glad you're here, Ellie."

"What is it? Is it Evan?"

"No. Evan is everything I ever thought he would be, including a wonderful lover."

"Well, good for you. I knew if I gave you those books, they'd help."

"They may help in that department, but there is so much more going on out there. Let's get out to the car. I can't talk about it with all of these people around."

Ellie's chocolate brown BMW waited for them in the parking lot. Jaycee relaxed against the soft leather of the interior, then fastened her seat belt. By the time they pulled out into traffic, Jaycee's words spilled out as easily as Noya's narration on the tape hours earlier.

"A past life," Ellie exclaimed, when Jaycee ran out of words.

"Sayo is the most frightening of all. He loved her so very much. He says only I can free him. His spirit is stuck here."

"I can't believe Evan encouraged you to leave. You must be very important to Round Tree."

"He knows how frightened I am. When we finished making love last night, he told me he was falling in love with me. The words no more than passed his lips when Sayo told me he always loved me. It was a terrifying experience. We agreed it would be best if I got away from everything, at least for the weekend. With me gone, maybe Sayo will give up."

"I doubt it. He sounds like a very determined man to me."

"He's not a man, Ellie. He's a spirit."

"Why don't you just tell him to go away, to go toward the light? Isn't that what spirits are supposed to do?"

"I can't. I tried it. He won't listen to me. He frightens me more than I care to think about. I'm afraid he's out to destroy me mentally."

Ellie reached across the seat and squeezed Jaycee's hand reassuringly. "You're safe here with Vern and me. I doubt even your wayward spirit will be able to find you at our house. So, why didn't you bring the hunk with you?"

Jaycee relaxed, even laughed at Ellie's straight forward question. "Evan wanted to come, but I said no. The weekends are a big deal at the dig. It's the only time he gets to talk to the tourists. It helps with the donations."

"What about the state funding? Can't he get it back?"

"That's another thing. I wanted to go the press with what we've uncovered, but Evan said no. He wants me to keep quiet, even knowing if I went to the press, he would surely get back the funding. Of course, it's not easy to prove that the visions or Sayo are real. Even if I told them about what I've been experiencing, they might not believe me."

"Maybe he wants to be the one to tell the press."

"He doesn't seem to want to do that either. I don't know what to make of it. I'm just glad to be away from it for a few days."

"If that's how it is, why go back? Tell Evan if he wants you, you'll be here. Under the circumstances he's sure to understand."

"I can't make Evan choose between Round Tree and me. Even if I could, Henry would hold it against me. He had a fit about me taking off the summer. He'd bust a gut if I didn't use the time to work on a dig. I have to continue, finish what I started."

"Of course, you do, but you know you're always welcome here."

Jaycee laughed. "It could get a little expensive. The only seat I could get was first class."

~ * ~

Evan returned to his apartment. It had been so hot at the dig, two of the volunteers were overcome before he sent everyone else back to the dorms. Stubbornly, he stayed a while longer, trying to make contact with Sayo. To his dismay, the spirit remained silent.

He stopped at the mailbox and retrieved the stack of letters. The tape on top, with the note from Jaycee, bothered him. Why did she go to Dr. Tess' office without him? What in the world was she thinking of?

By now, she's safely in New York. I won't have to worry about her for the weekend. With her gone, maybe Sayo will decide to talk to me.

He tossed the mail and the tape on the counter and went into the bathroom for a much-needed shower. As the water cascaded over his body, he dwelled on the problem with the air conditioning at the sorting shed. If he didn't know better, he would say it was struck by lightning, but there hadn't been a thunderstorm in over two weeks. Tuesday's rain came as a downpour, with no accompanying severe weather.

He closed his eyes and remembered what he saw when he climbed up to the roof to inspect the damage. The relay as well as the compressor was blown to bits. He certainly couldn't rule out sabotage even though the service tech assured him a power surge could have caused the damage. There were just too many problems cropping up at one time for him to accept logical explanations.

After his shower, Evan pulled on the shorts and tank top he wore to take Jaycee home the night before. Was it only hours ago when they made love? It seemed like days since he said good-bye to her after breakfast. Taking a beer from the refrigerator, he went into the living room to sort through his mail. The tape he picked up with the letters still bothered him. He read the note for a second time. From her wording, she must have listened to the session before dropping off the tape.

Absently, he put it into the tape player. Dr. Tess asked questions, the way she did two days earlier. It wasn't the questions, but the answers, that bothered Evan.

The voice, he recognized as Noya's, described the beatings she endured as a slave in the household of the high priestess, Dostra. It also hinted at the acts she was forced to perform with the men who came to visit her mistress. When she did become a woman, she described a ceremony in which Sayo took her virginity by using a stone penis covering, meant to break the hymen and inflict excruciating pain. Noya said Sayo told her it was necessary so the woman would fully appreciate her chosen husband. She also talked about Dostra's plans to send her to the house of pleasures, where she would live the life of a prostitute. She even elaborated on the tender moments she shared with Sayo.

When the tape ended, Evan cursed the members of this society, the people who so fascinated him for the past several years. As in most ancient civilizations, they sacrificed innocent people for any number of reasons. Before, he accepted this as fact. Now, however, it hit too close to home. It involved someone he loved.

Chapter Ten

Sounds of morning greeted Jaycee. It took a moment to realize she slept in Ellie's guest bedroom on Long Island and not the dorm at Round Tree. From the light streaming through the window, she knew it must be very late.

Raising herself on one elbow, Jaycee glanced at the bedside clock. Seeing it read ten, she laid back, with a satisfied sigh. She hadn't slept late in months. First it was Henry, then her obsession with Evan. Now it was the voice and image of Sayo.

The canopied bed put to rest all the fears and ghosts that plagued Jaycee's mind and robbed her of sleep.

The smell of coffee enticed Jaycee to get out of bed. Rather than dressing, she slipped on a robe before going to join Vern and Ellie in the kitchen.

"We figured you'd sleep all morning. Can I get you a cup of coffee?" Ellie greeted her. Jaycee nodded. "If I was at the dig, Evan would be insisting I eat enough to feed me for a week."

Ellie's husband, Vern, laughed out loud. "I can't imagine either of you girls eating breakfast."

Jaycee ignored the remark and Vern went back to reading his paper.

"I thought we'd go shopping and catch a matinee. It will take your mind off your handsome ghost."

Jaycee knew Ellie meant her statement as good-natured teasing, but the mention of Sayo sent a shiver of dread up her spine.

Vern looked up from his paper, a look of surprise on his face. "Listen to this. It looks like you're a real celebrity, even if they don't mention you by name."

"What are you talking about?" Jaycee demanded.

Vern spread the paper out on the table and began to read. "The problem plagued Round Tree Dig, headed by Dr. Evan Clark, got a needed shot in the arm this past week. An unnamed volunteer has reportedly been hearing voices and seeing visions of the people who inhabited the village being unearthed. It was reported the voices speak of ancient writings in a society with no written language. When these writings are finally found, state monies could be forth coming."

Vern looked up to assess the look on Jaycee's face. "It goes on. Do you want me to continue?"

Jaycee got up to stand behind Vern and look over his shoulder. The article continued describing, not only the visions, but also the words Sayo spoke and the rumor of the regression.

Beside the article, a picture of Evan smiled up at her. Jaycee wanted to cry, but found herself too angry to do anything but rant and rave.

"How could he? It's no wonder he didn't want me going to the local papers. He wanted to give the story to the Associated Press. I'm surprised he didn't tell them what I heard when we were in bed together."

Ellie placed a reassuring hand on Jaycee's shoulder. "Calm down, Jaycee. You don't know Evan gave the story to the press."

"Don't I? I should have known when he insisted that I come up here for the weekend. He wanted to get rid of me so he could bask in the glory of his revelation by himself."

"Aren't you being a bit too hasty?" Vern asked.

"I was too hasty when I allowed him to take me to bed. For the first time since I met Dr. Clark, I'm thinking straight. You offered to let me stay here for a while, Ellie. Does it still hold?"

"Of course, it does, but what about Evan and the dig?"

"This is what," Jaycee said, reaching for the phone.

Angrily, she pushed the buttons for Evan's home number.

"I'm sorry I can't take your call. Please leave a message at the tone," his machine greeted her.

"This is Dr. Jocelyn C. Grant. I will thank you to send my belongings to Makeover's By Ellie, 5342 Bly Street, New York. You can take my name off your list of volunteers. Oh, yes, you can keep your precious money. Just forget you ever heard of me. I can easily forget you, Round Tree and Sayo." She slammed down the receiver and turned to face a stunned Ellie.

"Let's go shopping. Who knows when or if I'll get my clothes?"

~ * ~

Evan made his way to the office. The last batch of tourists drained him with their questions. He no more than stepped into the cooler building before the phone began to ring.

"Round Tree Dig," he answered.

"Dr. Clark?" the man on the other end of the line inquired.

"This is Ronald Silverthorne. I represent the state. Based on the article in this morning's paper, we'd like to come down to Round Tree next week and talk about the possibility of reinstating your funding."

"What article? I didn't authorize any article."

"Well, someone did. The Associated Press doesn't make this stuff up. Can we meet with you on Monday morning?"

"Until I find out who gave an unauthorized interview to the press, you can go to hell."

Evan hung up the phone, realizing in his anger he had cut his own throat. He'd been downright rude, but with everything he had going on it was no wonder. He needed the funding Silverthorne promised. When the time was right, he planned to go to the press with Jaycee, but not until they found the writing and could prove Sayo right.

Before Evan could continue his thoughts, Bob barged into the office. "Have you seen this morning's paper? I thought you were going to wait to talk to the press."

Evan snatched the paper from Bob's hand. The headline jumped off the page at him.

Beleaguered Archaeological Dig Receives Help From The Spirit World

"How can you think I went to the press? I gave my word to Jaycee. I don't know how they got this story, but it didn't come from me."

"I believe you, but will Jaycee?"

"With luck, she won't see it."

"Don't count on it. Being an Associated Press release, it will hit every major paper. She's bound to see it. Maybe you can talk to her before she does."

"I would if I had a phone number. All I know is she's staying with her friend Ellie. I don't even know the woman's last name."

"Isn't there any way you can find out?"

"It's a shot in the dark, but maybe Henry Bennett knows. I hate to ask that son of a bitch for anything."

Evan knew Bob understood his reluctance to contact Henry.

Finding the card for Havelin in his roll-o-dex, Evan punched in the number for Henry's home. Bennett answered on the second ring.

"Henry, this is Evan Clark," he began.

"Evan? What's all this nonsense in this morning's paper? Does it have anything to do with Jocelyn?"

"I'm afraid it does. I'm wondering if you know the last name of her friend, Ellie."

"Why do you need to know her name?"

"Jaycee…ah…Jocelyn went to New York for the weekend. I have to talk to her."

"Give me a minute to think. Maybe my wife remembers who Ellie married."

Evan waited impatiently until Henry returned to the phone.

"Mable says its Vernon Dresden. They live on Long Island."

"Thank you," Evan said. He hung up without giving Henry a chance to ask further questions.

"Dresden," Bob read the name from the paper Evan wrote it on. "She's got some friends."

"What do you mean?"

"Get your head out of the sand, Evan. Can you honestly tell me you've never heard of Vernon Dresden?"

"How do you expect me to have heard of some guy in a city the size of New York?"

"He's only one of the best corporate lawyers in the country. I'm always reading about him and the cases he takes in the paper. He's called on to consult all over the world. They call him the boy genius. Sound like anyone else we know?"

Evan knew what Bob meant. For years his own colleagues used the term when they referred to him. Now no one even knew he existed. At least they didn't prior to the publication of this article.

"So, now you've got a name. How do you expect to get an address and phone number?"

"It's called directory assistance," Evan said, annoyed with Bob's tone.

"Go right ahead. Someone like Dresden will have an unlisted number."

Evan ignored Bob's comment then checked the phone book for the area code for Long Island. To his disappointment, the operator confirmed Bob's prediction.

"What now, Dick Tracy?" Bob asked.

"Maybe Jaycee has an address book at the dorm. We'll search her room."

"What's this 'we' stuff? I certainly don't want to be charged with breaking and entering."

"It won't be like that. Sandy is her roommate for Christ's sake. Now are you coming with me or am I going alone?"

"I guess someone has to go with you to keep you out of trouble."

Bob's smile calmed Evan a bit.

Sandy answered their knock, giving Evan a feeling of relief not to have to use his passkey like a thief in the night. "By any chance, do you know if Jaycee has an address book?" Evan asked.

"I think she does, but why do you want it, Dad?"

"I need to talk to her."

Evan watched as Sandy opened the drawer of the bedside table. He breathed a bit easier when she produced a book with a delicate floral pattern on the cover.

Under the letter D he found the names Vern and Ellie Dresden, along with a phone number and address.

"This has to be it," he announced.

"Why is it so important that you get hold of her? Is something wrong?" Sandy asked.

"Just a misunderstanding I need to clear up before Jaycee sees this morning's paper. I'll explain more later."

Evan left the dorm with Bob. "Now what?" he inquired.

"I go back home and give her a call. If you thought I leaked the story to the press, God only knows what she'll think. Damn Sayo. Why couldn't he stay out of things?"

"So now you're blaming our friendly neighborhood spirit. Why don't you just blame yourself? Jaycee wanted to go to the press the first of the week, but you wouldn't let her. Why couldn't you two work together on this? If you had, you wouldn't be in such a state over this."

"Drop it, Bob."

"Not on your life. I want to hear what you plan to say when you talk to her. Besides, you asked us to come over so we could listen to the tape. Remember? Amanda should already be there."

Evan nodded. He'd momentarily forgotten calling Bob and Amanda last night after hearing the narrative on the tape.

Noya's chilling words held no comparison to what Jaycee might think about the article he didn't authorize.

Bob followed Evan to the Jeep and got in. "Are you taking your truck?" Evan asked.

"Do you see it? Amanda took it to town for groceries. I told her I'd catch a ride with you."

At the apartment, they found Amanda waiting for them, "I thought you guys might like something to eat later. I picked up some pork steaks for the grill."

"Thanks," Evan muttered, as he unlocked the door.

Bob explained things, while Evan pulled three beers from the refrigerator. When he returned to the living room, he noticed two messages blinking on the machine. Almost afraid of what he might hear, Evan pushed the play button.

"Dr. Clark, this is Joe Campion. Call me when you get in at 555-4728."

A beep signaled the end of the message and the beginning of the next. Jaycee's icy tone mingled with her unnatural formality further depressed Evan. Ever since he first saw the article, he hoped she hadn't seen it, prayed he could talk to her and explain what happened. *So much for prayers,* he thought as he replayed the messages to jot down Campion's number.

Reluctant to erase Jaycee's message, Evan dialed the number on his paper.

"Just what in the hell did you think you were doing?" he demanded, when Joe answered.

"I called to try and explain. After I talked to you the other day, I talked to my editor and told him what we agreed on. This morning when I saw the article, I asked him what happened. He said this hotshot kid, someone we just hired, picked up on the story the same way I did. When the Gazette wouldn't publish it, he went to the wire services. It was a big mistake. It's certainly one the kid will regret for the rest of his life. He may have gotten a big story, but he lost his job over it. No newspaperman worth his salt runs a story blind."

Evan took a deep breath. He wanted to believe Campion. "I hate to see anyone lose their job over this, but the guy did screw up. Not only did he run an unauthorized story but also because of it, the volunteer involved has quit. If she doesn't come back, we'll never find the writings."

"I am sorry, Doc. I'd hate to think we jeopardized your project. Guess I can kiss my exclusive good-bye."

"It depends on whether we get our volunteer back. If we do, and if we find anything, I'll let you know."

"So?" Bob asked, when Evan hung up the phone.

"A hotshot kid wanted to make a name for himself. When the Gazette wouldn't publish his story, he went over their heads and ended his career. It's only right, but it doesn't bring Jaycee back. At least I have proof the story didn't come from me."

The look on Bob and Amanda's faces mirrored Evan's mood. Before calling New York, he slammed his beer and took another one from the refrigerator. "If this wasn't so serious," Evan mused, popping the top, "I'd say this was a good time for an all-night drink."

Amanda shook her head disapprovingly. "Drinking yourself silly won't change anything. Why don't you try talking to Jaycee instead?"

Evan nodded then entered the number from Jaycee's address book. "Is this the Dresden residence?" he asked, when a man answered.

"Yes, it is. How did you get this number?"

"It doesn't matter. Is Jaycee there?"

"Who is this?"

"It's Evan Clark, not that it should make any difference to you. Is Jaycee there?"

"I wouldn't let you talk to her if she was here, which she isn't. She doesn't want anything more to do with you, Clark. To be truthful, I don't blame her. Are you always a bastard or is this something you reserve for special occasions? I shouldn't tell you this, but Jaycee is terribly upset by what we read in the paper this morning."

"Look, Dresden, I didn't call to exchange obscenities with you. Will you at least tell her I called?"

"In a pig's eye. I'd sooner tell her I put a rattlesnake in her bed. Give it up, Clark. She doesn't want to hear from you. You can kiss your meal ticket good-bye. Jaycee isn't coming back to Round Tree."

The click on the other end of the line annoyed Evan further. "Bastard, he called me a bastard," he said, when he replaced the receiver.

"So, what do you plan to do now? Are you going to drop it?" Bob asked.

"Not on your life. I'm going to New York."

"New York? Are you crazy? What about the dig?"

"Right now, the dig is nothing compared to Jaycee. I need to face her, to talk to her and not over the phone."

Evan remembered feeling he needed to talk to her face to face at Havelin. At the time, he couldn't take a chance of her hanging up on him. It seemed like some things never changed.

"With the sorting shed shut down, Chris can oversee things at the site. You can handle the tourists. I'm catching a flight to New York tonight so I can drive out to Long Island first thing in the morning."

"I've got a better idea," Bob suggested. "You can catch an early flight tomorrow and I'll drive you to the airport. You're in no shape to go anywhere tonight. You probably couldn't get reservations anyway."

Evan slumped into a chair, defeated. Jaycee was avoiding him, the state offered him funding because of an unconfirmed article and his best friends were worried about him. Looking up, he saw Amanda pick up the phone. He momentarily wondered who she was calling, then dismissed the thought. He didn't care.

"I've booked you a flight for tomorrow and rented a car at the airport," Amanda said, when she hung up the phone. "I guaranteed it with the credit card for the dig."

"I can pay for my own damn flight," Evan said, defensively.

"I know you can, but this is important to the dig, to all of us. It's the least we can do. I'd give a month's pay to know who leaked the information to that reporter."

"Does it matter? If it does, you can blame all of us," Evan said reluctantly admitting the truth. "No one said this was something to be kept secret. It's exciting to talk about visions and voices. Anyone could have overheard us talking, even been in the sorting shed when Jaycee experienced the first visions. We can't change what happened."

"No, we can't, but it certainly doesn't make it any easier to accept," Bob conceded.

"Well, I've accepted it. When I go to New York in the morning, I don't plan to come back without Jaycee. Maybe you should have booked me a hotel room."

Amanda's smile told him he'd underestimated her, again. "I'm way ahead of you. I've already booked one."

Evan felt the burden lighten up, lifting a weight from his shoulders. Amanda thought of everything, just like she always did.

"Why don't you come over to our place and spend the night?" Bob suggested.

Amanda gave Evan no chance to answer. "Bob's right, you shouldn't stay here alone."

"What about the pork steaks you brought for the grill?"

"We've got a grill. Stop making excuses and pack a bag."

"You know what your problem is, Amanda? You need someone to mother, especially with the kids gone for the summer. Guess I'm as good a candidate as anyone."

~ * ~

"Are you going to church with us?" Ellie asked on Sunday morning.

"I don't think so," Jaycee replied. "I have a lot of things to put in perspective. This past life and regression thing goes against everything I've ever learned in church or anywhere else for that matter. I need to be alone for a while to think on it."

"Are you sure?" Vern inquired. "Maybe you should just put it out of your mind completely.

"Positive. I just want to stay here, listen to good music, and drown myself in coffee."

Vern put his arm around her shoulder and kissed her cheek. "Don't drink so much coffee you won't have an appetite left. When we get back, I'm taking you girls out to brunch. I made reservations at The Crystal Room."

"The Crystal Room? Isn't that kind of fancy for brunch?"

"They put on a good champagne brunch on Sunday. Fancy or not, I think you could use it. As for going to church, I do wish you'd come with us, but you know what's best for you. We'll see you when we get home."

Jaycee was certain Vern was right. She saw the worried expressions on their faces. The fact she was the reason for their concern, made her feel sorry she'd ever come to New York for the weekend.

Once they left, Jaycee selected several classical CD's and put them on to play, then went to the kitchen to start a pot of coffee. Watching the liquid drip through the basket into the pot, she could see Evan's face and feel his hands on her body as they made love.

What you are doing is wrong.

Jaycee turned, startled. She half expected to see someone standing in the room, even though she knew the voice that drowned out the music sounded only in her head. *What are you doing here?*

Now that I have found you, you cannot get away from me. The man loves you. You must know that I'm right.

The man loves Round Tree and he loves himself. Nothing more. I tell you what, why don't you go and haunt him for a while? Talk to him. I'm not going back there, so it does you no good to talk to me. I can't free you.

He cannot help me. Do you not think I have tried to communicate with him? It is impossible. It has to be you. The man gods have said so.

There is only one true God, Sayo. Your man gods were cruel and demanding. They died with your people. My God is compassionate. He lives forever.

I have learned of your God from your mind. He is very powerful, but so are the man gods. You are wrong to think they died with the people, for they will live until the end of time. They serve the One God whom is the same God you know. Now, will you come back with me?

I'm not going anywhere.

How can I make you understand I need you to come back?

I'm not ever going back.

Ever is a long time. I know. It has been my punishment, my penance.

Why were you being punished? What did you do to so anger the man gods?

I knew you carried my child. I tried to stop your sacrifice, but I could not stop Dostra. A woman with a child is sacred to the One God as well as the people. To sacrifice one is to sacrifice both. It is a sin.

Sayo paused and Jaycee couldn't stop the tears bathing her cheeks.

Please come back with me, Sayo pleaded, his voice faltering.

Before she could think of a reply, the doorbell rang, dissolving Sayo's voice, and allowing her to again hear the music playing in the other room. She had no idea who could be visiting when Vern and Ellie always went to church at this hour. Whoever it was she thanked them for silencing Sayo.

Her hand barely touched the doorknob, when the bell rang again. Opening the door, she saw Evan standing in front of her. She didn't know which she feared most, the spirit in her head or the man facing her. After a moment of indecision, she tried to close the door, but Evan stopped her.

"You are going to talk to me, Jaycee."

"I can't."

"Why not?"

"Haven't you seen the article?"

Evan pushed his say past her into the house. "Of course, I've seen it."

"In that case, you must be very proud of yourself. It makes you sound like a knight in shining armor."

"I didn't authorize it."

"Of course, you didn't. It only had Evan Clark written all over it. Give me more credit than that. I'm not blind. I can read. Not only what it says, but between the lines as well."

"What are you talking about?"

"I'm not a naive little school girl. I know what state funding means to you, to Round Tree. It's the reason I offered it to you, but you wouldn't take it from me. You had to make a big production out of it."

"I didn't make a production out of anything. I can prove it."

"How?"

"I've got a phone number in my pocket. All you need to do is call it, and you'll find out how the story got leaked to the press."

"Who will be on the other end of the line? Brandon, Sandy, Chris, or did you find someone else from the dig to play the part? Do you actually think I'd believe them? They'd only say what you told them to say."

"It's none of them. It's the home number for Joe Campion, the reporter I told you about. I got his message just before yours. It was a kid, a young reporter out to make a name for himself. I guess he did, because he lost his job over it."

"How did this *kid* get the story? It had to come from you. There are too many facts. Why didn't you tell him what I was like in bed? It would have made good reading."

"Jaycee, please, believe me, I'm not to blame. Anyone at the dig could have inadvertently given the reporter his story. Visions and voices make for a good topic of conversation. He could have heard about it anywhere, in a bar, a restaurant, even on the street. I can't blame anyone for talking about it. Someone could have even overheard us. We were seen, you know."

"We were? Where? Who?"

"Joe saw us at Montanelli's. He thought you were a student. That should flatter you."

"Do you think I'm looking for flattery? I told you in my message yesterday you can keep the money. You can keep your flattery, too. You have what you want. Eventually you'll find the writings. Once Sayo realizes I'm not coming back, maybe he'll start trying harder to talk to you."

"What do I have to say to make you realize the dig, even the writings, are meaningless without you?"

"I think you have it wrong. You and Sayo both think I have to come back to Round Tree to be useful to you. What neither of you understand is I don't want to be caught in the middle anymore."

"The two of us? Are you still hearing Sayo?"

Jaycee began to tremble. *Tell him. Tell him I will not leave you until you free me.*

She couldn't answer Sayo, couldn't confide in Evan. She wanted to run away, but to where? Sayo followed her to New York, so did Evan, would she ever be free?

From behind her, Evan's voice overruled Sayo's. "Jaycee, can you hear me? Answer me. Are you hearing Sayo now?"

Jaycee nodded.

"What did he say to you?"

Again, tears began to fall. Even though she willed herself to remain conscious, the warm blackness became a welcome haven.

~ * ~

Evan wondered if Jaycee even heard the question that he'd asked her. The terror in her eyes convinced him Sayo was present and invaded her mind. He wondered which one of them terrified her most, Sayo or him.

If he was such a prisoner, how could he follow her to New York? Why didn't he leave her alone? His questions came in conjunction with his realization that she was slipping away from him. He could only watch, helpless, as she slumped toward the floor. He caught her and gently lowered her the last few inches. Kneeling beside her, he pulled a pillow from the couch to put under her head. The sound of classical music now filled the silent room. Wishing he could face Sayo, Evan brushed his hand against Jaycee's cheek, softly repeating her name.

In the back of his mind, he heard a door open, but paid little attention. Concern for Jaycee consumed him to the point where nothing else mattered.

"What's going on in here?"

Evan looked up to see a man and woman standing in the doorway. To his shock, the man held a gun in his hand.

"I asked you a question. What is going on in here?" the man repeated.

Evan made no attempt to get to his feet. "It's Jaycee, she's fainted."

"What did you do to her?" the woman shrieked, rushing into the room.

"I-I didn't do anything to her," Evan replied.

From the look on the faces of the two people who just entered the room, he realized they wouldn't ever believe a word he had to say. Bob was right, Jaycee had some powerful friends, and the couple facing him attested to that conclusion.

The man motioned at Evan with the gun. "Get away from her."

"A gun? Really? Do you think this is necessary?"

"This is my home and the gun is for security. In this day and age, you can't be too careful when people invade your personal space."

Evan got to his feet slowly, his hands in the air. He cautioned himself not to make any quick moves to agitate the man. "I must assume you're Vernon Dresden."

"You assume right. I, on the other hand, don't have to assume anything. You have to be Evan Clark. You look just like that god-awful picture of you in yesterday's paper. Now that we have the pleasantries out of the way, move away from her and walk out into the foyer."

Evan glanced at the woman who knelt beside Jaycee's motionless body. He wanted to push the woman aside and gather Jaycee into his arms, to hold her until she came around.

"Ellie," the man said, never moving the gun pointed at Evan. "Call 911. Have them send over an ambulance for Jaycee and an officer."

The request shocked Evan. "An officer? Why?"

"Isn't it obvious? I'm having you arrested."

"For what?"

"Trespassing," Vern announced calmly.

"You're out of your mind."

"I'm not out of my mind, but I think you are. Now, we're going to wait right here for the police."

Evan stood in the hallway, glancing nervously between the gun and Jaycee. Although only minutes passed, it seemed like hours before sirens sounded.

The bell rang and Vern backed toward the door, never lowering his gun. "I want this man arrested for trespassing."

"Are you Mr. Dresden?"

"Of course, I am."

The officer turned to Evan. "Who are you?"

"I'm Dr. Evan Clark and I'm not trespassing. I came here to see Dr. Grant, to talk to her. She let me in the house."

He knew it was only a half-truth. He forced his way into the house in order to talk to Jaycee.

"Dr. Clark, you are under arrest. You have the right to remain silent. Anything you say can and will be used against you in a court of law. If you cannot afford an attorney, one will be appointed for you."

"This is the most asinine thing I've ever heard of. I'm not trespassing. If you'll put away your toy pea shooter, Dresden, we can talk about this."

"There's nothing to talk about."

Turning to the officers, he continued. "As soon as I'm comfortable with my house guest's condition, I'll come down and fill out the necessary papers."

"I can't believe any of this is happening," Evan said, as the officers roughly pulled his hands behind his back and cuffed them.

"Do you have some identification, Dr. Clark?" the officer asked.

"It's in my back pocket, only I can't get to it."

"Is there anything in your pockets that will harm me?"

"Oh sure, I carry a poisonous snake back there all the time just for occasions like this. Of course, there is nothing in there that will harm you."

The officer reached into Evan's back pocket, making him feel almost violated, and produced his wallet. "You're not from New York, are you?"

Even held his temper in check. "No, I'm Dr. Evan Clark, head archaeologist at the Round Tree Dig. You've heard of it, haven't you?"

"I can't say as I have."

"Look Dresden, I know what's going on with Jaycee. Let me stay here and explain it to the EMT's"

"We'll explain things."

"How can you when you weren't here? She'll be just fine."

"She will? What makes you think so?"

"It's happened before. She'll come around and be perfectly all right."

"Add aggravated assault to the charges."

"Aggravated assault? I never even touched her."

"Well, someone did. Look, Clark, take some professional advice. Keep your mouth shut until you get a lawyer, if you can get a lawyer. I certainly wouldn't represent you. Not with everything Jaycee has told me."

"Just what did she tell you?"

"I know how you've been treating her. How did you convince her she's hearing voices and seeing visions? I think you're trying to drive her crazy, but I don't know why."

"She's not the one who is crazy and neither am I. You, on the other hand, are the one who has lost his mind."

Vern purposely turned from Evan. "Take him away, Officer. I can't stand the sight of him."

Evan turned toward the door, to see two EMT's enter the house.

He could only stand and listen as Vern explained the situation to them. "Your patient is in the next room. She's a thirty-five-year-old woman, in relatively good health and she's unconscious."

Evan wanted to stay, but the officers prodded him toward the door. Outside, they pushed him into the patrol car. All the way to the police station, Evan fumed. "Do I at least get a phone call?"

"You do, as soon as we finish the paperwork."

"Don't you mean as soon as you book me? What do I have to go through? Finger prints, mug shots, strip search? Good god, I'm not the one who was holding the gun. I'm not a criminal."

"Calm down, Dr. Clark. Charges have been filed. We're only doing our duty."

"I demand a phone call," Evan continued, refusing to be quiet.

"All right, if it will shut you up, you'll get your phone call."

Once inside the station, the officer took him to a private room. Taking off the cuffs, he motioned toward a phone. Evan picked up the receiver then remembered the officer still had his wallet with his calling card. Completely defeated, he called Bob collect.

"Evan?" Bob questioned, after accepting the charges. "Where are you?"

"I've been arrested. It's a long story. Get hold of Dr. Tess. Tell her Jaycee needs her up here now. For that matter, I need you and get me a lawyer while you're at it."

"What happened? Did you get to see Jaycee?"

"Yes, and that's when all the trouble started. We were talking and Sayo sort of interrupted things. You know what happened at the site. She just stood there, crying. I couldn't get her to answer me. When she did acknowledge me, I knew I was going to lose her."

"Did she pass out again?"

"Do you even have to ask the question? Of course, she did. That's why I need Dr. Tess here. She knows what's going on. At least she can talk to these people, tell them what's happening."

"What did they arrest you for? I'll need to know for the lawyer."

"Jaycee's friend, Dresden, had me arrested for trespassing and aggravated assault."

"Aggravated assault?"

"There's not a mark on her and he thinks I beat her up."

"Let me talk to someone in charge, so I know where to come and what to bring for bail money."

"To hell with the bail. This will all be academic once Jaycee comes around and tells them what actually happened."

"I don't know. She's not very happy with you right now. Don't forget, I heard the message she left on your machine."

"The tapes, you'd better go over to my place and get the tapes Dr. Tess gave her. You'll find an extra key in the knothole of the tree in the front yard. Both of them are labeled. One is in the tape deck. The other is on the entertainment center."

"I'm sorry, Dr. Clark," the officer who monitored the conversations said. "You've had more than enough time."

Evan looked up. "My friend wants to talk to someone about where to come and what he needs to bring for bail money."

A detective entered the room and took the phone from Evan, answering Bob's questions. When the man finished, they took Evan back to the main room. There he saw Vern talking to the sergeant at the desk.

"How is she?" Evan asked.

"What do you care?"

"I care enough to come up here to talk to her. Now, how is she?"

"She was still unconscious when they took her in the ambulance. They were giving her oxygen."

"The unconsciousness lasts about half an hour."

"You seem to know a lot about it."

Vern's accusatory comment made Evan's blood boil. Of course, he knew a lot about it. He'd been on this entire journey with Jaycee. He knew how hearing Sayo's voice affected her.

"I saw it happen before. I prayed it would never happen again. You've got to believe me. I didn't hurt her. I came here to convince her I love her."

"You have a strange way of showing your feelings, Clark."

Vern turned toward the desk sergeant. "I want this man charged with aggravated assault and trespassing on my property."

"You are a bastard."

"They're going to get you booked, Clark. If I have my way about it, they'll throw away the damn key. Believe me, I'll move heaven and earth to keep you away from Jaycee."

"I only wanted to tell her I love her," Evan said slowly, emphasizing the word love.

Vern shook his head. It was evident he didn't believe a word Evan just said.

"We'll see what she says when she regains consciousness. In the meantime, I want to know where the hell you are. I want to be assured you won't be able to get anywhere near her for a while."

"Gee, thanks."

"Do you have a lawyer, Dr. Clark?" the man at the desk asked.

"Of course, I don't have a lawyer, I just arrived in New York at seven this morning."

"Can you afford a lawyer?"

"Yes, I can afford a lawyer. I have a friend coming up who will engage one for me."

"We might not be able to do much until tomorrow, so you might as well make yourself comfortable."

"Tomorrow? What about due process of law and innocent until proven guilty?"

Chapter Eleven

Consciousness returned slowly, as the sound of sirens assaulted Jaycee's ears.

"Dr. Grant, Dr. Grant, can you hear me?"

Jaycee opened her eyes and took in, not only the woman checking her blood pressure, but the interior of the ambulance. She raised her free hand and brushed against an oxygen tube in her nose,

"Yes, I can hear you. Who are you?"

"I'm an EMT. We're taking you to the hospital."

With consciousness came memory. She recalled being with Evan before her confrontation with Sayo. Certainly, he hadn't called an ambulance. He witnessed this happen before. The memory prompted her to question the woman further. "Where is Evan?"

Before the woman answered her question, the sirens died down and the vehicle stopped. The back doors opened and another EMT entered Jaycee's line of vision. He helped to take the gurney into the emergency room.

Inside one of the small cubicles, the EMT's transferred her to a bed and a nurse began to check her vitals.

"Has this happened to you before, Dr. Grant?" the woman asked.

Jaycee nodded, unable to speak for the thermometer in her mouth.

"Do you know what caused it?"

Jaycee removed the thermometer. "It's not physical," she said, handing it back to the nurse. "I'm fine. I want to talk to Evan and ask him why he brought me here when he knows it's unnecessary."

"I don't know who you're talking about. The report we received was that you fainted at the Dresden residence and they called the EMT's."

"What about Ellie Dresden? Where is she?"

"She's been sent to the main desk to fill out your admittance papers."

"Admittance papers? Don't be ridiculous. I want to see Ellie."

"You will, soon. The doctor will be with you shortly."

"I don't see why. This is a waste of time, energy and money," she continued, even though no one remained with her.

Before the doctor arrived, Ellie came to Jaycee's bedside.

The worried expression on Ellie's face upset her. "Don't look so down, Ellie." She hoped her tone sounded reassuring. "All you have to do is go out there and tell them this is a bunch of nonsense. I'm fine."

"Fine? How can you tell me you're fine? You were unconsciousness when we got home from church. That horrible Dr. Clark was bending over you. Good God, Jaycee, what did he do to you?"

"Evan didn't *do* anything to me. He must have told you what happened. Where is he? Did you leave him out in the hallway?"

"He's in jail," Ellie said emphatically.

"He's where?" Jaycee questioned, a wave of panic rising within her.

"In jail. Oh, Jaycee, we had no idea what happened. Vern had him arrested and plans to press charges."

"What kind of charges?" Jaycee continued, unable to comprehend Vern or anyone doing such a thing to Evan.

"Trespassing and aggravated assault."

"Aggravated what?" Jaycee sat up and swung her legs over the side of the bed in an attempt to get up.

"Please Jaycee, lie back and let them check you over. I've been worried sick about you. You've been unconscious for much too long for it to be nothing."

"How long have I been out? It's been about a half an hour, right? That's how long it was before. Believe me Ellie, I'm fine. I told you...no, I guess I didn't, but this happened before. I can't say I understand it, but I do know what I'm talking about."

"When did this happen? Where were you? Why didn't you tell me?"

"With everything that has been going on, it seemed pretty minor. It happened right after I arrived at the dig. I went out to the site and started to hear Sayo's voice. It's all his fault."

Ellie noticeably tensed. "I'm sorry, I can't, I won't believe in either this ghost of yours or this past life nonsense. Vern thinks Evan has brainwashed you to defraud the state and get the funding he needs."

"For God's sake, Ellie, I'm telling you the truth. Can you find someone who understands me?"

"Why don't you try me, Dr. Grant?"

Jaycee looked up to see a young doctor standing by her bed.

"I'm Dr. White. Do you want to tell me what happened?"

"Why? So, you can agree with my friends and tell me I'm crazy?"

"No, so I can get you the help you need."

Jaycee sighed deeply. She realized she had no choice but to do what this man wanted her to do. "I've been working on an archaeological dig," she began.

As she related her experiences, she prayed Dr. White would understand.

"Clark's dig? Round Tree? Are you the volunteer they wrote about in the paper?"

"Yes, I am," Jaycee said, relieved to find someone who she thought understood.

"Has this happened before?"

"Yes, it has, and when I regained consciousness, I was just fine. It's the same this time. Now, why don't you let me go back home and consider today a false alarm?"

"Not so fast." Dr. White put his hand on her shoulder. "Healthy thirty-five-year-old women don't faint without reason. I'm admitting you for further tests. We're going to keep you here over night. Are you seeing a doctor we should contact?"

Jaycee knew it would do no good to argue about being admitted to the hospital.

"I'm seeing Dr. Sharon Tess."

"What is Dr. Tess' specialty?

"She's a psychiatrist."

She knew her admission would only fortify this man's opinion of her condition.

"Are you telling me she doesn't think this is something to be concerned about?"

"She also specializes in past life regressions. She's a hypnotist."

"How can we reach this Dr. Tess?"

"I don't know." Jaycee fought to control her tears of frustration. "If you call Bob Matelin, at Round Tree, he can give you her home phone number. She can tell you I'm not sick or crazy."

"We'll get in touch with her right after we get you admitted."

"What if I say no? What if I refuse to allow you to admit me?"

Ellie took Jaycee's hand in hers. The look in Ellie's eyes was one of concern.

"Please, Jaycee, don't fight this. Vern will be here soon. He'll make you understand this is all for the best."

"The best? Evan's in jail and you're committing me to a hospital. If this is what you call the best, I'd hate to see the worst. Oh, hell, why not? You can run your tests and waste my insurance company's money. When you find nothing wrong, I'll tell you, I told you so."

Jaycee lay back and allowed a nurse to help her into a gown. Lying in the bed, her clothes taken away, she felt naked and exposed to the world, even though the scratchy garment, with its back open, covered the front of her body.

Technicians came into the cubicle and took blood, while other doctors and nurses continued to poke and probe. Finally, they took her to a room.

Miraculously, Ellie was nowhere to be found. *She probably wants to get as far away from me as possible.*

Damn you Sayo. Are you happy? Evan is facing criminal charges. I've alienated my best friend and the doctors think I'm crazy. This is entirely your fault. I wish I never heard your voice.

You do not wish such a thing, Little One. I frustrate you, but at the same time I fascinate you. When the time is right, you will have all the answers you seek. For now, you must rest.

Jaycee closed her eyes and willed Sayo to be silent, to go away and leave her alone. When she again opened them, a woman stood beside the bed.

"I'm Dr. Norris. Dr. White suggested I come up and see you. Do you want to talk?"

"Talk? I must assume you're a psychiatrist. I don't know what good this will do. How do I even begin to explain what's happened to me this past week? I want to see Evan."

"Considering Clark is in custody, I don't think it's going to happen within the near future," Vern's voice sounded.

Jaycee looked past Dr. Norris to see Vern and Ellie standing in the doorway.

"What is going on? Please, Vern, tell me what's happening here."

"I pressed charges against a man I found in my house kneeling over your unconscious body. A man, I might add, who you told me you never wanted to see again. I had no idea what he did to you, but I had to do something to protect you from him."

"Why is it no one will listen to me?"

"Why is it you won't listen to yourself? You want people to believe you and yet you insist on blaming Sayo for this. Really Jaycee, couldn't you be more original than to conjure up a ghost?"

"Damn you, Vern. I thought if I could talk to anyone it would be you and Ellie. How can you blame Evan for something he didn't do? Until I can see Evan, I don't want to talk to you. Contrary to what you might think, I am not crazy."

"Look, Jaycee, no one thinks you're crazy. I do think Evan Clark can be very persuasive. Sayo doesn't exist, except in Evan's mind."

"You're wrong, Sayo is a spirit. He speaks to me and only to me. Until I told Evan about him, the man had no idea he even existed." By the time she finished, the tone of her voice had risen noticeably.

Dr. Norris stepped between Jaycee and Vern. "I must ask you to leave, Mr. Dresden. I'm here to help Jaycee, not allow you to aggravate her further."

Jaycee watched as Vern turned to leave the room. "Thank you."

"I'd like to talk about Sayo," Dr. Norris pressed. "When do you hear him?"

Jaycee resigned herself to answering this woman's questions. "At first it was only when I held an artifact. Now he comes to me whenever he pleases. He spoke to me just before you came into the room."

"Dr. White told me you've been seeing Sharon Tess. Sharon and I went to school together. I called her before I came up to see you. She asked me to sedate you until she can get here."

"Sedate me? Why?"

"She wants you to rest. She did ask me if you listened to the tape of your last regression."

Noya's words echoed in Jaycee's mind. "Yes, I did, even though she advised me not to listen to it alone. Do you know what it's like to be curious?"

"Yes, I'm afraid I do. I'm only going to give you a mild sedative. It will allow you the rest you need."

Unable to protest, Jaycee accepted the capsule Dr. Norris gave her. Within a matter of minutes, she could feel her eyelids begin to become heavy, as sleep crept over her body.

~ * ~

Evan paced the length of the small cell where they took him when they finished with fingerprints, mug shots and paperwork. He never felt so degraded as when the officer took his belongings, including his clothes, as well as his cell phone, and gave him a pair of orange coveralls to wear.

Thoughts of Jaycee, lying motionless on the floor, flooded his mind. Did anyone tell her where he'd been taken? Was she upset when she regained consciousness and he wasn't beside her? He almost laughed at the questions he posed. She hadn't been exactly pleased to see him at the door. Perhaps she would even agree with Dresden about the arrest.

"Pacing ain't gonna change nothin', Doc," the man who introduced himself as Donovan Freeland said. "They ain't gonna do nothin' with you 'til tomorrow. This is Sunday. Ain't a lawyer in this city gonna talk to anyone until nine, maybe ten in the morning. You might as well make the best of a bad situation."

Evan assessed the man. Long stringy hair, looking as though it hadn't been washed in weeks, topped an unshaven face with cold blue eyes staring from beneath heavy brows. An offensive odor wafted from the other side of the cell. The smell of an unwashed body made Evan want to vomit.

"Don't they ever feed us?"

"You missed lunch. This ain't no fancy hotel. They don't cater to high society folks like you. You never did tell me, Doc, what they got you in here for?"

"Does it matter?"

"'Course it matters, Doc, you're innocent, right? Just like me. Only the cops caught me beatin' the shit out of my old lady. I would have gotten away with it, too, if it wasn't for all the publicity this crap is gettin' lately. Things sure have changed since I went into the joint. Just got out last month."

"You were in prison?"

The man nodded. "It seems they don't look too kindly on you when you sell dope to a cop. The dumb son of a bitch didn't tell me he was the heat. If he had, I wouldn't have sold it to him."

"You're a drug dealer?"

"Only when it's necessary. I had a little stash and I needed some money. The bastards made a federal case out of it."

"They should have," Evan said, moving closer to the wall, never taking his eyes from Donovan.

"What's the matter, Doc? Are you afraid I might try and screw you up the ass? Don't worry I never got into that sort of thing, especially after one of the ladies in the joint did it to me. I'm still a good old boy who likes his old ladies to have a crack between their legs and a good pair of tits."

Evan continued to stand as far away as he could possibly get.

"Don't act so high and mighty with me, Doc. Since you're in here, you ain't pure as no driven snow. I told you my story. Why don't you tell me yours? It should make the time go faster."

"They arrested me for trespassing and aggravated assault," Evan finally said, embarrassed by the words.

He swallowed down the gall in his throat at the memory of Dresden holding a gun on him and the officers handcuffing him.

"Who the hell did you pop?"

"I didn't pop anybody. There was a misunderstanding concerning a house guest at the Dresden residence."

He didn't know why he mentioned Dresden's name. It wouldn't

mean anything to this low life. It just seemed to slip out.

"Dresden? Vern Dresden? The fat cat lawyer?"

Evan nodded. "Do you know him?"

"We don't exactly travel in the same social circles, if that's what you mean. My cellmate in the joint did though. Dresden was the lawyer for his company. They caught him with his fingers in the till and the bastard decided to make him an example. The poor son of a bitch got twenty years in the joint for takin' a measly hundred grand. Shit man, you got Dresden against you and you ain't got a snowball's chance in Hell. You better kiss whatever you had before good-bye. All that man has to do is snap his fingers and he gets what he wants. Money talks and he's got plenty of it."

"Guess it does," Evan said, knowing Donovan made sense.

"What kind of a Doc are you? I mean if I get sick, can you take care of me?"

"No. I'm a Doctor of Archaeology."

"Archaeology? What the hell is that?"

"The study of ancient civilizations."

"Don't see where you can make much money doin' that. You'd be better off studyin' people's brains or pullin' babies out of old ladies."

"I probably would, but those things aren't in my chosen field."

"Well, Doc, you'd better start lookin' for a different field. How do you feel about license plates or laundry?"

Evan ignored the remark, even if he couldn't ignore Donovan's laughter.

"You have a visitor, Clark," an officer said, as he came up to the cell.

Evan glanced at the man lying on the bunk. Donovan's smirking smile bothered him.

"Hope they don't keep you past supper, Doc. It's a hell of a long time before they serve breakfast around here."

The guard escorted Evan through a series of hallways to an office with a closed door. Once inside, he saw Dresden sitting at a table with Bob.

"Are you alright, Evan?" Bob asked, getting to his feet.

"Oh, sure, I'm just peachy," Evan snapped. "I've just spent the last few hours in the enlightening company of a convicted drug dealer who beats his wife. It's been an experience I'll never forget. I heard wonderful things about Dresden, too."

"Watch it, Evan," Bob cautioned.

"What am I supposed to watch? The way I talk, how I feel? What more can he do to me? He's already locked me up. No one will tell me what's going on with Jaycee. I'm in here with the scum of the world and I haven't had anything to eat since they gave me coffee and peanuts on the plane."

"I've dropped the charges," Vern said, his voice barely audible, as though the words made him sick.

"You've what?"

Vern cleared his throat. "I've dropped the charges."

"How magnanimous of you. What changed your mind?"

"I did it for Jaycee. She needed to calm down. I figured it would be best for her if I dropped them. Now, I'm asking you to go back to Round Tree and leave her alone."

"Leave her alone? You must know I can't do that. I have to talk to her."

"You think you do, but I want you out of her life so she can forget all this bull about Sayo and past lives you've been feeding her."

"I haven't been feeding her anything. If you want to get rid of someone, find a way to make Sayo disappear. Has she asked about me?"

"You really do have an inflated opinion of yourself, don't you?"

"You didn't answer my question. Has she asked about me?"

"Yes. She says she wants to see you, but I don't think it would be good for her."

"I want to see her," Evan pressed.

"It's a free country. I can't stop you, but I will be there to look out for her interests."

"Look Dresden, we've both got the same interests in mind. If you listened to Bob, you must know I wouldn't hurt her."

Before Vern could say anything in reply to Evan's statement, the guard returned with Evan's street clothes and belongings.

With no regard for Dresden or Bob, Evan stripped off the offensive orange coveralls. After dressing in his own clothing, he took inventory of his wallet, keys, comb, change, cell phone and airline ticket. Finding everything intact, he turned toward the door.

"I'll see what I can do to get you past the reporters," Vern said, following Evan closely.

"Reporters?"

"It hit the news," Bob answered.

"What hit the news?"

"Your arrest, Jaycee's collapse," Vern explained. "The press put two and two together and linked it with yesterday's newspaper article."

"If that's the case, I want to talk to them. Someone needs to set the record straight."

Chapter Twelve

Jaycee awoke from her sedated sleep. Seeing Dr. Tess sitting across the room caused her to smile.

"I told Jean to mildly sedate you," Sharon greeted her. "What did she give you? They tell me you've been sleeping soundly ever since you took the medication."

"I don't know what it was, but at least it silenced Sayo. He followed me, just like you said he might. He's spoken to me more here than he ever did at Round Tree."

"I gathered as much, from what Bob told me."

"What about Evan?" Jaycee asked, hungry for information and not wanting to pursue the subject of Sayo further.

"Bob went over to the police station. I don't know what's been going on, though. I have your tapes with me. If Evan isn't released soon, Bob says he may take them to the press. I did play them for Jean. She agrees with me about your past life. They'll be releasing you in the morning, on her recommendation. Before they do, I want to regress you."

"I don't think I can go through it again. What more can you possibly learn?"

"I need to try to contact Sayo."

This woman wants to talk to me. Why?

"Jaycee, what's wrong?"

"It's Sayo. He's here. He wants to know why you need to talk to him."

"I want to plead with him to go away and leave you alone."

Tell her it will not happen. Not until you free me.

Oh, Sayo, I want to free you. Just tell me what to do and I'll do it now.

The time has not yet come. It will happen soon. As for the man, you can believe him. He would never harm you.

156

Jaycee waited for Sayo to say more, but he didn't. "He won't go away. I told him I would do anything in my power to free him right here and now, but he said the time isn't right."

"Sayo," Dr. Tess said firmly. "You're frightening Jaycee terribly. I know you're desperate, but can't you see what you are doing to her?"

The woman does not understand. I am doing nothing to you. What is happening is what you are doing to yourself. You become frightened every time I speak to you, but you should not because I love you. In another time, you clung to me for love and protection. I hurt you then and destroyed my people. I will never harm you again. It will be over in due time. When it is, you will understand everything.

How can I not be frightened of you?

Think of me as a tender lover and not an evil spirit. Allow me to caress your mind as I once caressed your body. Please grant me this wish.

"Are you alright?" Dr. Tess asked, once the voice in Jaycee's mind became silent.

Jaycee nodded.

"Sayo has disturbed you deeply. Can you talk about it?"

"I have to learn not to be so frightened of him. He says my body is doing this to me because I am afraid. He wants me to think of him as a tender lover who would never harm me."

"Why do you think you passed out today?"

"Exhaustion. I haven't slept well since all of this began. Even though you told me he could follow me, I didn't think he would do it. When he spoke to me, I became startled. I didn't expect to hear him in Ellie's kitchen, to say nothing of experiencing a three-way shouting match between Sayo, Evan and me."

"Can I come in?"

Jaycee looked up to see Evan standing in the doorway, with Bob beside him. Seeing them brought to mind all the events of the past few days. She couldn't control the tears running down her cheeks.

"I didn't mean to upset you," Evan said, hurrying to her side to take her in his arms.

She buried her head against his chest and sobbed until the tears no longer flowed. "Sayo told me none of this is your fault. I'm sorry I jumped to the wrong conclusions. You have to admit it looked…"

"I know. It looked pretty bad, but I didn't give the story to the paper."

"How did you get here? Did they set bail? Did you get a lawyer?"

"Your friend, Dresden, dropped the charges about two hours ago. I have to admit, it was an interesting experience spending the better part of the day in jail. Everything was worth it to see you conscious and talking. I only wish you'd been in this condition when Dresden came home from church."

"You really shouldn't blame Vern. He's only concerned about me."

"I can understand why. He's known you a lot longer than I have, the lucky devil."

"Have you met Ellie?" she asked, desperately wanting to change the subject.

The admiration in Evan's voice made her uneasy. Even though she said she believed he didn't leak the story, she knew she only said what he wanted to hear. In her heart, she still harbored doubts.

"Very briefly. It wasn't a cordial meeting with Dresden holding his gun on me."

With a light rap, the door opened and Vern and Ellie entered the room.

"Ellie, this is Evan," Jaycee said, anxious to break the tension she sensed building between Vern and Evan.

"I don't know if I should say I'm pleased to meet you, Dr. Clark." Ellie tentatively held out her hand.

Jaycee watched as Evan took a step toward Ellie, causing her to withdraw her hand and pull back.

"Jaycee's a very special lady. In your place, I might have reacted in much the same way."

Jaycee wondered if Evan meant the words he uttered or only said what he thought Ellie wanted to hear.

"I hope you won't hold this against us." Ellie edged closer to Vern, as if for protection.

"I should, but I don't have time for such nonsense. Jaycee and I have to get back to Round Tree as soon as possible."

"Oh, Jaycee, you can't be considering going back," Ellie pleaded.

Jaycee swallowed hard. She wanted to stay in New York and yet she knew she needed to return to Round Tree. "I have to go back, eventually. I took the summer to work a dig. With all of the digs in the world, I picked the one with Sayo. He needs me to come back."

Vern's expression became stern and the veins in his neck bulged out in anger. "There you go again with that nonsense. When are you going to realize what this-this bastard is doing to you in the quest for his precious funding?"

Jaycee cringed at the sound of Vern's voice, the implication in his tone.

"It's not nonsense, Mr. Dresden," Sharon intervened. "Jaycee has been reliving a past life. Sayo is part of it. He was her lover, the father of her child."

"I don't believe you people. How can you call yourselves educated and still believe in reincarnation? I could understand if you were uneducated and superstitious, but you've all gone through years of schooling. You're hardly what I'd call good candidates for either of those things."

"Stop it, Vern." Jaycee put her hands over her ears in a childlike manner. "We aren't crazy. I'm sick and tired of everyone questioning my sanity."

"Calm yourself, Jaycee," Sharon cautioned, gently taking Jaycee's hands from her ears. "It's always easy for people who don't understand what's going on to condemn those of us who do. It's like you becoming frightened when Sayo talks to you."

Jaycee lay back, soothed by Sharon's voice and the touch of her hands.

"Good. Now if you remain calm, I won't have to order a sedative. I think the best medicine I can prescribe is for you and Evan to talk this thing out."

~ * ~

Evan glared at Vern. Although Evan completely understood Vern's need to protect Jaycee, his obvious ignorance of her predicament seemed overstated. Evan turned his attention back to Jaycee and watched her relax as she listened to Dr. Tess' voice. He loved Jaycee too much to make a move to jeopardize her recovery. He admitted his love for her over and over again in the last week, even though he fought it at first. He wanted her in his life, in his arms. Looking back, he'd been attracted to her when they first met.

It was Dr. Tess who tried to defuse the situation. "I think Evan and Jaycee need to talk, alone. Why don't we go down to the cafeteria for something to eat, Bob?"

"We're not leaving," Vern declared.

Evan could hardly believe Vern's continued hostility. "Good God, Dresden, cut me some slack. You already know I don't intend to hurt her."

"Please, Vern, for me," Jaycee pleaded.

"Not even for you, Jaycee. I don't trust this bastard any further than I can throw him. I only dropped the charges because of you. Somehow, I don't believe you willingly invited him into the house."

"Maybe not, but I didn't willingly invite you into my room earlier. As I recall, I didn't charge you with trespassing."

Evan could see Jaycee beginning to become agitated again. Although he wanted to stay and talk to her, he questioned the prudence of doing so. "Maybe I should go back to the hotel. You need your rest."

Jaycee clasped his hand tightly. "No. Vern, please, take Ellie down to the cafeteria. I'll be alright. Honestly I will."

"I'm doing this against my better judgment. So, help me, Clark, you lay one hand on her and you'll be sorry. If I hear one negative thing, I'll make sure you spend a long time getting to know that drug dealer you spent the afternoon with."

"I won't touch her."

He watched as Ellie went to the bed to give Jaycee a hug. Vern made no move to do likewise. When at last they left, Evan closed the door, relieved to be alone with Jaycee.

"What did he mean you spent the afternoon with a drug dealer?"

"It's nothing for you to worry about."

Jaycee laid back against the pillow as if in frustration. "This is so ridiculous. It was just like what happened at the site. After I heard Sayo's voice, even though he didn't say much when you were there, I was so exhausted I couldn't remain conscious. When I came to, I was fine. They brought in a psychiatrist. They think I'm crazy. Thank God she knew Dr. Tess. What I don't understand is how Bob got here?"

"I called him from the police station and asked him to come and bring Dr. Tess with him. Of course, the doctor here called her first."

"What about the dig?"

"Amanda and Chris will run things until we get back. If we have to, we'll close it down for a few days."

"You can't. Sayo says..."

"Haven't we talked enough about him? I don't care about Sayo. I only care about you. Without you, Round Tree, anything I might ever try to do in my life for that matter, is meaningless. If you don't come back to the dig, I'll close it down and not come back next year."

"Why?"

"Because everything I do or see there revolves around you lately."

"It's only been a week, Evan. How can you be so certain in such a short time?"

"Maybe it's only been a week, but it seems like a lifetime. Sayo has known you forever and I'm envious of him."

"I thought we weren't going to talk about Sayo."

"Sorry."

Evan paused, wishing she'd ask him to hold her. When she didn't, he continued. "I'm afraid everyone at Round Tree will know who you are now."

"I'm sure they will. I think it's for the best. It was unrealistic of me to expect to remain unknown. I know too much about archaeology not to be found out sooner or later."

"Sounds like you're setting yourself on a pretty high pedestal."

"It's not a pedestal. I am knowledgeable. I do want to come back, but I don't know if I can."

"What about Sayo? If you don't come back, you won't silence him. He followed you here."

"Funny, so did you."

"Yes, I guess I did. Isn't it strange how the two men who love you can't seem to leave you alone?"

"Strange and wonderful. Please Evan, be up front with me. Do you love me or do you love what I can do for you? I'm certain you know what I mean."

"Of course, I do. I love the idea of making love to you and I can't stand the thought of facing life without you. It's been a long time since I've experienced anything like this. Once upon a time, a long time ago, I felt the same way about Kathryn. My involvement with Round Tree killed it."

"What about Round Tree?"

"Like I said, without you, it means nothing. If by staying at Round Tree I lose you, I'll walk away tomorrow."

"I don't know if I can be as positive as you, in light of all that's happened."

"I don't blame you. I can't begin to understand all that has happened to you these past few days, but this has to have been one of the hardest weekends of your life."

"It's right up there in the top ten. Vern and Ellie are my best friends. I can't blame Vern for his reaction. I don't know what I would have done if I'd walked in and found you bending over an unconscious Ellie. I don't think I would have had you arrested, though."

"I hope this won't jeopardize your relationship with them. Good friends are hard to find."

"We'll work past it."

"I'm sure you will. He did drop the charges and got me out of jail."

"Only because I threatened him."

She knew her voice sounded depressed.

"You're a powerful woman, Jocelyn Grant. You take on the head of a school like Havelin, you contend with a stubborn spirit along with a lovesick archaeologist and you tell one of the most powerful corporate attorneys in the country what to do. What other hidden talents do you have?"

"I think you've just about covered them all."

Evan enjoyed the smile on her face. "Does this mean you'll come back with me?"

He pulled a chair closer to the bed.

"I think so."

"What do you mean you think so?" Evan questioned, unable to mask his disappointment in her statement.

"I want to, but I don't know if I'm strong enough yet. This episode has taken its toll on me. Even Dr. Tess was surprised by how quickly the mild sedative Dr. Norris gave me worked, and how soundly I slept. I think it's because I'm exhausted. I need to stay here and rest for a few more days."

"Don't you mean stay here and be influenced by Vern?" Evan asked. "I'm sorry, I shouldn't have said that. It's been a trying day for both of us."

She could tell he was trying, unsuccessfully, to control his anger at her statement.

"I'm not influenced by anyone, not Vern and not you. I do what I want, when I want. Right now, I need to be here, alone and away from Round Tree."

"How will you deal with Sayo?"

"He told me I should believe you. He also says he'd never hurt me. The only harm to come to me has been through the fright of my own body. I'm beginning to believe he's right. If I stay here for a little while, I'll be able to deal with him when he comes to me again."

"Aren't you really saying you won't be coming back, no matter what Sayo says or does?"

"I'll be back. Just don't press me as to when. I need to make some decisions in my life. I have to come to some conclusion as to what to do after..."

"After what?"

"After I set Sayo free."

~ * ~

Evan didn't know if Jaycee's statement relieved him or upset him further. She didn't mention their relationship, only the debt she owed Sayo.

"He says the time will come, very soon, when I have to decide where I want to be and what I want to do."

He took her hand and pressed it to his lips. "I hope you'll want to be with me."

"I can't say what or when I'll decide."

"I can wait. Just remember one thing, no matter what you decide, I love you."

Jaycee's silence said more than her words. Her indecision rang loud and clear.

"It is now eight o'clock. Visiting hours are over," a woman's voice sounded over the public address system.

"You look tired. It's been a long day for me, as well. I'm going back to the hotel. I'll be here in the morning, before you're discharged."

Leaning across the bed he kissed her good night. She put her arms around his neck and ran her tongue over his lips. He fought the urge to pull her into his arms and allow his body to respond to hers. This wasn't the time or the place. They were both tired. He certainly didn't want to push her into anything she wasn't prepared to handle.

He moved his chair back to where it originally stood. When he turned back, Jaycee's eyelids were drooping.

"Sleep well."

Before leaving, he again bent to kiss her.

"I'll see you in the morning." The words no more than passed her lips than she began to yawn broadly.

"You bet you will."

After pulling the door shut, Evan shoved his hands into his pants pockets. Jaycee responded to his kiss. Did she only do what she thought he wanted or did she care for him? Her reluctance to return to Round Tree with him ate at the back of his mind. Even though she said she believed he didn't leak the newspaper article, he questioned her statement.

He wanted to blame all of this on Sayo, but he couldn't. No matter what happened, Evan knew he had to admit to his share of the blame. He'd give anything to do everything differently where Jaycee was concerned. The only thing he wouldn't change was the hours Jaycee spent in his bed, in his arms. The memory of that night would remain fresh in his mind for the rest of his life.

Once he returned to the hospital lobby, Evan saw Bob talking to the Dresdens.

"How's Jaycee?" Ellie asked.

"She's asleep. At least, she was very close to being asleep when I left."

Vern tightened his arm around her waist pulling her closer to him "I told you she needed to rest, honey. It's time we went home. We'll need to be back early tomorrow morning to get Jaycee."

"I'll be here, too. You aren't going to keep me from seeing her."

Vern's brows knotted in a frown. "I figured as much. We've had a long talk with your friend, as well as Dr. Tess. Maybe I was hasty, but Jaycee is very important to us."

"I can understand why. I told her I didn't want this to jeopardize your relationship. Take it from me I know the value of a good friend. Once this is behind us, maybe we can put aside our differences, for Jaycee's sake."

"We'll see you in the morning, then. About the other, I have my doubts, but time will tell."

Evan watched them leave, before he addressed Bob. "Where is Dr. Tess?"

"She took my rental car back to the hotel. She said she needed to get to bed. She has a six o'clock flight to catch tomorrow so she can make office hours. Since we were able to get your car out of the police impound lot, we aren't without transportation. As for you, my friend, I think you could use a good stiff drink."

"I've never heard a better suggestion. Were you able to get a room at the hotel?"

"Didn't I tell you? I'm bunking in with you tonight. I couldn't see paying for two rooms."

"It's just as well. For a while I didn't know if I'd be able to use it. Do we have to get your bag from the car?"

"No. I told them at the desk, I'd be joining you. They sent it up to your room."

"You were certainly sure of yourself."

"You know me. I usually look out for the finances. Give me your keys. I don't think you're in any shape to drive."

Evan agreed, and fished in his pocket for the keys to the car he rented earlier. He liked the way Bob took charge when things got rough. They'd become instant friends when Bob took his course at Utah and Round Tree further cemented their relationship. In the years when he was growing up, Evan could never remember having a best friend. It was hard when you were a child genius, thrown in with adults.

"So, what happened between you and Jaycee?" Bob asked, once they left the hospital.

"She's not coming back to the dig with us."

"Why not?"

"She says she needs more time. I think she needs to rest, but I wish she was willing to do it at Round Tree rather than the Dresdens."

"Don't worry, she'll be back."

"How can you be so certain?"

"I just am. Would you like to make a bet on it?"

Evan laughed. "I don't think it's wise to bet on anything concerning Jaycee. Didn't you say something about a drink?"

They turned toward the hotel and Evan relaxed. Once at the bar, he asked for a brandy old fashioned sweet.

While they waited for their drinks, Bob voiced the thoughts running through Evan's head. "It's been quite a day. Was it only last night when you first heard the message from Jaycee?"

"It feels like weeks ago. I certainly wouldn't ever want to repeat it."

"Look at it this way, being thrown in jail will spice up your life story."

"I'd just as soon no one ever mentioned it again."

"Considering the press was waiting for you when you were released, I doubt it will remain much of a secret."

Evan nodded, exhaustion overshadowing irritation. He quickly finished his drink. "Let's get out of here. I think we both need to get some sleep."

They left the bar and drove the short distance to the hotel. "When do you plan to go back?" Evan asked.

"I thought I'd catch a mid-morning flight. You don't need me here.

How long are you staying?"

"At least until I get Jaycee settled at Dresden's place, if he'll even let me go out there. I'll probably fly out late tomorrow afternoon."

Bob parked the car and together they entered the hotel lobby. "I'm Dr. Clark in room 2543. Do I have any messages?"

The young man checked the box for their room. "There's a message for you, as well as one for Mr. Matelin."

Evan fingered the envelope then decided to wait until they were in their room to read what it had to say.

Bob took his envelope from the clerk. "How about that. Amanda misses me already. When we were on the road last winter, she never sent me love notes. I guess it makes a difference when the kids are gone."

In the room, Evan opened his envelope. "My God," he gasped.

"What's wrong?"

"Emergency at Round Tree. Call me immediately. Chris. What does yours say?"

Evan watched Bob open his envelope. "If you get in before Evan, call me right away. It's also from Chris. What do you think happened?"

"I don't know, but I intend to find out," Evan said, picking up the phone. He paid little attention to Bob as he entered the number for the dorm and asked for Chris' room.

"Chris, it's Evan, what's going on down there?"

"We had a fire in the office. Amanda and Brandon are in the hospital."

Evan sank down onto the bed. "How bad?"

"We had a bad storm here. It all came up quite suddenly. Bob left for the airport about twelve-thirty, so Amanda called Brandon and me to help with the tourists. We were just closing down for the day when it hit. I was out at the site and hightailed it for my car, but Amanda and Brandon were at the compound. They went into the office to get out of the rain. We won't know what happened for sure, until the Fire Marshall finishes his investigation, but Brandon thinks the electrical service took a direct lightning hit. He says he remembers an explosion. Both of them were knocked unconscious. We got them out, but we couldn't save the building. It went up like a torch."

"How badly are they hurt?"

"Brandon has burns on his hands and arms. So does Amanda. They're both suffering from smoke inhalation. We're lucky everything on the computer is backed up and in the safe at the lab. Thank God, we didn't lose the dining hall and kitchen. I'm shutting Round Tree down for a couple of days."

"Was anyone else hurt?"

"Only one of the tourists who helped get them out. He's got some burns, but they already released him from the hospital. None of the other volunteers were working. "What about you and Jaycee?"

"I'm out of jail, if that's what you mean. As for Jaycee, she's in the hospital. She'll be getting out in the morning. They've assured me she'll be just fine."

"Look Evan, I know you want to stay there with her, but I need you here. Everything is falling apart. We have investigators crawling all over the place. Shit, they got here almost before the fire was out. To make matters worse, we're lousy with reporters."

Evan took a deep breath. "It's too late to get a flight tonight, but we can take one at six tomorrow morning."

"Do you need me to pick you up?"

"No, Bob has a vehicle at the airport."

"I'm sorry about all of this, Evan."

"So am I," Evan replied.

He felt guilty about being away, about pulling Bob away, when they were both needed.

"With the questions they're asking, it sounds like they think we're trying to scam the insurance company. Hell, they're even asking questions about the air conditioning going out. As if that had anything to do with lightning hitting the office."

Evan ended the conversation then turned to Bob.

"What is it?" Bob asked, almost before Evan hung up the phone.

"You'd better sit down," Evan said, postponing telling Bob as long as possible. "We had a fire at Round tree. The office is a total loss. I'm afraid Amanda and Brandon are in the hospital."

The color drained from Bob's face. "Is she...?" he began.

"No, she'll be fine. It was a lightning strike. The storm came up after you left. They were in the office closing things down. There was an explosion. It knocked them out. They're both burned and are suffering from smoke inhalation."

Evan hated the feeling of helplessness, as he watched Bob pulled out his phone to call the hospital for an update on Amanda's condition. Not wanting to intrude on Bob's private conversation, Evan went into the bathroom.

As he splashed cold water on his face, he couldn't help but silently rail at Sayo. *What are you doing to us, Sayo? It's as though you don't want us to find the writings or to learn about your people.*

His pleas met with silence.

In frustration, he flicked off the light and returned to the room. "How is she?" he asked, when he saw Bob was off the phone.

"She's having some trouble breathing, but the nurse assured me she's resting comfortably. The drugs they gave her are keeping her stable. I called the airport and changed our flights to tomorrow morning."

Evan sat down on the bed and picked up the phone. "I'll have to try and explain this to Jaycee."

"Good luck. You did tell her you'd be there before she is discharged in the morning."

"I know, but once I explain, she'll understand. She has the Dresdens, they'll take good care of her."

"I hope so."

Evan dialed the number for the hospital. The phone on the other end rang several times before someone at the desk answered.

"I'm sorry, it's too late for us to put a call through to Dr. Grant's room."

"This is an emergency," Evan insisted.

"There are no exceptions, Sir. Calls cannot be put through to the patients between the hours of ten in the evening and seven in the morning."

The click on the other end of the line signaled the break in the connection. In frustration, Evan shoved his cell phone back into his pocket. "Damn, what time is it, anyway?"

"Are you talking to me?" Bob asked, coming out of the bathroom.

"No, I'm just muttering to myself. I guess I didn't realize how late it was. They won't put a call through to Jaycee."

"So, now what?"

"I bite the bullet and call Dresden. Thank goodness, I brought his home number along with me."

Evan recognized Vern's voice when he answered. "Vern, this is Evan."

"Now what?" Vern demanded.

"There's been an emergency at Round Tree. I have to fly back first thing in the morning."

"So, you won't be at the hospital after all. I knew she couldn't depend on you."

"It's not that way. Tell her I'll call her tomorrow night and explain. It would be foolish for her to call me. She'd only get a machine. The dig is closed down. There's a lot going on there."

"Whatever you say, Clark. Just don't expect her to wait around for you. Eventually she'll see you only want her for what she can do for you."

"I hope not. Between the two of us we'll prove you wrong. I promised her to try and get along with you. Believe me, it won't be easy. Just give her my message."

Evan lay back against the pillows. In his entire life, he never hated anyone the way he did Vern. If Jaycee did come back to Round Tree, he wondered if she would be poisoned against him.

Although Evan fell asleep almost instantly, he awoke with a start. The lighted digital clock on the bedside table read two-thirty. Turning over, he saw Bob silhouetted by the window, staring out into the night.

"Have you had any sleep?"

"No. I just wish it would be morning and I could get on that plane. I'm worried about Amanda. They wouldn't let me talk to her."

Evan got out of bed to join Bob at the window. "I know what you mean. I feel like this is my fault. If you hadn't come up here to bail me out, none of this would have happened."

"Stop it, Evan. You weren't responsible for this any more than you were responsible for losing the funding or for the power surge that took out the air conditioner. It's nothing any of us could have stopped. I'm beginning to think we're cursed."

"I've been thinking the same thing myself. I even tried to get Sayo to talk to me, but he's having none of it."

Chapter Thirteen

Evan settled into the aisle seat of the plane. Bob purposely took the window seat, leaving the middle for Dr. Tess.

"I'm sure everything will be alright," Sharon said.

Evan knew she wanted to divert Bob's attention from his dark thoughts.

Bob's answer came without any diversion from the clouds he was staring at. "I hope so. I called the hospital this morning. They said she's still having trouble breathing."

"What about your son, Evan?"

"About the same as Amanda. The explosion knocked both of them unconscious. The smoke got to them before anyone could get them out. Thank God some tourists were just leaving when the explosion happened. They saw Brandon and Amanda go in and stayed to help."

"Is it a total loss?"

"Chris says it is. I'm surprised the press didn't track us down in New York. They were all over everyone at the dig yesterday."

Bob turned from the window to join the conversation. "I can only think of one positive thing to say, at least now people know what and where Round Tree is."

~ * ~

Jaycee brushed her hair and dressed in the shorts and top she wore the day before.

Ellie entered the room, her smile unable to hide the concern behind her blue eyes. "Are you ready to go? They said you could be released."

"I told you the same thing yesterday. Is Evan with you? Did you leave him out in the hall? He told me he would be here."

"He left for Round Tree on the first flight this morning. He called us last night and said he had to go back."

"Why?"

"Some kind of emergency, I guess. He didn't go into much detail."

Jaycee felt betrayed. "Why did he call you and not me?"

"It was too late. The hospital won't put through calls after ten. He called much later than that."

She lowered herself into the wheelchair Ellie held. Under normal circumstances, Jaycee knew she would have bristled at the suggestion she use it. Now she felt the fight drain from her body.

"Vern took the day off. He's downstairs finishing the paperwork. He said I should tell you there are several reporters waiting for you. We'll try to get you past them."

"Why would reporters care about me?"

"They were waiting for Evan yesterday when they let him out of jail. The fact all of this happened at our house makes it news. Vern is a very important man. Anything he does is news. Couple it with the report in Saturday's paper and you've got a story."

Jaycee nodded. "I still can't understand why Evan didn't try harder to reach me."

"He told Vern he did try, but hospital policy stopped him. With his plane leaving so early, they wouldn't put his call through this morning, either."

"It certainly is convenient how he didn't know he had to go back until it was too late to call me. He must have had second thoughts. I can see now, everything he told me yesterday was a lie."

"What did he say?"

"He fed me a line about loving me, not wanting to continue on Round Tree without me. When the chips were down, he chose the dig over me. I think I can do quite nicely without his kind of love."

~ * ~

Jaycee changed into the swimsuit Ellie loaned her. She looked forward to lying around the pool and forgetting Round Tree ever existed.

On the way home, Vern stopped at a restaurant. At his insistence,

Jaycee ordered a sandwich she didn't want. All through their lunch, every question she posed about Evan met with stony silence. After several such one-sided inquiries, Jaycee stopped asking.

In her mind, she questioned an emergency at the dig. She wondered what could have been so pressing. At last, she decided it didn't matter. Whatever it was, it told her where she stood. As she told Bob, less than a week earlier, she could, in no way, compete with Round Tree.

Ellie waited for Jaycee at the pool. To her surprise Vern was nowhere in sight. "Where is Vern? I figured he'd already be swimming laps."

"He said he'd be right out. He has to call his office to get his messages. Come over and join me." Ellie motioned toward the chaise lounge in the sun.

"I think I'll swim a few laps first."

"Do you think you should?"

Jaycee chaffed at Ellie's question. "Of course, I should. I'm not an invalid. When are you going to understand what happened to me isn't physical?"

"It looked pretty physical to me. Let's drop the subject, altogether."

"Agreed. Come and join me in the pool."

"You go ahead. I don't get into physical things so early in the morning."

"Early in the morning? It's afternoon."

"I usually don't go swimming at all. I just like to lie out here and catch rays."

"You don't even know what you have here, do you? You have a husband who adores you, a thriving business and a beautiful home. You don't have to contend with the dating scene or what Evan thinks."

"Do you actually care what he thinks, at this point?"

"I don't know what I care about anymore. He said he loves me. I want to hate him for what he's done, I really do, but I can't."

"Why?"

"I don't expect you to understand, but I've been in love with him for a long time."

"You've admired him. You can't love someone you don't know."

"I know a lot about him."

"On paper, yes, but you don't know the man. When it really counted, he left you here and went back to Round Tree."

"Let's find a different topic of conversation."

"You're going back there, aren't you?"

Jaycee wanted to put Ellie's mind at ease and tell her what she wanted to hear, but she couldn't lie. "I have to. It's the only way to silence Sayo."

Without saying more, she dove into the pool and swam vigorous laps. Hoisting herself onto the side of the pool, she saw Vern sitting next to Ellie, drinking an iced tea.

"We're all invited out to dinner tonight."

"What do you mean all?" Jaycee grabbed a towel and dried off before setting down to enjoy her tea.

"There's a client I've wanted to get together with. He called the office. It seems he's in New York and wants to take us to dinner. I told him we had a houseguest and he said he knew. He's been following the stories about you in the paper, as well as on television."

"I understand. You want me to be the side show freak at dinner." Jaycee knew her voice sounded sarcastic.

"It's not like that. He has his family with him. He wants you to be a dinner companion for his son."

"Of course, this son is conveniently unmarried. You're good, Vern. How hard did you have to talk to get these people to take us out?"

"Get off it, Jaycee. Dinner was the client's idea, not mine. His son not being married has nothing to do with it. Besides, it will do you good to get out with real people. It's not healthy for you to associate only with people like Clark and Matelin."

Ellie looked at Jaycee, her eyes pleading. "Please, Jaycee. This is a very important client."

Jaycee dropped her arguments. "Does this client have a name?"

Vern began to smile at what Jaycee knew he thought was her acceptance. "It's Phil Garland. Does it mean anything to you?"

"It should, he's an alumnus of Havelin and donates very heavily. It's strange, though, he's never been overly anxious to meet me before. I guess it's the least I can do for you. What about Evan? What if he calls?"

Ellie's expression turned to one of surprise. "What makes you think he'll call?"

Before Jaycee could answer, Vern put her fears to rest. "The machine is on. He can leave a message. He certainly can't expect you to wait around for a call that might not come. If he does leave a message, you can call him back."

"I guess it won't hurt me to hobnob with Garland for an evening."

"That's my girl. I knew you wouldn't let me down."

Jaycee finished her tea then dove into the pool to again swim laps and hopefully vent her frustrations at the situation. She didn't want to meet Phil Garland and his son. As a matter of fact, she knew Dan Garland, even considered herself taken with him during her freshman year at Havelin. Being a senior, he considered her nothing more than an irritation, someone to be avoided. She eventually came to view him as a stuck-up snob. She doubted if he'd changed much with age.

~ * ~

They met the Garlands at an intimate bar, located in their hotel, at six. Dan immediately monopolized Jaycee's attention. "You've changed over the years. You've turned into a very attractive woman. Even the picture in the school directory doesn't do you justice."

Jaycee chafed at his unwelcome compliment. "Thank you, Dan. Ellie insisted I have one of her makeovers last winter."

"What about all this nonsense in the paper, concerning visions and voices? How much truth is there in it?"

"A lot."

"If that's the case, why didn't *you* go to the press?"

"Because Evan and I made a pact not to do it until we found the writings."

"There probably aren't any. This is all a publicity stunt, you know."

Jaycee could hear Vern voicing the same sentiments. She wondered when he had time to talk to Dan about suitable dinner conversation to sway Jaycee's position on Round Tree and Sayo. "Do I?"

"Maybe not. It seems as though Clark has somehow managed to

brainwash you into thinking you hear voices."

Jaycee tried to keep her anger in check. "I don't think I hear voices, Sayo is real. When we find the writings, everyone will understand."

The hostess called their name and led them to a large corner table in the dining room. Jaycee waited while Dan held her chair, then seated himself next to her. Once their orders were taken, Dan rested his hand on her knee, making her even more uncomfortable than he did with his verbal compliments.

Without so much as a break in his train of thought, Dan returned to their original conversation. "From what I've read, Clark's project can use all the help it can get. I even felt sorry for him and donated a grand."

"How generous."

She hoped her annoyance at Dan's self-centered attitude didn't sound in her voice.

"My accountant suggested I could use a good deduction."

Jaycee again felt her dislike for Dan threaten to surface. A tax write off was all Round Tree meant to him. Inwardly, she chided herself. Her own ten-thousand-dollar gift was a bribe to Uncle Sam, or at least that's what she told Evan and Bob on the night they first met.

"Did you hear what I just asked you, Jaycee?" Dan inquired.

"I'm sorry. I guess I was somewhere else. What did you say?"

"I asked why they let you come to New York for the weekend if you're so important to Round Tree."

"Evan was concerned about everything I experienced. He insisted I get away for a while. We had a minor problem in the area where I was working, so I was able to leave early on Friday."

Dan moved his hand further up her leg. Shocked, she discretely pushed it away.

"The man shows real concern. First, he insists you get away to rest, then he tracks you down, breaks into Vern's house and assaults you."

"You shouldn't believe everything you read or hear for that matter, Dan." Jaycee found herself unable to mask her annoyance any longer. "Evan didn't assault me. Vern dropped the charges. It's all over, past history. Why don't we try to find something else to talk about?"

"Whatever you say. You know I remember people calling you Jaycee in college, but when I checked the school directory, you were listed as J. C. Grant. What do the initials stand for?"

"Jocelyn Christine, but I prefer Jaycee when I'm with friends. My colleagues call me Jocelyn. My students call me Dr. Grant. I find both names much too formal."

The entrees were served and Dan asked no more probing questions. She gratefully allowed the conversation to flow around her, answering questions only when they were posed directly to her.

"I'd like to see you again," Dan said, when dinner finally ended.

"You might have some difficulty in doing so. I'll be going back to Round Tree soon."

"Perhaps after school starts. I'm sure I can find some reason to get to Havelin."

"I'm certain you can, but I won't be there. I've taken a year's sabbatical. I'll be spending the winter in Peru, working another dig."

Dan put his arm around her shoulder. "I guess I'll just have to make a trip to Round Tree so I can convince you to find your pleasures in the present, with me."

Unexpectedly, he pulled her into his arms and kissed her. "Think about it, Jaycee. I'm only a phone call away. I'm certain we would make a great couple, if you just give us a chance."

As much as she wanted to slap his face, she refrained. It would do her no good to make a scene in front of Vern and Ellie.

"I'll think about it, Dan. Just don't put your life on hold for me."

You are not being fair to the man. Sayo's voice invaded her mind as Vern pulled out into traffic. *In our society, a man's woman would never kiss another man or allow him to so brazenly fondle her.*

I'm not in your society. What you don't understand is I'm not Evan's woman. He isn't even here. He thought it more important to return to Round Tree than to honor his promise to be with me.

In time, you will understand.

Please, Sayo, leave me alone for a while. I need to rest.

The time is coming when you must return. You cannot change what the man gods say will happen.

"Well, that was a profitable evening. I signed Garland, and you relaxed for a while." Vern's comment silenced Sayo's voice.

"I don't know if I'd call it relaxing. Dan Garland makes me feel like a mouse being played with by a cat."

"You're just out of the habit of dating. You'll get the hang of it. Are you going to see him again?"

"I doubt it. I didn't like his egotistical behavior seventeen years ago and I certainly don't like it now. I'm not impressed by his money or his inflated opinion of himself."

Vern made no comment, for which Jaycee was grateful.

As soon as they were in the house, Ellie went into the family room to turn on the TV. "I'm going to catch the news. Why don't you join me, Jaycee?"

Vern almost pushed Jaycee toward the family room. "Go ahead. I just checked the answering machine. Clark didn't leave any messages. Of course, I didn't expect him to call."

I did, Jaycee silently added, as she followed Ellie to the family room.

Ellie turned on Headline News and Jaycee watched as the camera focused on the sign for Round Tree Dig. In the background, the phone rang, but she paid no attention.

~ * ~

Evan left the hospital much later than he originally planned. Kathryn's surprise appearance led to a bitter exchange of words. He dwelled on it, as he drove from the hospital to his apartment.

"Just what were you thinking of, running off to New York to chase one of your little volunteers? I saw you on TV after you got yourself arrested. What kind of an example are you setting for the children?"

"A better one than you've set with your parade of lovers. Jaycee is the first woman I've been interested in since the divorce. Can you say as much? Can you honestly say there have been no other men than what's his name?"

"We aren't discussing my lifestyle. I never put the children in danger. Because of your obsession with this woman, Brandon is in the hospital, fighting for his life."

"Don't be so melodramatic, Kathryn. Brandon isn't fighting for his life."

"Maybe not, but I intend to insist Sandra return to Los Angeles with me tomorrow."

"I don't think she'll be interested in going. I must assume you asked Brandon to go back with you. What kind of an answer did he give you?"

"He refused to come with me. Of course, he's bullheaded, just like his father."

"So, where are you staying?" he remembered asking, in an attempt to lead the conversation to more neutral ground.

"I'm in a hotel in town."

"Good. Stay away from me, and Round Tree. You didn't want to be here when I first came here. You don't need to be here now."

"You're so right. I don't want to be here now. Unfortunately, when you put my son's life in danger, I had no recourse but to come."

"He's my son, too. I can't remember anything like Immaculate Conception happening twenty-three years ago. What happened yesterday was an accident, an act of God. A lightning strike could happen at your place, or his apartment, for that matter."

"Only it didn't. It happened at Round Tree, while you were in New York, getting arrested for trespassing and aggravated assault."

"Those charges were dropped."

"Probably because that little twit you were chasing insisted that they be dropped. Speaking of her, I saw her on TV this morning. She was leaving the hospital. They were pushing her in a wheelchair. It made her look so helpless and innocent. She didn't even have the decency to wear a dress. She had on shorts and a revealing top."

Evan remembered the shorts and tube top with an open blouse Jaycee wore when he went to see her. "She only wore what she had on yesterday when they took her to the hospital. I'm sure no one thought to bring along a complete wardrobe so she'd look good for the press."

"I think you could do better, Evan, but it's no concern of mine. I'll see you tomorrow, before I leave."

"I hope not," Evan said.

His statement caused her to turn and storm out of the lobby.

When he finally made it to Brandon's room, he was still reeling from the confrontation.

Brandon reassured him about what the plans for the remainder of the summer entailed. "Sandy and I signed on for the summer, Dad. We're here for the duration. What about Jaycee, is she coming back?"

The question echoed in Evan's mind as he parked in front of his apartment and got out of the Jeep. He wondered now about his answer to Brandon's questions. He told his son Jaycee would be back, but what kind of lies would Vern tell her.

Not wanting to dwell on negative thoughts, Evan shoved his key into the lock and opened the door to his apartment. His answering machine blinked, advising him he'd received two messages. He wondered whom they could be from, considering he insisted Jaycee not call. He pressed the button only to be greeted by, first, Kathryn's irritating voice, announcing her arrival, then an annoying hang up. Quickly, he erased both messages.

Tossing the mail he held in his hand on the table, he picked up the phone and dialed the number for the Dresden residence.

To his dismay it was Vern who answered. "It's Evan, I'd like to talk to Jaycee."

"I don't think it's such a good idea, Clark."

"Are you telling me you're going to keep me from talking to her?"

"Look, I'm considering a restraining order against you. It's very tempting to keep you from calling or seeing her. It's even more tempting to have a good reason to slap your ass back in jail."

"I said it before, you're a real pal. Now, let me talk to Jaycee."

"What if she doesn't want to talk to you?"

Before he could reply, Evan heard Jaycee begin to scream, then sob hysterically. "What's going on? What's happening with Jaycee?"

His question met with a click on the other end as Dresden hung up the phone.

Evan angrily pressed the redial button. This time, Ellie answered. "Ellie, it's Evan, what is going on with Jaycee?"

"We just heard about the fire at Round Tree, on the news. I'm so sorry. We didn't know what kind of emergency you had down there. How is your son?"

"He'll be alright. Things look better today than they did yesterday."

It galled him to be making small talk when he wanted to be talking to Jaycee.

"What about Bob's wife?"

"Amanda will be in the hospital longer than Brandon. They plan to keep her until the end of the week. Now, can I talk to Jaycee?"

He waited a moment before Jaycee came on the line. "Evan, how are they?"

From the sound of her voice, he knew she fought to keep from crying. Evan repeated everything he just told Ellie, hardly able to believe the tragic turn of events.

"I'm coming down. I'll leave in the morning."

"Do you want me to meet your plane?"

"There's no need. My car is parked at the airport. I don't know when I'll be able to get a flight. I'll see you when I get in."

"Are you sure you're strong enough to come back? There's nothing you can do here. Maybe you should stay put and rest for a few more days. Just hearing your voice is enough to put my mind at ease. After this morning, I doubt if I'm ranking very high on your list. I'm sorry about not being there for you."

"I must admit, I was mad at you this morning. Of course, I didn't know about the fire yet. Ellie said it was an emergency. I thought it was a good excuse to avoid me. I know Round Tree is very important to you."

"Not as important as you are." He paused, in the hopes what he said would soften what he intended to say next. "This might not be the best time for you to come down."

"Why?"

"Kathryn is here. I'm afraid she's been making some very derogatory remarks about us."

"It doesn't matter. I need to be there, Evan. I've been taking a beating from Sayo for staying in New York. I finally begged him to leave me alone and let me deal with this by myself."

"Was he receptive to your suggestion? I've spent the last two days asking him to talk to me, but he isn't having anything to do with me."

"You know he won't talk to you."

"I guess I do. I don't care if he ever talks to me, as long as you do."

"Even if we don't have a chance, I can't shut you out. I need to be at Round Tree, to be with Amanda and Brandon, even to be with you. Please don't ask me to stay away."

"Whatever you say. I'll see you tomorrow."

Evan hung up the phone, his emotions churning. On one hand, the prospect of Jaycee returning elated him, on the other hand, her statement about them not having a chance depressed him. How would he deal with seeing her again if things didn't work out?

Tomorrow she would arrive at the site. Tomorrow he would convince her how much she meant to him. Tomorrow he would be able to work again.

Thinking about going back to work, Evan turned his thoughts to the beleaguered dig. The air conditioning at the sorting shed was working again and no other buildings were damaged in the fire, although the outer wall of the dining hall stood as a grim reminder of what happened on Sunday. Throughout the day, he talked with several volunteers who came to help with the cleanup. Everyone seemed undaunted by the unfortunate chain of events.

"Well, Sayo, you haven't won yet. If you thought this would scare everyone away, you were wrong."

Chapter Fourteen

Ellie took Jaycee to the airport. While they waited for the flight to be called, they discussed the happenings of the past weekend.

"I don't like you going back there. It's not healthy."

"You don't understand. I have to go back. I don't know if Evan and I have a chance, but I have to try. He's been unaware of my feelings for him in the past, but these last few days I've been unable to conceal them."

"Just remember, our door is always opened to you."

Once seated on the plane, Jaycee wondered if she was doing the right thing. It would be easy to believe everything Vern told her. Only Evan's voice, his tone, made her realize why she wanted to go back to Round Tree. After deplaning, Jaycee went directly to her car. With the intense heat of the last week broken by Sunday's storm, the outside air seemed pleasingly cool compared to the oppressive temperature inside the car. She quickly rolled down the windows and enjoyed the breeze kissing her cheek as she drove toward Round Tree.

Stopping at the dorm only to leave off her bag and change clothes, Jaycee hurried down to the sorting shed.

Chris was the first to greet her. "Jaycee, how are you? Evan didn't tell me you were coming back today."

"There's no need to look so concerned. I'm fine. From the look of things around here, you're running short handed. Put me to work."

"Are you sure? There's not a volunteer on the dig that doesn't know who you are and what you do for a living. Can you handle it?"

"I can now. It was foolish of me to try such a charade in the first place. For the time being, I need to work with my hands. This sitting around isn't for me."

By noon, Jaycee reluctantly sat aside the piece of pottery she'd been working on to go down to the dining hall. Although several people greeted her warmly, she couldn't mask her disappointment at not seeing

Evan. After lunch, she again worked on the piece she started in the morning. Obsession pushed her to work frantically to finish it before quitting time.

Chris's hands on her shoulders surprised her. "Put it down, Jaycee. Tomorrow is another day."

"I know, but I wanted to finish it."

"Not today. Tomorrow will be soon enough. Have you had any visions from this stuff?"

"No. I think Sayo decided to leave me alone for a while."

"Good. What are you doing for dinner tonight?"

The question surprised her. "I don't know. Maybe I'll drive into town and grab a burger."

"Let me take you out."

"It isn't necessary. You don't have to entertain me. I want to see Sandy and maybe go to the hospital. I do thank you for the invitation, though."

She found Sandy waiting for her at the dorm. "I saw your suitcase. Dad told me you were coming back today."

"I wasn't until I saw the news report about the fire. When I talked to Evan, I knew I couldn't stay away."

"I'm glad you're back. You and Dad certainly have been through hell this past weekend. Did you resolve anything?"

"Not really. I'm sort of caught in the middle. You know, your dad and Sayo are on one side. While my friends are on the other."

"I can't believe anyone would think Dad could hurt you."

Jaycee agreed. The memory of Vern's accusatory statements burned in her mind. "They don't know him. I'd be hard put to know how I would have reacted if I found someone who didn't belong in the house bending over my best friend, who was unconscious."

She paused, giving Sandy a chance to digest what she just said.

"Is anything new happening at the site?"

"Not really. Dad seems to have lost interest. He's preoccupied with Brandon and with good reason. Of course, Mom was here and you could have cut the tension between them with a knife. Thank goodness she left this morning. She kept insisting I go back with her, but I said no. She

185

doesn't understand the magnetism of this place."

Jaycee contemplated Sandy's words. How appropriate to describe the feeling for Round Tree as magnetism. "Your father told me she was here. He even suggested I stay away rather than clash with her."

"He had good reason. They exchanged words. Of course, when it comes to Round Tree, they always fight."

"I'm afraid this time it had nothing to do with Round Tree. What he told me was she made some derogatory remarks about our relationship."

"Well, whatever it was, she wanted Brandon and me to pack up PDQ. She kept insisting we fly back to Los Angeles. We both told her no."

Jaycee could understand Brandon and Sandy's devotion to this project. She felt the same way herself.

"How do you feel about my dad?"

"You're asking a loaded question."

"You were getting very close before you went to New York. Do you think you can pick up the pieces and try again?"

"I can't honestly say. We've been through a lot this past week. It seems like I've been connected with Round Tree and your father forever. What I don't know is if we have a chance of ever becoming more than good friends."

"Did Dad really break into your friend's house?"

"Do you want the truth, or the story I told Vern?"

"The truth."

"He pushed his way in. I wouldn't call it trespassing, though."

"Did he assault you?"

"Good heavens no. I lost consciousness after I heard Sayo. He has a tendency to frighten and exhaust me. In the hospital, he made me see it's my body working against me rather than anything he's doing. As for your dad and me, we have a lot to work past."

"I can understand why. Let's change the subject. A bunch of us are going out for pizza. Do you want to join us?"

Jaycee thought for only a moment. Pizza with some other volunteers sounded much better than a quick burger on the run.

"It sounds good."

"I'm surprised."

"Why? Don't you think I eat pizza? Well, I'll tell you a little secret. I drink beer, too."

"That's not what surprises me. Everyone knows who you are. I thought you might be reluctant to spend the evening with us."

"So, Chris reminded me when I went to the sorting shed this morning. It doesn't matter anymore. The important thing is finding the writings. When I first arrived, I expected a summer of fun working the dig. Now I realize why I came here in the first place."

~ * ~

Jaycee seated herself at one of the two long tables pushed together to accommodate several people. Before she could acknowledge those around her, three fourteen-inch pizzas were delivered to the table.

Across from her, one of the volunteers she'd seen in passing pushed a plate in her direction. "Don't be bashful, Jaycee, help yourself."

Jaycee picked up a slice of pizza, loaded with several toppings, well aware these people would soon want an explanation for her deception.

"You and Dr. Clark certainly caused a stir this weekend," a young man Jaycee only saw at mealtime commented.

"We didn't mean to. Things seemed to get out of hand."

"Are you really a professor?" someone else asked.

Jaycee nodded, unable to speak for the pizza in her mouth.

"Why didn't you tell anybody?"

"I thought it would be fun to be just another volunteer for the summer. Unfortunately, things didn't work out the way I planned."

"So, what's going on between you and Dr. Clark?"

Jaycee looked to where Sandy sat, hoping her roommate wouldn't mention any of the things they talked about earlier.

"Dr. Clark is the head of the dig. I'm a volunteer."

"Is that all that's going on?"

Jaycee turned to see Evan standing behind her. She felt her heart pound a little harder when she saw how tired he looked. "For the time being."

"Sit down and join us, Doc," the young man who questioned Jaycee earlier suggested.

"Do you mind if I join you, Jaycee?" Evan asked.

"Of course not," she said, as he pulled a chair from the table behind them to sit next to her.

"I looked for your car in the parking lot. When I didn't see it, I took a chance you'd be here. Sandy assured me she'd get you to come with her."

"I didn't want to drive tonight. I came over with Sandy and her friends."

"In that case, you can ride back with me."

"Help yourself to pizza, Doc," the young man who asked Evan to join them offered.

Jaycee silently thanked the boy for giving her time to analyze the situation.

"Not only will I help myself, but I'll save you kids some money and pick up the tab for supper."

Jaycee looked across the table to Sandy. "Did you set me up?"

Sandy smiled broadly. "Of course, I did. I figured someone had to do it. I'm as good a matchmaker as anyone. You and my dad are cut out of the same pattern. You're both stubborn. If I waited for you two to do something, it might take all summer. I told Dad to let me handle things."

"I thought Sandy had a good idea, so I agreed to it."

Evan reached under the table to take Jaycee's hand in his. The gesture caused her heart to skip a beat. All day she promised herself to keep Evan at arms' length, to not let her emotions complicate things. Evan's dedication to Round Tree was commendable, but she wondered if she could accept the role of his second love.

With supper completed, Evan suggested they leave. For some unexplained reason, Jaycee panicked. She wanted to be alone with Evan, but she worried about her reaction to him. Could she keep her emotions at bay, keep from blurting out things she might regret later?

After parking in the dorm parking lot, Evan turned to face her. "Are you back for good?"

"For a while."

"I don't know what kind of line Vern fed you about me. I did tell him

I'd be calling and wanted to talk to you."

Jaycee chewed on her lower lip, remembering Vern trying to convince her Evan wouldn't call. "He didn't tell me."

"I figured as much when he said you didn't want to talk to me."

"Did you try to call earlier in the evening?"

"No. Like I told you last night, I had a run-in with Kathryn at the hospital. I didn't get out of there until much later than I originally planned."

"She seems like an interesting study."

Jaycee almost wished she could have confronted the woman who so upset Evan.

"She is."

"Aren't all exes? It's a shame I didn't get to meet her. Sandy told me she went back to California today."

"Thank goodness she did. I didn't want you to meet her. She's not a very nice person."

"Come on, Evan, you were married to her for a long time. You only divorced a few years ago. You must have loved her to stay married to her."

"At one time I did, but it wasn't enough to keep the relationship going."

"You mentioned she made some not so nice comments about us. Can you tell me what they were?"

"Do you really want to know?"

"I wouldn't have asked if I didn't."

Jaycee watched Evan's features tense, as though he found it hard to repeat Kathryn's comments.

"She said I put Brandon's life in danger because of you."

"Maybe you did. If you hadn't come to New York, they might have had to pull you out of the fire instead of him."

"If I hadn't come to New York, you wouldn't be here now. I have to weigh one against the other. It was an accident. I'm a firm believer in things happening for a reason."

"Like you getting thrown in jail?"

"Maybe. It certainly pulled down my inflated opinion of myself.

Let's drop the subject. You said something last night that's still bothering me."

"Such as?"

"You said, and I quote, 'Sayo has been beating me up about staying in New York.' Do you want to talk about it?"

Jaycee searched her mind. She hardly remembered mentioning it, "I guess so. Vern arranged a dinner companion for me last night. Someone I knew in college. He spent most of the evening trying to tell me you brainwashed me about Sayo and Noya."

"I wonder where anyone would get the idea, I brainwashed you?" Evan's tone sounded sarcastic.

"It doesn't matter. Before I went back to Vern and Ellie's, he asked me if he could see me again."

"What are you trying to tell me? Is this your way of saying 'Get lost'?"

"Of course not. You should have let me finish. I told him I didn't want to see him again then he kissed me. It really angered Sayo."

"It must have. I think he's jealous of me. What must he think of someone else? For a while, I thought he was so jealous he put a curse on us. Of course, the technician confirmed the air conditioning went out due to a power surge and the Fire Marshall said the office took a direct lightning strike. I guess none of it was a curse."

"I think we can find something else to talk about. Speculating about Sayo makes me nervous."

"So, what subject won't make you nervous?"

"The article in Saturday's paper. Maybe we should confirm it."

"I think we've already done that. Between you making no statement to the press when you were released from the hospital, and me practically telling them what's been going on here when I got out of jail, I think they get the idea. At least the state did."

"What do you mean?"

"Their representative arrived today. When and if we find the writings, they're prepared to reinstate our funding."

"Oh, Evan, that's wonderful. I'm so pleased for you."

"For me? What are you saying? Are you pleased enough to stay?"

Jaycee considered her answer. Her heart pushed her to profess her feelings, her mind cautioned her to keep her distance. "Pleased enough to consider it."

She knew it wasn't the answer Evan wanted, but it was the only one she felt comfortable giving.

"It's funny, the people who have come out of the woodwork over this. I even had a call from your friend, Henry. He wants to come here and see you. He misses you. I don't blame him. He says you're the best and he doesn't know how he'll get along without you for a year. I told him things would go just fine. I even assured him you wouldn't have left Petersen in charge if you didn't believe in him. Do you believe in me?"

Evan's question bewildered Jaycee. "You know I wouldn't be here if I didn't believe in Round Tree."

"I didn't ask you about the project. Do you believe in me?"

"Believe in you about what?"

"The way I feel about you. Can you honestly tell me you don't care?"

Jaycee lowered her eyes. She couldn't honestly tell Evan anything. She admitted her feelings to Ellie yesterday, but she wasn't ready to tell Evan of them just yet. She needed to be sure of him before she committed herself.

"We have all summer to make a commitment. It's getting late. Maybe you should take me home. I shouldn't break curfew again. It wouldn't set a good example."

"I'd like to take you to my home."

"What, and have Sayo all over me again? I think not."

"When can I stop competing with him?" Evan's voice was tinged with anger.

"When he's gone. When he no longer invades my thoughts."

They rode in silence for several moments until Evan pulled into the parking lot next to Jaycee's car. "I don't want you to go in."

His statement made her heart pound so loudly she prayed he wouldn't hear it. "Unfortunately, I have to. It's been a long day."

Evan pulled her into his embrace. When he covered her mouth with his, she felt all questions and concerns dissolve from her mind.

"I want you, but I'm willing to wait until you're ready. I'll see you tomorrow."

Although she didn't want Evan to leave her, Jaycee made no reply. The promise of tomorrow made her heart leap with joy.

Wasn't it better with this man than the person you were with last night? Sayo questioned, as Evan drove away.

Yes, Sayo, it was better with Evan than with Dan, but I'm not Evan's woman.

I think you are. Can you not see how much he cares for you?

I know what he says, but what about Round Tree?

This is his work. Just as teaching is your work. Do you care less for him because of what you do with your life? Together the two of you will do great things.

I thought you said you couldn't predict the future.

I cannot look beyond today. If I could, I would have never been able to endure these long years of imprisonment, each day I've prayed to the man gods to allow you to return, to end their cruel punishment for what I did to you.

I'm sorry about your punishment. What will we learn from your writings?

Perhaps you will deem them as only the ramblings of a lonely and desperate man. In my futile race to save my dying people I chronicled my experiments in great detail. When, at last, I thought I found a cure, it became more of a curse. After my failure, I realized it was too late.

Jaycee stood for a moment, trying to understand Sayo's meaning. When his voice no longer sounded in her mind, she entered the dorm and went to bed.

Chapter Fifteen

Jaycee slept soundly, dreamless, until Sayo's voice awakened her.

The time has come, Little One. We have only hours until the time is right for you to free me. I can allow you no more rest.

It's late, Sayo. Can't this wait until morning?

I am afraid it cannot. The man gods have told me the window is open. I did not expect it to happen so soon. I wanted more time with you, but it is not to be. Get dressed, quietly, so as not to awaken the one who sleeps.

She got out of bed and looked first at Sandy then the clock. The digital numbers read four-fifteen. She wondered when Sandy got in. Could she have been sleeping so soundly she didn't even hear the door close?

As quietly as possible, she dressed in shorts and a tee shirt, not even taking the time to find underwear or a bra.

Are you ready, Little One?

Almost.

Before you go, take the torch, which needs no fire to cast its light.

She smiled at his description of her flashlight. She grabbed it and her keys from the dresser before silently closing the door behind her.

Where are we going?

To the machine you call a car.

Once outside, she again questioned him. *Where are you taking me?*

To the temple, to where I first fell in love with you and made love to you to make you my own. You must begin the journey with me.

What journey?

My journey. You must come with me for at least a little while.

Jaycee drove the car to the dig, then across the open field, to the place Sayo indicated.

Your machine can go no further. From here you must walk as you walked with me so very long ago.

Following Sayo's instructions, Jaycee picked up the flashlight and got out of the car. Without turning it on, she walked toward the top of the knoll. Unexpectedly, she lost her footing and tumbled down the embankment. She lay for a moment, stunned.

You are not injured, merely bruised. Get up and light the torch. We still have a way to go and little time to do it in.

Where are you taking me?

To where you have been before.

Realizing arguing with Sayo would do no good, she switched on the flashlight and began to walk down the dry streambed. As though she had no control over her hands, the flashlight scanned the hillside. At last, the beam rested on a growth of bush that looked out of place on the lush grass of the embankment.

This is what we seek, Little One.

Without comment, she laboriously climbed the steep hillside and worked at removing the brush, breaking off branches and throwing them aside. When she finished, the first rays of dawn were streaking the sky. To her amazement, in the dim light of morning, the mouth of a cave stood in front of her.

Inside, the beam of her flashlight fell on a stone altar. Her heart pounded as she noticed an altar table standing to one side. On it, she saw a stone sheath resembling a man's penis, along with a stone knife. Beside the table lay a skeleton.

This is where you were sacrificed, not once, but twice. You have no need to be afraid. This place will never harm you again. Instead, it shall be a place of enlightenment.

Stunned by his words, she rested the light beam on the skeleton.

Gaze upon it, Little One. Once I am gone from this place, once you free me, this is all that will remain as a reminder of me. Only the bones, which once supported my body, bones that could belong to any man, will be all that will attest to the fact I was here.

Why are you showing me this?

Because if you will do as I ask, the man gods will allow me to once more take physical form and enjoy your body before I am released from this prison. Even though I will never again love you, in the normal way, my hands will serve to satisfy the needs that will no longer be important once I am free.

Jaycee stood numbly, listening to him. What should have been a relief to her manifested itself as tears at his words.

What must I do?

Open your mind to the knowledge I need to impart to you. Allow me to tell you my secrets, so you can share them with the man.

With Evan? You would approve of me sharing this with him?

He is a good man and he loves you. Alas for me, you love him as well. I prayed I would be the only love in your life, but how foolish that is. Soon I will be gone, freed from this prison, while you go on with our life, as is only right. Will you open your mind to me, Jaycee?

She gasped. For the first time Sayo called her by her name, rather than Little One. Every time he spoke to her, she longed to have him use her name. *I will open my mind to you, Sayo.*

Before her eyes, the apparition of a man appeared. His bronze skin portrayed a young healthy body, with rippling muscles. His dark eyes acted like pools, reflecting his love. His face was handsome, framed with black hair. He wore only a breechcloth and the very sight of him made her gasp with baited expectation in anticipation of his phantom touch.

A cool breeze blew through the cavern as if from some unseen chamber, as Sayo's hands reached beneath her clothing to caress her body. Wherever he moved his hands, warmth spread until her entire body felt as though it was on fire. His fingers kneaded the mounds of her breasts and teased her nipples to full arousal before he moved his hands down her belly to the tuft of hair at the juncture of her thighs.

Lost in the pleasure of his touch, she moaned softly as the warmth spread between her legs, to the heart of her woman's soul.

Oh, that I could love you fully. Now that I have fulfilled my selfish desires, I will impart to you, my knowledge. With it, part of me will live on through you. I loved you deeply before. I love you with even more intensity now. Your destiny is with the man you call Evan. For now, Little One, you must sleep. Rest and when you awaken, you will remember all of what I will tell you

~ * ~

Evan fell asleep immediately. In his dreams, he wondered if he slept because of exhaustion or because he felt the tension drain from his body when Jaycee so easily returned his kiss. As the dream progressed, he held her in his arms and stroked her hair, while he professed his love. He even went so far as to tell her he would give up Round Tree to possess her.

The ringing of the phone jolted him from sleep, from his dream. "Hello," he said, still shaking the remnants of sleep from his mind.

"Dad, it's Sandy. Jaycee's gone."

Evan sat bolt upright in bed. "Gone?"

"She was asleep when I came in, so I didn't wake her. A little while ago, I heard her get up, although I don't know why. I thought she was just going to use the bathroom. I was almost asleep when I heard the door open. I called her name, a couple of times, but she didn't answer me. I watched from the window while she got into her car and drove out of the lot, toward the site. I'm worried."

Evan felt a chill run through his body as soon as he realized what happened. Sayo came to Jaycee to tell her this was the time he waited for. Although Jaycee insisted Sayo wouldn't harm her, Evan panicked.

"You did the right thing in calling me, Honey. Don't worry, I'll find her."

Pulling on his clothes, he wished he felt as confident about finding Jaycee as he sounded on the phone. Before leaving the apartment, he grabbed the fluorescent lantern. Being still dark, he realized he would need it to find her.

Who am I kidding? She could be anywhere. This dig covers hundreds of acres. I can only guess where to begin.

Driving directly to the site, he prayed for divine guidance. As he pulled into the gravel lot, he saw tire tracks leading across the grassy field. Without stopping, he turned his vehicle to follow them. Ahead of him, he saw Jaycee's car, the headlights shining out across the open expanse of the ravine. Pulling up next to it, he noticed the driver's door standing open and heard the engine running.

Flicking off the ignition of the Jeep, he hurried to the running car.

His heart pounded wildly when he could see Jaycee was not anywhere to be found. With no clues to her whereabouts, Evan turned out the lights and flipped the key to off. In exasperation, he ran his fingers through his hair, before getting his lantern from the Jeep and turning it on.

Shining it out across the area, he saw a spot, at the top of the hill, where someone apparently lost their footing and tumbled down. Instinctively, he knew it had to have been Jaycee. Shining his light down the ravine, he noticed how the dew-laden grass remained bent where she must have fallen.

Evan hurried down the slope until he reached the bottom. A well-used track spread out in either direction. He wondered if animals or young lovers wore the path as he chose a direction to follow.

He picked his way along, shining his light to either side. Above him, the sun crested the horizon, but shed only long shadows into the ravine, making his lantern a necessary tool. Evan became so lost in his thoughts he almost missed the mouth of the cave beckoning him from the hillside. He wondered why, in all the times he walked this ravine, he'd never seen it. This had to be where he would find Jaycee.

Scrambling up the embankment, he made his way to the opening. Once inside, he blinked his eyes several times to adjust them to the light reflecting from his lantern onto the artifacts in the cavern. Amid the treasures, he saw Jaycee standing by a stone altar, oblivious to his presence. His mouth dropped open in shock, as he saw the apparition of a man standing in front of her. It could only be Sayo. The man's perfectly formed body exceeded any expectations he harbored about the people he'd studied for the past years.

No closer, a voice sounded in his head.

"No closer?" Evan questioned aloud.

You need not speak to me. I can hear your thoughts.

What are you doing to her?

For the last time, I am loving her. Before I leave, I will impart to her all of my knowledge. When I do, I will entrust her and the knowledge, as well as everything in this sanctuary, to you. You are not aware of it, but we have been good friends for longer than you can imagine.

If I've been such a good friend, why didn't you confide in me before this?

Because I could not. As soon as this woman came to you, I knew the time was right and she was the one I once loved. You have no idea of the powers she carries. She will become very important to both you as well as your work, but only if you treat her with love. The moment you stop loving her, the knowledge I give to her will cease to be of value and will be viewed as a hoax.

I could never stop loving her.

The apparition smiled broadly. *I feel the same way about her. Although your Jaycee is not my Noya, she was born of the same spirit, the same personality. Any man, once captivated by her, is destined to love her beyond this earthly life. How I envy you. Treat her with kindness. Love her completely.*

I will. Before his eyes, the apparition disappeared. When he no longer supported her, Evan saw Jaycee slump toward the floor of the cave. As he had, on two previous occasions, he cradled her in his arms. Seating himself on the floor, content to stroke her hair and face until she regained consciousness, he thought about what just occurred. He wondered if he only imagined it, or if her face actually glowed.

"What did Sayo tell you? What is this secret he's been guarding so carefully?"

In his arms, Jaycee began to stir. Once she opened her eyes, they mirrored her confusion. "Oh, Evan, I saw him. Sayo was here."

"I know. I saw him, too."

"You saw him. You really saw him?"

"Yes, but he's gone now."

"I know. He's free, at last."

"Yes, free, but at what cost to you. He told me he empowered you with his knowledge." Evan could feel Jaycee shudder in his arms.

"So, he said. It was wonderful and at the same time terrifying."

"He made love to you, didn't he?

"Yes."

Evan could feel a wave of jealousy wash over him. Did Jaycee sense it? He hoped not.

"He loved me with his hands, his eyes and his mind. He wants you to finish what the man gods would not allow him to do. He wants you to love me, now, and in this place."

Jaycee hoisted herself into an upright position and put her arms around Evan's neck. "Make love to me. Finish what Sayo started."

"Are you certain?"

"Yes. It is one of the things Sayo asked of me. He knew you would come looking for me. He wanted you to experience what he could not."

Rather than answer verbally, Evan pulled Jaycee into his arms and kissed her. Turning her onto her back, he began to caress every inch of her. When at last he removed her clothing and entered her body, he felt as though he was eighteen again, loving a woman for the first time.

To his surprise, Jaycee arched against him as though she was afraid that he wouldn't penetrate her fully.

Their lovemaking took on the properties of the marriage ceremony Jaycee described under hypnosis. Sayo prepared her, but not as harshly as he did the virgins of his village. It was up to Evan to play the part of being loving and tender, to show her the joy of being with a man.

It pleased him when she was receptive. "I love you Jaycee," he whispered, pulling her even closer as they climaxed.

"I love you, too, Evan. Sayo knew what I couldn't admit. The project is your work, it has nothing to do with us and yet it has everything to do with us. Without it, I would have never found you."

"Nor I you."

"Don't ever let me go."

"Not if I can help it," he said, withdrawing from her and rolling to one side.

"Evan, Jaycee," Bob called from outside the cave.

Evan quickly straightened his clothing. "Somebody must be worried about us."

His hand caressed her face while she also dressed. When he did, he realized he'd used no protection, but he didn't care. He wanted Jaycee to have his child, if not nine months from today, sometime in the near future. As soon as he could, he planned to find a minister.

"We're in here," he called, once Jaycee finished dressing.

Against the bright sunlight outside of the cavern, he recognized Bob and Chris.

Bob hurried to where they stood. "We've been worried sick. Sandy called me. I got hold of Chris. She told me she talked to you hours ago."

"What time is it?"

"Almost noon. She told me she called you at four-thirty. What's going on?"

"More than we can ever tell you about in the matter of a few minutes."

"Look at this place," Chris exclaimed.

For the first time, Evan flashed his lantern around the cavern and took inventory of its furnishings. Stone carvings of animals stood everywhere, each covered with gold or silver along with a strange purple metal, sporting large pieces of jade in place of their eyes. Stone jars stood against the walls and on shelves. It all seemed like a scene from Raiders of the Lost Ark. Knowing no one gazed on these things in centuries made him stare in awe.

~ * ~

While Evan explained to Bob and Chris what happened, Jaycee looked around the cavern. The light from Evan's lantern illuminated the altar table. To Jaycee's surprise, her flashlight sat on it, out of place amid the ancient artifacts. She didn't remember placing it on the table, but there it stood, alien, not belonging with the rest of the things. The knife and stone sheath both belonged, but something was missing.

She closed her eyes trying to see the table, as it once was the way Sayo remembered it. When she did, she saw the bowl she put together on the first afternoon. As the memory continued, she saw Sayo take the bowl from the temple to Dostra's home. There he confronted his mother with what she did to Noya. He accused her, loudly, of killing the one person he ever loved, the woman who carried his child, the joy of his heart. Jaycee could hear him admonish Dostra for committing such an unforgivable sin. In his anger, he raised the bowl over his head and threw it to the ground. *There will be no more human sacrifices. I forbid it.* Jaycee shuddered at the memory.

She picked up her flashlight and switched it on, moving the beam around the cavern until it rested on a stone shelf. On it sat three small urns. The first held a medication for the ravages of old age, known now as arthritis. The second, herbs to be brewed into a tea to help with the pain of childbirth. The third mysteriously sealed, brought flashes of pain to her mind. Determined to know what it contained, she worked past them, until she realized this is what Sayo worked on so desperately before his death. She could see him working long hours to find a cure for his dying people. She could see them, their bodies covered with running sores, pleading for a cure. In his experiments, he tried to find the proper mixture of herbs to give them relief.

She realized he thought he'd found the miracle he sought within this jar. When he first gave it to the people, they seemed to get better, until they started to vomit and lose their hair.

"Oh, dear Lord," Jaycee said aloud.

Almost instantly, Evan was at her side. "What is it?"

"This jar contains the last medication Sayo worked on before he died. I think we should have it analyzed."

"How can you know what it contains? It's sealed with wax."

"Sayo imparted his knowledge to me. I know what every jar contains."

"What do you think it is?" Chris inquired, joining their conversation.

"It's the forerunner to Chemotherapy."

Jaycee watched the expressions on the faces of the three men who stood beside her.

"Are you certain?" Bob asked.

Jaycee nodded. "Sayo's people were very ill. I think they contracted some sort of cancer. They had running sores and were emaciated. He gave them this medication. At first it helped but then they began to vomit and lost their hair. What does it sound like to you?"

Beside her, Evan nodded. "Exactly what you say it is. What about the writings? Did he tell you where they are?"

Jaycee moved the beam of her flashlight around the cavern until it fell on several stone jars. "The first one contains grain, the second nuts, and the third dried fruit. The writings are in the fourth jar."

"Why would he put them there?" Bob questioned.

"Because only Sayo and Noya knew of their existence."

"Why?" Chris asked.

"There was no written language for these people, just as you suspected. Zandar, the man god who fathered Sayo, told him he needed to learn the language of writing, in order to leave a written record for the future."

"We'll never be able to decipher them," Bob lamented.

Jaycee began to smile broadly. "Yes, we will. Sayo left me with his knowledge. It will take a while, but eventually we'll know what they say."

She watched Evan lift the stone cover from the top of the fourth jar, all the while holding her breath. From it, he pulled several well-tanned skins each rolled tightly to resemble a scroll and tied with leather thongs. Jaycee's heart raced as Evan untied the fastenings and unrolled the writings on top of the altar table. Before her eyes, markings appeared on the skin and with them a vision of Sayo bent over this very table laboriously printing the symbols, the story of the people who once inhabited the area.

Evan busied himself rerolling the leather. "We'll take these back with us. If you think you can read them, we'll let you have one of the offices in the lab where you can do it in privacy."

"We'd better be getting back. Everyone at the dig is worried about you," Chris reminded them.

"Why?" Jaycee questioned.

"Did you hear us when we told you it's past noon?" Bob asked. "You and Evan have been missing for eight hours. Sandy said you left the room just a little after four. She called Evan at four-thirty and me at eight."

Jaycee gasped in disbelief. "It can't be so late. We haven't been gone that long, have we Evan?"

"It doesn't seem like it to us, but I'm afraid Bob is right. If the truth be known, I'm getting hungry. You should be, too."

Jaycee glanced at the stone jars. "We could eat nuts and berries."

"I think we need something more substantial than food that is hundreds of years old."

Jaycee enjoyed the easy tone of Evan's voice, the feel of his hand as he slipped it around her waist.

Chris stood in front of her, his hand outstretched. "Give me your keys, Jaycee. I'll drive your car back. You can ride with Evan."

For a moment panic overtook Jaycee as she reached into the pocket of her shorts. "I don't know where they are." She couldn't keep the bewilderment from her voice.

"They're in the ignition of her car," Evan said.

"They are?"

"You not only left it running, but you didn't turn off the lights."

"Are you certain? I don't remember."

"Positive. Just trust me. I took care of it. At least you won't be out of gas or have a dead battery."

Jaycee smiled at the thought of Evan taking the time to do something especially for her.

"Before we leave here, I think we should cover the entrance to the cave with brush. I don't want just anybody coming in. At least not until we get these things photographed and cataloged. I don't want this place exploited, like King Tut's tomb or any of the other tombs of the pharaohs."

"You make it sound like this place is a tomb," Bob said.

Jaycee watched as Evan glanced toward the skeleton. "It is. It's Sayo's tomb. Only there won't be any evil spirits hovering around to harm us. Sayo isn't evil. He told me he's been watching over our project."

"He told you?" Chris echoed.

"It's a long story. It may take weeks, even years, for it all to come out, but yes, I did talk to Sayo. I even saw him."

"Did you see him, Jaycee?" Bob questioned.

"Yes, but it wasn't the first time. I've been seeing him in my dreams for several days now. I saw the same man today. He's very handsome. He would have made Noya a wonderful husband. Instead, their relationship, their love, destroyed these people."

"I don't understand," Bob said.

Jaycee began to smile before she gave Bob a sly wink. "You will. It's all in the writings."

Chapter Sixteen

Evan could hardly wait for Jaycee to decipher the symbols on the leather scrolls. Once the writings were translated, they could get back to the business of loving each other.

"I hope you're not sorry about what happened at the cave," Jaycee said, as they drove toward the dining hall.

"How could I ever regret loving you?"

"Sayo told me you loved me. I didn't know if I could believe him."

"Aren't you the one who told me he hasn't lied to you yet? He even cautioned me about the ramifications if I should ever stop loving you."

"Does that mean he did talk to you?"

"Loud and clear. I can see why you were frightened. His voice is very gentle, yet filled with authority."

"Isn't that an oxymoron?"

"I don't think so."

He drove in silence, allowing her a moment to think about the happenings of the morning. "How about you? Do you think you can put this behind you?"

"It will never be behind me. The knowledge Sayo gave me will always be a part of my life."

"Just how much knowledge did he impart to you?"

"More than I ever thought possible. I began getting bits and pieces of it when I looked around the sanctuary. It's almost as frightening as hearing Sayo's voice for the first time. What about you? How do you feel about our friend, Sayo?"

"I think he's spooky, but as you say, he's part of our lives now."

"Our lives?"

"Yes. What happened today is what he watched every time he sacrificed a woman's virginity. It was an ancient marriage ceremony."

Evan waited for Jaycee to answer, but she remained silent.

Back at the sanctuary she begged me to make love to her. I wonder if when she made her request, she remained under Sayo's spell. Did she mean the words of love she spoke or were they Sayo's words? Was she only echoing the things he said to her?

"It's hard to believe Sayo lived in the cave so long after Noya died," Jaycee said, as though she hadn't heard what Evan said about the marriage ceremony.

"What do you mean?"

"If his memories are correct, he lived there for about three years. His people were sick and he was trying, desperately, to find a cure. Unfortunately, everything he tried ended in disaster. It's as though the man gods deemed him to fail."

"You're talking about primitive gods. It's as though you think they're real. You can't believe in them?"

"I don't, but Sayo did. It's his memories I'm contending with. They don't change my personal beliefs. If we want to understand these people, we must listen to the knowledge he gave me. I know there is only one true God, but what else can I say? If God hadn't approved of what Sayo told me, he wouldn't have allowed it to happen."

This time it was Evan who sat silently. He could think of nothing else to say. Jaycee made sense, but he wondered about the prudence of her logic.

When he parked the Jeep in front of the dining hall, Jaycee turned to face him. "Have I upset you?"

"Of course not. I only hope Sayo's legacy won't extract too high a price from you."

"It won't," she assured him.

Evan inhaled deeply. He knew his concern was laced with enthusiasm for the impact of Jaycee's newfound knowledge on Round Tree. As they entered the building, the buzz of conversation ceased. All of the volunteers were gathered there. They immediately turned toward them as they entered the room.

Sandy was the first to reach their side and embrace them. "We've been worried sick."

Evan noticed Brandon following behind her closely. In all of the confusion, he'd forgotten his son would be released from the hospital this morning.

"I'm sorry if we gave you cause for concern. I could only do what Sayo commanded."

"Did you find the writings?"

Evan looked up to see Ron Silverthorne coming toward him. He stood, for a moment, staring at the man, wondering if he should confirm what they just experienced.

Jaycee took the decision from his hands. "Yes, we did."

"What did they say?"

"Give us a chance to decipher them." Evan knew his tone was more like a snapping dog than a seasoned professional. "These are ancient writings, in an unknown script. You must understand, it won't be like picking up a novel and reading it all the way through. It won't happen overnight. There are at least fifty large scrolls, each filled with very small pictures and symbols. Give us a chance to do our work."

Ron nodded. "Of course. I don't know what I was thinking of asking you something like that."

"I do."

Evan turned to see Joe Campion coming over to join them.

"Something told me to come out here today and talk to you. Guess it's a good thing I did. Otherwise, I wouldn't be getting the exclusive you promised me."

Evan's blood boiled at Joe's statement. The only thing the artifacts in the cave meant to him was an exclusive news story. In the same light, Ron was looking for a coup with his superiors. Couldn't either of them see the impact of this important find?

"Look, Doc," Joe continued, when Evan remained mute. "This is news. It's a hell of a lot better for your project than the crap they had on TV last weekend. It's better than the story about you getting thrown in jail."

The comment brought laughter from everyone in the room, breaking the tension. Evan felt himself relax. Round Tree could certainly use some positive publicity.

"Give us a chance to catch our breath," Jaycee said. "This has taken us as much by surprise as it did you. As Evan said, transcribing the writings will take time. I only hope everyone will understand and not pressure us."

Both Joe and Ron nodded then turned to Evan. "You have to admit, we have reason to be excited about this," Ron agreed.

"Of course, you do, but right now, both Jaycee and I need some lunch. It's been a long time since either of us had anything to eat. Once we're finished, we'll begin to put all of this in perspective. When we do, you'll both get what you want."

Taking Jaycee's arm, he guided her toward a table where Bob and Chris were already sitting. He smiled to see two extra plates, each filled with food, waiting for them.

"This time you can't blame me for forcing you to eat."

Jaycee smiled at his comment. "This time, I appreciate a full plate. Suddenly, I'm very hungry."

"So, now what?" Bob asked.

"We'll have to make some sort of statement about what we found this morning. Once that's done, we'll get back to work. You'll both need to get your departments up and running. I want Jaycee to work on the writings in the office at the lab. I'm taking Brandon and Sandy back to the cave with me. We need to start photographing and cataloging what we found out there."

"Let me come with you," Chris suggested. "I can run the flood lights for you. Jason has been here for the last two years. He can take over at the sorting shed."

"It sounds like a plan," Evan agreed. "The volunteers from the site, as well as the cataloging department, can be divided up between your two areas."

"Will you have enough time?" Jaycee asked. "It's already after three."

"Don't worry about us. We'll get a few pictures, something we can start working on. Besides, now that we've found this, I want to secure some of the smaller pieces."

Jaycee nodded her agreement. "Whatever you say. I just thought it was going to get too late on you. By the time you eat and get back, it will be well after four. What can you do in so short a time?"

Chris was quick to reply. "A lot, actually. We do have to secure the artifacts. We all know what happened in Egypt. We can't let it happen here. Relax Jaycee, this is all necessary."

Will Jaycee see this as necessary, or will she think I'm deserting her again? Evan worried.

After settling Jaycee at the lab, Evan went back to the cave. Leaving her alone with the small recorder to translate the writing made him ache. He wanted to be with her, but he knew the artifacts in the cave required his attention.

With Chris, Brandon, and Sandy, Evan walked toward the mouth of the cavern. "Is it as magnificent as it sounds, Dad?" Sandy asked.

"Beyond our wildest expectations."

Just saying the words brought flashes of the treasures Evan saw earlier in the day. The thought of what sat, only a matter of feet ahead of him, pushed all other concerns from his mind.

"Are you alright?" Brandon asked. Evan realized the excitement of the moment took over his thoughts, removing him from those around him.

"Of course, I am. I was just remembering what we saw this morning. You'll understand, when you see it for yourselves."

Evan could feel the spark of excitement generated by his statement. "You're good with the camera, Brandon. I want you to take pictures of everything you see, from every conceivable angle. When Chris gets the lights set up, it will help. Sandy, I want you to catalog everything. Keep track of what Brandon shoots. It's going to be a big job, but it's necessary. Jaycee's part is to decipher the writings."

"You want to be with her, don't you, Evan?" Chris asked.

Evan didn't answer, couldn't answer. Of course, he wanted to be with Jaycee, but he wanted to be here, as well. For the first time in the past years, he damned Round Tree. He wanted to chuck it all and whisk Jaycee away from here, yet he knew he couldn't. Round Tree was too important to him to walk away. With what they found this morning, he knew, within hours, the whole world would recognize the name of Round Tree Dig and equate it with Dr. Evan Clark. Damn it, it was important to him. For now, the recognition was more important than anything else in the world, even

Jaycee.

They pulled away the brush from the entrance and Evan flashed his lantern around the interior. To his relief, the artifacts were all as he left them hours ago, as Sayo left them centuries earlier.

"Do you intend to take some of this stuff out of here?" Chris asked.

"I think so. If we leave the smaller items, we could easily lose them. This location is so remote anyone could come in and walk away with everything they can carry, without detection. I certainly don't want something like that to happen."

"What do you want to take?"

Evan looked around the interior. "Let's see, we definitely want those small jars. You know, the ones Jaycee said contained medicine. We'll also take the pieces from the altar table and as many statues as we can carry. The large jars and bigger statues will have to stay, they're just too hard to get out of here without additional help."

Chris went to work, setting up the generator-powered lights. When he turned them on, Evan gasped at the beauty before his eyes. "There's more here than we thought. It's hard to tell what else this cave holds. This is only the main chamber. Look at that opening in the back. God only knows what we'll find, once we explore the passageway."

While Brandon took pictures and Sandy made notes, Evan and Chris worked with their hand-held recorders making observations about everything they saw. Together they examined each artifact.

"Where did they get all of this metal?" Chris asked, as he examined a small deer made of gold, its hooves covered with the strange purple metal they noticed earlier in the day.

"Maybe by trading with other peoples," Evan observed. "We'll know more when Jaycee finishes with the writings. The gold and silver, even the jade are things they could have traded for, but I have no idea where this purple stuff came from. It's not like anything I've ever seen before."

It seemed as though very little time elapsed, when Brandon approached them. "That does it, I'm out of film."

"Already? Are you sure? I thought we brought along more than we needed."

"We've been at this for hours, Dad. I've already shot ten rolls of thirty-six exposures each and I haven't even scratched the surface. I've only photographed the stuff we want to take back with us tonight and a few of the larger pieces."

Evan nodded. "There's just too much here. This will definitely take weeks, if not years. I'm anxious to get the carbon dating done on some of these things."

"What about the skeleton?" Sandy asked, kneeling beside the remains.

"It belongs to Sayo. I don't want him disturbed. This was his temple, as well as his tomb. He guarded it well. Jaycee says he lived here for about three years after Noya's death. Can you imagine spending your life in this chamber?"

Chris joined their conversation. "We'd better pack up, it's after eight."

Evan looked outside at the long shadows cast across the ravine. Where had the past several hours gone? It seemed as though they'd been in the sanctuary only a matter of minutes. Time virtually seemed to have slipped away unnoticed. He glanced at his watch and realized it read eight in the evening. With it being high summer, the sun was just beginning to set.

"We could stay here for years, working day and night, and still not find everything."

Chris laughed at Evan's observation. "I think they call it job security. With all of this security, I vote we go back to town and get something to eat. Archaeologists cannot live by artifacts alone. Once in a while we have to eat something or we'll all end up looking like our friend, Sayo."

"Very funny. Of course, you're right. Tomorrow is another day, but when will I get to see Jaycee?"

"Relax Dad. You have to learn how to slow down and take some time for yourself. We have years to find everything."

"Do we? The state wants answers and they want them now."

"With everything I shot on these rolls of film, I think they'll get the message. These pictures should pacify them for a while. They'll have to understand we can't rush through this or we'll overlook something important."

Evan nodded, then began to pack up the artifacts to take back with them. "Did you photograph the altar and altar table?"

"Yes, even though I don't understand what it all meant. What is this thing?" Brandon picked up the penis covering.

"Jaycee talked about it in her regression. It's a penis covering. Sayo put it on when he sacrificed the virginity of the young women before giving them to their husbands. The harshness of the act was meant to be in direct contrast to the tender lovemaking of marriage. It was all part of the ceremony, first she endured the brutal sacrifice of her virginity then she learned the joy of loving a man."

Sandy picked up the penis covering and ran her hand over it as though testing its texture. "It's one hell of a condom. I'll take latex any day."

Sandy's comment upset Evan. He knew she was more than likely sexually active, even still, he didn't like to hear her voice her opinion so strongly. More upsetting to him was the memory of having unprotected sex with Jaycee earlier in the day. He remembered her ignoring his comment about a marriage ceremony. How would she react if she learned this morning started an unwanted pregnancy?

Brandon was saying something and Evan forced himself to listen. "Did you and Jaycee see a ghost in here this morning?"

"We saw a Spirit, an apparition. Sayo isn't a ghost. I honestly believe he wasn't here to haunt, but to teach. I do worry about Jaycee, though. The amount of knowledge he imparted to her must have been astronomical."

Evan felt a hand on his shoulder and turned to see Chris standing behind him. "Come on, Evan, let's finish packing up here. We all need to get some rest and something to eat. Maybe by the time we get back, Jaycee will have some of the writings deciphered and can shed some more light on all of this. Once you're able to talk to her, you can put your mind at ease."

Evan agreed. He was definitely anxious to get back and see what, if anything, Jaycee uncovered. By leaving the lights and generator, they were able to pack several small pieces in the cases.

Once back at the lab, Evan couldn't mask his disappointment when they found it deserted. After carefully unpacking their treasures, Evan tried the door to the office where he left Jaycee earlier in the afternoon. The resistance he found in the locked door defeated him.

"Don't you have a key, Dad?" Sandy asked.

"Bob has it. This is his area. I wonder where he could be."

"He's probably at the hospital with Amanda." Chris no more than said the words when they saw Bob pull into the parking lot.

"I was wondering when you guys would get back. Have you had anything to eat?"

Evan shook his head.

"I can only imagine what you found out there."

"We never got out of the main chamber. We could have spent all night there. Maybe it's a good thing we ran out of film. We found more statues, hundreds of them, all covered in gold, silver and that strange purple stuff we saw earlier. How about Jaycee? Was she able to decipher any of the writings?"

"If you're up to it, we could go in and listen to the tape."

"I'm up to it. Speaking of Jaycee, where is she?"

"She wanted to go the hospital and see Amanda. Afterward, she was so tired I dropped her off at the dorm. She's probably asleep by now. I did get her to eat something."

Brandon interrupted their conversation. "We're starved, Dad. I think we'll pass on the tape and go into town to grab a bite, before we crash."

Evan knew he should join them. The adrenaline pumping through his veins drove hunger and exhaustion from his body. More than anything else, he wanted to hear Jaycee speak the words Sayo wrote eons ago.

Once Brandon, Sandy and Chris left, Evan followed Bob to the office. His heart pounded wildly, while Bob unlocked the door.

"Have you heard the tape?" Evan questioned, as Bob turned on the light.

"No. Jaycee wanted me to hear it with you. She insisted I wait."

Evan sat down on one of the chairs and watched Bob turn on the recorder.

My name is Sayo, I am the high priest of the people.

After all of these generations the man gods have commanded me to leave a written record of our history.

This is against the laws of the people. If the wrong people were to find out, it would result in my death. My life does not matter. Although the stories are meant to be told by the storytellers, I have been told the day will come where there are no longer any storytellers left. Someday, in the future, when we are no more, others will read my words. At that time, they know who and what we were. I feel compelled to use the language devised by the man gods to tell of our existence.

In the beginning, the man gods came down from the heavens, in their craft. With them they brought the people and when they found this area, they deemed it good. They gave the people knowledge of the land and the commands by which to live. When a woman has her first bleeding, she must be presented to the priest, at the temple. There, her virginity will be sacrificed. When the priest is done, her chosen husband, who will watch, will love her before the man gods and the priest, to show her the beauty of loving a man. He will be tender with her. If he should ever beat his wife, he will be likewise beaten.

A husband shall love his wife and only his wife, except for the time when she is in the house of the women or is carrying his child. At those times she is unclean. During those times, he is allowed to love a slave of his household or a woman in the house of pleasures. If he has the means to support more than one wife, it is his decision whether to take another woman into his household. This can be done, only with the approval of his first wife.

It is a woman's duty to keep the house and raise the children. Her husband will provide for her every need. Women shall be gatherers of grain, nuts, and fruit. Men shall be hunters of the game abundant in this area.

Any child left without parents, any woman left without

a husband, will become a slave. They will work for those better than themselves in return for food and lodging.

The metal of the gods shall be used in our sacred statues. It shall be there as a reminder of where we came from and how we got here. The knowledge of the man gods shall be part of us forever. To betray the man gods or disobey their commands is punishable by death.

Human sacrifices will be made, to satisfy the man gods at the time of the planting and the time of the harvest, to ensure fertility and give thanks. Those slated for sacrifice will be from among the enemies who we have captured and the slaves.

To kill a woman who carries a child, either for sacrifice or malice is the greatest sin of all. It will bring down the wrath of the man gods upon the people.

The recording ended and Evan took a deep breath. "The commandments given by the man gods. If we can believe this, the man gods came from outer space. They brought these people here and left them in what they perceived as paradise."

"The metal of the gods?" Bob asked, making the statement into a question. "What do you think it means?"

"It has to be the purple metal we found on the statues. At least that much of the mystery is explained. Where do you think they got the gold, silver, and jade?"

"Maybe the rest of the writings will give us the answer. You saw how many there are. Jaycee has only translated a minute portion of one scroll. We'll have to be patient, but I'm sure we'll get all the answers we need, in time."

"Time? I don't want time. I want answers."

"You'll get them. I feel of all the scrolls, this one is the most important."

"How did she choose this particular one?"

"She didn't choose it, you did. It's the one you unrolled at the cave. Maybe Sayo guided your hand. However, you picked it, I think this is only the tip of a very large iceberg. I believe he wrote it, bit by bit, in order to enlighten future people about the beliefs of this civilization."

Evan rewound the tape and began to play it. *In the beginning, the man gods came down from the heavens in their craft.* Jaycee's voice repeated the words. Evan pushed the stop and rewind buttons, replaying the sentence over and over again.

"This is something right out of Star Trek."

Bob nodded. "I'm sure this will be something people will argue over for years. We should let it rest for tonight, though. We've got a lifetime of tomorrows to find the answers we want."

Evan agreed. He took one last look at the pile of scrolls and realized their translations would take weeks, months, even years.

After her silent reaction to his mention of a primitive marriage ceremony, he wondered if Jaycee would be content to dedicate the rest of her life to Round Tree and Evan Clark.

Chapter Seventeen

Unable to sleep any longer, Jaycee got out of bed, picked up the clothes she laid out the night before and went to the bathroom.

"Did the alarm go off?" Sandy asked, groggily.

"No. Go back to sleep. I'm going to get dressed and go out for a walk."

"Are you alright?"

"I'm fine. There's no need to worry. Sayo's gone. He won't be bothering me anymore."

"Good," Sandy muttered before she turned over.

By her even breathing, Jaycee knew the girl fell back asleep immediately.

Once dressed, Jaycee went outside. Being too early to go to the dining hall, she walked away from the buildings. The first rays of morning light streaked across the sky, much like it must have appeared twenty-four hours earlier, when she took no note.

You slept well, Little One.

Jaycee jumped, startled by the sound of Sayo's voice in her mind. *I released you. Why aren't you gone?*

I am free to leave or to remain where I want to be. Where I want to be at this point in time is with you. At least until you finish deciphering the writings. How did you think you read them so easily?

From the knowledge you gave me.

Yes, the knowledge, but without me, you would have encountered more trouble. I will never be far from you.

Oh, Sayo, you disturb me.

I love you. You will understand as you learn more. Why we did what we did to survive will become clear. Our lives went from peaceful and serene to a nightmare that I thought would not end. It was terrible.

I am certain it was. I have to know, Sayo, why wasn't Dostra taken

216

as a slave when your father died?

Dostra was of the Gods and not subject to the laws of the people. I had not a father, in the normal sense. As one with the Gods, only a man god could father her children. Zandar was that man god, but he was only in our village for short periods of time. He came with the man gods every three or four turnings of the seasons and left as soon as they deemed everything to be in order with the people. He fathered me. Three turnings of the seasons later he fathered my sister Yasma. She would have become the next high priestess, if the man gods had not taken her away. They, Dostra and Yasma, were the most powerful of all the people. As high priest, I possessed power, but not equal to theirs. My sin, in my eyes, was falling in love with Noya. In the eyes of the man gods, it was not doing everything within my power to protect her and our unborn child.

Jaycee could feel Sayo's presence fill the space around her.

Will you tell the man I have come to you?

No. I am afraid it would upset him.

Perhaps you are right. I should not have made my presence known to you.

I'm glad you did. Your voice is becoming comforting to me. I was afraid I would miss hearing you. I doubt if Evan will ever understand my feelings. Will I ever see you again?

I will not invade your dreams nor will I appear to you again, but you will see me. Once I am assured you understand, I will be gone, free to be reincarnated. Once that happens, I am certain our paths will cross again. For you it will be a joyful reunion, but you must know I will remember none of this. Of course, I speak of things yet to come. I will not leave you until I am certain you understand the legacy of which I have left for you.

Jaycee could feel her brows knot, her stomach churn. She didn't understand, didn't believe in reincarnation, even with the evidence she now had about her own past life.

I know what you are thinking, Little One. You still do not believe in reincarnation, do you?

It's alien to everything I've always believed.

How different from our beliefs. For us the greatest accomplishment we could hope to achieve was to be reincarnated again and again, until we reached the perfection we craved. Being free, I have learned of the reincarnation of many of those who inhabited my village. Most of them became good people in other societies. Ones that did not believe in second life. These people never knew who they once were. For the anguish it has caused you, I am sorry. I wish you would never have had to learn of it, but it was necessary.

I know and I do understand. How much more will we find?

Many caverns lie beyond the temple and the man will find them.

I meant in the writings.

I know you did. I will not disclose their content. It would take away my joy in watching you discover them for yourself. I will only guide your mind and make them clear. Why did you choose the great scroll?

Evan chose it. It's the one he unrolled in the cave.

It is the most important one of all as it tells of our origins. It also tells of our demise. I kept it, especially, to keep track of our history. As I told you before, the others are little more than the mad ramblings of a lonely man.

Do you have any idea what you discovered in the last medicine, the one sealed with wax?

At first, he didn't answer, then his voice became strained almost saddened. *I discovered a nightmare.*

Not a nightmare, Sayo. What you discovered is called Chemotherapy today. Your people had a cancer. I don't know why they contracted it, but they did. What you discovered is now being used as a cure.

You must be wrong. How could a cure make the people so very sick?

Patients today become sick, just as your people did. If you are free, go to the hospitals and see how this drug is used. The patients lose their hair and they vomit. In the end they do get well. If your people had given the medication more time, they would have realized you found the cure.

Alas, they became frightened and the predictions of the man gods came true. Those taken away were never returned. I was forced to die a lonely and broken man.

What do you mean, the ones who were taken away?

It is in the writings. I grow weary of this conversation.

In that case, look beyond this place, beyond me. See what wonders your Chemotherapy has brought about.

It is hard to believe the drug I sealed away so it would harm no one else, is such a godsend to mankind. I will see this for myself, but I will also return to you, Little One. I want to help you in your quest for knowledge.

Sayo's voice silenced. Jaycee stood for a moment, trying to calm her nerves and adjust her mind to his return. At last, she went to the dining hall in hopes of seeing Evan. Instead, she found Bob waiting for her and the building virtually deserted.

"Where have you been?" Bob greeted her.

"I only went for a walk.

"For four hours?"

"Four hours? What time is it?"

"It's after nine. What's going on?"

The memory of her conversation with Sayo sent up warning flags in her mind. Like Evan, Jaycee knew Bob wouldn't understand. "Nothing is going on. I just lost track of time. Where's Evan? I thought he would be waiting for me."

"He's already taken Brandon, Chris and Sandy out to the cave."

Jaycee felt as though a weight suddenly attached itself to her heart. No matter what he said, or did, it came down to the same thing. Evan's first priority would always be Round Tree and the notoriety he would gain from the find they made at the cave.

She realized Bob was saying something to her and jerked her mind back to the present. "What?"

"I said, after Evan heard the tape last night, he wanted to see what more he could find at the cave."

"Evan heard the tape? Did you hear it, too?"

"Yes. We listened to it when he got back. We would have called you, but I figured you were already asleep. We both agreed you needed to sleep more than you needed to be with us."

"You're right. I did need the rest."

"As I was saying, Evan wanted to explore further into the cave. He was especially interested in your description of the metal of the gods. The statues at the cave are all covered with a strange purple substance. He doesn't know what it is."

"He won't. It's alien to this planet. Sayo refers to it as the metal of the gods, because it came from the craft the man gods used to bring the people here."

"Did you hear what you just said? How do you know this?"

Jaycee looked up at Bob, shrugging at his inquiry. "I just know it."

"Was it written down? Is it something you read and didn't put on the tapes?"

"No. I know it from the knowledge Sayo gave me. I know it the way the storytellers told it. 'And when the Man Gods brought the people to this place, they commanded the craft be dismantled and the metal used in all of the sacred statues and artifacts.'"

She smiled at the look of bewilderment on Bob's face. "The man gods, from whatever planet they came from, deemed it necessary to leave these people here, with no means of escape. They meant for the people to stay here forever, but events made it necessary to take them all away. They broke the commandments. How lucky we are to believe in a God who doesn't destroy us when we break His commandments."

"Maybe our God did dispose of His people. Don't forget the Garden of Eden. It sounds like these people were put here, much like Adam and Eve and driven out in much the same manner. The only difference is, Adam and Eve were allowed to continue outside the garden."

"I guess you're right. Maybe these people continued to live somewhere other than here, but still on this planet."

She took a drink of her coffee, while she contemplated the path the conversation seemed to be taking. "I still can't believe Evan didn't wait for me."

The change in subject came from the thoughts foremost in her mind.

"I think you ought to see this," Bob said, ignoring her earlier statement and picking up a newspaper. "Joe wrote a full report, just as you and Evan told it to him. After the article last weekend, I'm certain he contacted the Associated Press as well. We'd better be prepared to give statements. Evan doesn't deal with the media well. I think it's the main reason he wanted to get out of here early. He took off like a shot right after he read it."

"Jaycee," one of the volunteers called, before she could respond. "They just put a call through for you from the dorm."

She got up from the table and hurried to the black wall phone, unable to imagine who would be calling her here.

"Jaycee," Ellie's voice greeted. "We've been listening to the news reports on the radio and television all morning. Did you really find the writings?"

"Yes, we did."

She wondered why she said we when she knew Evan only watched her find them.

"Vern and I are coming down."

"Do you think that's wise? Vern and Evan don't particularly get along."

"Vern wants to apologize."

"Whatever. I don't suppose I can change your minds. You have to understand, though, I don't have any place to put you up."

"We know. We already have reservations made at a hotel. Our flight will be taking off shortly. We figure we owe you two a big apology."

"I guess I'll be seeing you later today."

"How about you?" Ellie pressed, not allowing Jaycee to end the conversation. "How are you holding up?"

"I'm holding up just fine," she said, realizing she just told a big lie.

In fact, she wasn't holding up at all. Evan was at the cave and Sayo wouldn't go away. "There's a lot of work to do here. It's been a trying few hours."

"I'm sure it has. We'll see you soon."

Jaycee returned to the table where Bob waited for her. "This ought to be interesting."

"Ellie and Vern?"

Jaycee nodded. "They booked a room in town."

"I'm sure they're some of the lucky ones. Unless I've misread the media, no one will be able to get a room within a hundred miles of here by tonight."

The phone rang another time. Again, one of the volunteers summoned Jaycee to answer it.

"Jocelyn," Henry's voice came across the wire. "You're all over the media. What's going on down there?"

"We found the writings."

Jaycee's comment met with a momentary silence. "I want to see you," he finally said.

Jaycee signed deeply, wondering how she would handle two explosive situations at the same time. Keeping Vern and Evan from each other's throats was one thing but holding her temper around Henry was another. "I can't stop you. It's a free country."

"Good. I'll be there sometime this afternoon."

Jaycee stared at the phone for several seconds before returning to the table. She finished her now cold coffee, then pushed aside her untouched breakfast. "Let's get out of here before anyone else calls."

"Who was it this time?"

"Henry. He's on his way. I can't stop him, just as I couldn't stop Vern and Ellie."

"He's the last person you need here."

"I know he is, but if I want to keep my job at Havelin, I can't antagonize him too much. Let's get over to the lab. Did Evan bring in any artifacts last night?"

Bob nodded. "I thought you'd like to see them this morning before I go and get Amanda."

When they left the building, a barrage of reporters and cameramen greeted them.

They'd hardly taken three steps before the first reporter reached them. "Dr. Grant, will you comment on what you and Dr. Clark found yesterday?"

"I have no comment at this time."

"Funny, you and Dr. Clark were talking to someone yesterday. Are you going to deny this release, like you did the one last weekend?"

Jaycee knew she was trapped. "I won't deny the interview we granted to Mr. Campion yesterday. We promised him an exclusive, when and if we found anything. I can say what we found will require a lot of study before we know what we have. I haven't seen most of the artifacts or the photos yet."

"What about the writings? They've caused the greatest stir and speculation in this case."

"This isn't a case. You make it sound like we're committing a crime."

"You know what I mean, Doctor."

"Yes, I do. We did find the writings."

"What do they say?"

"Give us a chance to decipher them. They're in an ancient script. One neither I, nor Dr. Clark has ever seen. It isn't recorded anywhere in the modern world. We'll need time to break the code."

"What can you tell us about the artifacts, Mr. Matelin?" another reporter asked Bob. Jaycee couldn't help feeling relieved not to have to answer.

"Until they are photographed, examined, cataloged and carbon dated, absolutely nothing. You'll have to wait until Dr. Clark is ready to comment."

"When will Dr. Clark make this comment?"

"Why don't you ask him?"

"Because we've been told, he's already gone out to where you made the find."

"Yes, he did go out to the site early this morning."

"Where he's been digging before?"

"I'm not at liberty to divulge the location of the site. Until we can be certain about what we have, we won't allow this to be exploited. Now, if you will excuse us, Dr. Grant has work to do and I have to get to the hospital to pick up my wife."

"In all of the excitement, I'm afraid we've forgotten to inquire about your wife's condition. How is she doing?"

"Very well. She's being released today and is anxious to get back to work, especially in light of yesterday's findings. She wants to be here, but not without the consent of her doctors."

"Thank you, Mr. Matelin, and we do wish your wife well. We will be here, waiting for any news."

"I'm sure you will. I'll be certain to tell Evan."

Jaycee relaxed when Bob guided her away from the reporters toward the lab. "I didn't expect to have to deal with reporters this morning."

Bob smiled. "Evan did. As I said, it's one of the reasons he insisted on leaving for the cave so early. He doesn't deal well with the press, but you certainly do."

Jaycee replayed the answers she gave in her head, trying to understand what Bob meant. "Years of dealing with Henry," she replied.

Bob held open the door to the lab and Jaycee stepped into the air-conditioned comfort of the building.

"When Evan and I listened to the tape last night, we couldn't get over how chilling it was."

"I know. It struck me the same way."

Several volunteers turned to watch them as they entered. After nodding their greetings, everyone went back to work.

Instead of going to the office Jaycee used the day before, Bob took her to another room. Once inside, Jaycee gasped at the number of artifacts it contained. Her eyes fell on a perfectly crafted deer, its body formed of gold, its eyes of jade and the metal of the gods on its hooves.

I was making this for you. I began to work on it when you first came to live with Dostra. Your name, Noya, means little deer. I thought it fitting. I didn't intend to put the metal of the gods on it. When the man gods came back, to dole out their punishments for what we did, they saw the deer. They said it was only proper for it to be left in the temple as a memorial to you and should contain the sacred metal. What I once intended as a gift to you has turned into a grim reminder of what I have lost.

It's beautiful. I'm certain Noya would have been honored to receive it. Its beauty amazes me, but I'm not Noya.

You need not remind me, for I am painfully aware of it.

Good, because I'm only a modern woman, seeking the knowledge of the ages, the knowledge you left behind.

I am aware of who you are. Noya exists only in my memory.

"Jaycee, can you hear me?"

The panic in Bob's voice silenced Sayo.

"I was so engrossed in the beauty of this piece. I didn't hear you."

She hoped he wouldn't guess the true reason she was oblivious to her surroundings.

"No, you weren't. Evan's described the look you have when Sayo takes control. He's not gone, is he?"

"Of course, he is."

She prayed the sound of her voice wouldn't betray her lie.

Bob put his finger under her chin and tilted her head so their eyes could meet. "Tell me the truth, Jaycee. Is Sayo gone?"

She couldn't give voice to her answer. All she could do was shake her head.

"How long has he been back?"

"I doubt if he ever left. After being a prisoner for so long, I think his freedom frightens him. He says he wants to help me translate the writings."

"I'm worried about you."

"Don't be. He promised not to appear to me or to enter my dreams. I feel comfortable with his presence. It's enough for me."

"Yes, but is it enough for Evan?"

"I hope so, but I don't intend to tell him, not now at least."

"Why not?"

"It will upset him. He's so excited about this project I can't put a damper on it. Besides, Sayo isn't a permanent fixture. He's promised to leave as soon as we have an understanding of the writings."

"Some promise. Understanding everything could take years, a lifetime. How can you keep this from Evan that long?"

Jaycee didn't answer. Evan's absence this morning, bothered her. Yesterday his kiss was full of promise, this morning the promise seemed empty. Her first instincts about competing with Round Tree pushed themselves to the forefront of her mind.

"Trust me. I do know what's best."

"Whatever you say. Just remember, I respect your decision, but I certainly don't agree with you. I'm going to the hospital now. When we get back, we'll pick you up and go out to the cave. I promised Evan, I'd take them out lunch."

"I won't be going with you."

"Why not?"

"There's too much to do here. It's ridiculous to start, only to be interrupted. My work is here. I'm certain Evan would agree with me."

A young man came into the room, giving Bob no chance to respond to her comment. "Do you want to see the pictures, Bob? I just finished developing the film."

Bob turned from Jaycee, focusing his attention on the young man. The gesture made Jaycee more comfortable. Once engrossed in the photos from the cave, she prayed he would forget about her decision not to accompany him when he went to see Evan.

Bob took the pictures and seated himself on the edge of the table. Jaycee could see the excitement in his eyes, the same excitement she felt when she touched the writings, the same excitement Evan generated every time he mentioned Round Tree.

She took each photo Bob handed her and gasped at the beauty they depicted. "If this doesn't satisfy the state, nothing will. They're magnificent. I can't believe the detail in these animals."

Jaycee paused when she looked at the photo of the altar table. She stared at it for a long time, trying to picture it in tact with the bowl in place. As she did, she focused on the knife.

"Did Evan bring back the knife?"

"I'm sure he did. Why do you ask?"

"I want to see it. There's something here I didn't notice yesterday."

Bob put down the pictures and searched through the artifacts, many still packed away in the camera bags. At last, he produced the knife.

Tentatively, Jaycee took it from him. Before she could focus on the intricate design on the blade, she experienced an overwhelming fear. Flashes of a woman standing over her assaulted her eyes. The woman's face appeared to be distorted with anger as she plunged the knife toward her terrified victim.

Jaycee closed her eyes to block out the vision, only she couldn't rid herself of the fear. She could only shake. Bob's comforting arms encircled her, calming her fear with his strength.

"What are you seeing, Jaycee?"

"The end of Noya's life. Dostra is plunging the knife into her chest."

"Should I call Sharon Tess?"

The vision began to disappear and the shaking she experienced ceased. "No, I'm alright, just put the knife away. It provokes such terrible memories. I can't stand it."

Bob took the knife from her hand then guided her from the room. "Maybe you should come to the hospital with me."

Jaycee shook her head. "I need to stay here, to decipher the writings. I made a mistake in touching the knife. It holds too many terrifying memories for Noya."

"Noya is dead. You've said it yourself."

"Yes, but she's been reborn in me and is making me remember the end of her life so I can better understand the writings. By reliving her nightmare, I know why Sayo smashed the bowl in the courtyard of Dostra's home. For the first time, he saw the sacrifices for what they were, premeditated murder. In his anger, he denounced the sacrifices and literally sealed his future."

"All the more reason for you to come with me and forget about the writings for today."

"I'll be fine. If you stand around here talking to me much longer, Amanda will sue me for alienation of affections."

Once Jaycee sat alone in the office, she ran her hands over the leather of the scroll. Before she again began translating, she turned on the recorder and started making notes on a legal pad. For each symbol, each picture, Jaycee wrote a corresponding word or letter. As she did, she devised a dictionary of sorts. When she finished it, she could walk away from Round Tree and forget everything she experienced this summer. Once a key was devised, anyone could translate the remainder of the writings. She wouldn't be needed. Evan wouldn't even notice she was gone.

~ * ~

At the cave, Brandon began photographing, while Sandy cataloged and Chris described each piece aloud into his recorder. Feeling like a fifth wheel, Evan picked up a lantern and started down the passageway toward the back chambers.

After passing through a twenty-foot-long corridor, he entered the first chamber. What took him by surprise was the contents of the room. Stone benches with tools and ancient dust reminded Evan of the workshop he kept in the basement of the house in Utah.

In front of him sat a small statue of a naked woman. Picking it up, he gasped as he recognized the face of the statue as belonging to Jaycee. He ran his fingers over the perfectly shaped body. Full breasts with prominent nipples gave way to the slight bulge of the woman's belly. Evan tuned over the little statue to see the strands of hair reaching to her rounded buttocks.

Could this be Noya?

You are very perceptive.

Evan jumped at the sound of Sayo's voice. *It can't be. You're gone.*

The woman voiced the same words this morning. I asked if she would tell you of my return, but she said no. It is the reason I came to you.

Why return? Why not leave? You're free. It's what you wanted.

How do you know what I want? More than freedom, I want the woman to learn the secrets contained in the writings. Since the markings on the scrolls are my own creation, I must assist her in reading them. I intend to help her and you.

Why me? You certainly aren't pleased with my relationship with her.

No longer do I begrudge you your feelings. I lingered long enough yesterday to see how gently you loved her. She is a receptive lover. You were tender as a husband should be.

I don't know if she wants me for a husband.

It is strange you should think such a thing. I wonder if you want her for a wife.

What do you mean?

You left this morning without seeing her. You planted the seeds of doubt when you showed no concern about her disappearance.

You can read my thoughts. You must know my biggest fault is considering no one but myself. For the past several years I have been responsible to no one, with the exception of Round Tree and myself. Old habits are hard to break.

It will be difficult, but necessary. She needs you with her. She needs to be loved. For now, she is safe. Go to her. Make your feelings known.

Only do it slowly and with much thought, for she is vulnerable as well as doubtful. When she found you were not waiting for her, she became confused.

Evan panicked at Sayo's words. *I should go to her.*

Give her time. As I said, I came for you as well as for her. You want to know about this room and its significance. Here is where the statues you so admire were created as gifts to the man gods.

Did you create all of them?

Hardly. The high priests who came before me made most of them. It took many turnings of the seasons to perfect our craft. I follow only in their footsteps and do as the man gods direct.

In this as well as the sacrifices.

Yes, until I felt the loss of my beloved Noya.

With Sayo's mention of Noya, Evan experienced a vision. A young girl appeared before his eyes. Her features were so like Jaycee's he wanted to reach out and pull her toward him. Breasts beginning to swell with pregnancy reminded him of the blissful lovemaking he shared with Jaycee. The girl stood in the middle of the stream, beckoning to a young man to join her.

As soon as the vision appeared, it dissolved.

She looks so much like Jaycee.

It is how I knew this woman was whom I waited for. She carries so many of the same features as Noya, I tend to confuse the two of them. Even her body feels much the same. I realize she is much older than my beloved. Among my people, she would be a grandmother by now, perhaps even dead. What is still considered young in your culture would be ancient in mine.

How old did you live to be?

I ended my life by my own hand. I was seventeen turnings of the seasons when the man gods left me with the old and dying. They were thirty possibly thirty-five turnings of the seasons, of an age ready for death and yet not ready to accept it. They did not deserve to die the horrible, painful deaths they endured. They were innocent people who were destroyed for Dostar's sin. Without her here, they blamed me and with good reason. It was I who sinned first by my love for Noya. Life has strange twists.

It certainly does, Evan agreed.

He waited for Sayo to continue, but he didn't.

Evan wondered if he would lose consciousness the way Jaycee did whenever she fell under Sayo's hypnotic spell. Although he felt weak, he didn't pass out.

He lowered himself onto the stone workbench, the figurine of Noya still clutched in his hands. Although he tried, he could feel no presence at all, not like when he first saw the apparition or when Sayo entered his conscious thoughts. Evan found himself in awe of the man who so easily invaded Jaycee's dreams as well as her mind. Sayo seemed to have a way of making time slip past without knowing it happened. For the first time, Evan knew how Jaycee must feel whenever she encountered Sayo.

"Evan, are you in there?"

Evan turned to see Bob standing in the doorway. "I didn't know how far back you might have gone. This is only the first chamber. Chris said you've been gone for hours."

"Yes, I have…I guess."

"What do you mean, you guess?"

"It's a long story. This is the workroom, the place where Sayo and the priests before him fashioned the statues." Evan held out the figurine he picked up before Sayo invaded his senses. "This is Noya," he said.

"How do you know?"

"Sayo told me, but he wouldn't have had to. Look at her face."

"My god, it is Jaycee."

"No, it's Noya. Sayo told me it's how he knew Jaycee was the one. She's beautiful, isn't she?"

Bob turned the statue over in his hand, studying it carefully. "Yes, she is."

Evan felt Bob's hand on his shoulder. "Sayo was here, wasn't he?"

Evan nodded. "He says he wants to help us."

"Why do you think he came to you?"

"To admonish me."

Bob's bewildered expression asked the question before he voiced it. "What are you talking about?"

"He told me he doesn't think I care for her enough, since I didn't wait for her to get back this morning. She did finally come back, didn't she?"

"Of course, she did. She's confused, though. I'm sure she thought you'd be there when she arrived."

"So, Sayo told me. He's very protective of her."

"I think someone should be. The next few hours could get rough."

"What do you mean?"

"She's expecting company."

"Company?"

"She got two phone calls this morning, one from the Dresdens, the other from Henry Bennett. They're all on their way here."

"They're the last people she needs here."

"You're right. What she needs now is you, only you're off playing archaeologist. Sayo's right, maybe you don't care enough. I think it's time you put Round Tree aside and looked after Jaycee."

"I do, too."

"Good. I brought out some lunch. Why don't you grab a sandwich before you go back to the lab?"

"No. I'll go back right away. I need to talk to her."

"Since you're going back, why don't you take Brandon with you?"

"Any particular reason?"

"He looks pretty tired. Amanda can take over with the camera. I'll stick around to make sure she doesn't overdo. I brought along more film with lunch. As soon as I saw Brandon, I insisted he sit down and eat right away."

Evan put his hand on his friend's shoulder. "What would we do without you, Bob? You're the old mother hen of this group."

"Someone has to look out for you. If not me, who?"

"It's a good question. You can take care of things here. I'll get Brandon and take off."

They left the workroom and went back into the main chamber. Evan took particular note of his son. Brandon did look tired. Evan should have never allowed the boy to come out again today, but Brandon's excitement overruled Evan's judgment.

"Why?" Brandon protested, when Evan insisted that he should return to the dorm.

"Because you're exhausted. I should have been more considerate and not even brought you with us today."

"You're going to cut me out of this, aren't you? How can you do it?"

"Because it's for your own good."

"If I promise to sit around and watch, can I stay? I'll give Amanda the camera, if you want."

"What do you think, Bob?" Evan asked.

"The kid's got a mind of his own. He must be related to you. We might as well let him stay. I'll keep my eye on him."

"Thanks Bob. I didn't mean to go against you, Dad, but I want to be here."

Evan could understand why. This morning he didn't consider anything but finding the treasures here. After his encounter with Sayo, he realized without Jaycee they didn't matter.

"Before you go, you should know we're lousy with reporters."

"I expected as much, considering the article in this morning's paper."

"They already cornered Jaycee."

Evan felt his stomach begin to churn. Jaycee having to deal with the press was the last thing he needed. "How did she handle it?"

"Like a pro. She made a statement, didn't say much of anything, and they think she gave them the royal jewels. She's exactly the person we need to deal with the press."

Evan smiled. He needed Jaycee all right, only not to deal with the press.

Chapter Eighteen

Reporters swarmed at the entrance to the lab. To avoid them, Evan drove to the back parking lot and entered through the service door.

He stopped first at the room where he put the artifacts less than twenty-four hours earlier. Kendra Williams, from the university, sat examining the ancient pieces. She looked up when he entered the room. "I can't believe what you have here, Evan. This has to be the biggest find of the twenty-first century."

"I'm glad you agree with me. Have you seen Jaycee this morning?"

"Do you mean Dr. Grant?"

Evan nodded.

"Only briefly. When I first came in, she was already at work in the other office. I didn't want to disturb her."

"Have you met her?" Evan asked.

He tried to keep things light, not to let his feelings show.

"Once at a seminar about two maybe three years ago at Havelin. You're very lucky to have someone of her caliber working at Round Tree."

"I know I am. Have you eaten lunch yet?"

Kendra nodded. "One of the volunteers brought over a sandwich. I didn't want to have to face the reporters."

"Good. As long as you've had something to eat, I guess I'll go and see if Jaycee wants some lunch. You didn't see her go already, did you?"

Kendra thought for a moment. "I've been busy here, but I doubt if she's gone. The door to the office she's using is right across the hall. I haven't seen her leave all morning."

Kendra held up the knife Evan retrieved from the altar.

"Do you have any idea what this purple stuff is?" she asked.

"The metal of the gods is what the writings call it."

"Does that mean Dr. Grant has been able to do some translating?"

"A minuscule portion, enough to tell us why they practiced human sacrifice and to talk about the metal of the gods. Enough to whet our appetites for more."

~ * ~

Jaycee put aside the book she now referred to, in her mind, as her dictionary. Tears stung her eyes at the thought of someone else transcribing the multitude of writing using her copious notes.

How can I leave this? How can I hope to forget Round Tree and the feelings for Evan I can't express?

Why must you leave?

You wouldn't understand, Sayo. You're content to stay here, but I can't.

I understand more than you think. You ache for the neglect of the man. Give it time, Little One.

Just what are you doing back here? I thought you were going to go to the hospitals and see the wonders of modern medicine.

In time. For now, I am never far away. Are you ready to learn more? If you are, I will show you where to begin.

Why can't I just continue on? Why can't I read from the beginning to the end?

There will be time to continue on later, time to learn all of what this says. You know the beginning and now you must read of the end.

The end? Oh, Sayo, I don't think I want to read of the end just yet.

You must read the last words I wrote.

Jaycee looked down at the scroll spread out on the table. To her surprise, the markings appeared blurred. At last, her eyes focused on what looked like the shaky writings of an older person. She picked up a new cassette and slipped it in the recorder, then began to read.

The end is coming closer for me. It has been three turnings of the seasons since the sacrifice of my beloved Noya. Much of what has happened stems from my sin. My punishment is what I deserve. Of course, I am getting ahead of myself.

Noya was a slave in my mother's household and I fell in love with her. I think I loved her from the first moment I saw her. It only increased when I sacrificed her virginity. It seemed so cruel for her to be there alone with me, with no mother and father looking on, no husband waiting to complete the marriage ceremony. When I finished the sacrifice, I became the tender lover, the man to show her the way a man loves a woman.

I planned it to happen only once, for it was sinful for me to be with a woman, even if she was the joy of my heart. Me, who was created by the Gods, realized once would never be enough for me. We were to meet time and time again, until she told me she carried my child. In my ignorance I denied the child could be mine and accused her of coupling with another man from the village. Noya ran from me and was pursued by the hunters. When they found her, a prisoner in a neighboring village, they brought her back to Dostra.

Although Ustro and I planned to change her status from slave destined for the house of pleasures to healer, her frightened flight from us prohibited it. Instead, she was returned to the one person who hated her.

On the day of the sacrifice of the harvest, Dostra brought Noya to the sanctuary. No matter what argument I gave her, I could not make her believe Noya carried my child, nor any child for that matter. We struggled over the knife. Dostra was stronger and had the advantage of her weight. In the altercation, I lost my footing and fell, hitting my head on the altar table.

When I regained consciousness, I heard Noya's screams, then a stony silence. By the time I got to my feet, Dostra had put Noya's heart into the bowl designated for that purpose and was collecting her blood. Once she finished, she ripped open Noya's womb to show me my error in believing a slave. To her horror, she found the body of a perfectly formed girl child cradled within Noya's womb. She threw up her hands and screamed in terror over what she did. The knife clattered to the floor and she ran from the sanctuary, as though being chased by demons.

She left the disposal of Noya's body to me. I could not entertain the thought of leaving her as food for the scavengers, nor could I envision her eyes being plucked out by the ravens. Instead, I prepared her, as I would prepare one of the leaders. I used the herbs and spices designed for this purpose to fill the now empty cavity of her body then closed the wound. I continued to cleanse her skin before I applied the oil of the dead. Later, after I confronted Dostra with what she did and forbid the practice of human sacrifice, I returned to the sanctuary. Through my mind, I heard my father, Zandar, tell me to take her body to the chamber of the dead. There it would always be close to me and away from any who sought it.

It took one more turning of the seasons for the man gods to return. During that time, I had very little communication from my father. He seemed to be shunning me for what occurred. When the man gods finally returned, I learned why I had not heard his voice in my head. The high council had been discussing my fate as well as the fate of the people. Dostra was the first to be accused. When she denied their charges, they became very angry with her. At last, she confessed and before my very eyes, they produced their terrible weapon and destroyed her.

When they turned their attention to my sister, Yasma, I feared for her life as well as her spirit. I could not stand by and allow them to destroy her. They told me she would be spared. She, along with all of the young and healthy people of the village, would be taken away. I would be left in the village with the old and dying. Because of what happened, I would be stripped of my immortality. As punishment for the sacrifice of Noya, I would not be able to be reincarnated until such time as a future reincarnation of Noya came to free me. My only redemption would come if within the next three turnings of the seasons, I could find a cure for the terrible disease, which would be visited upon the people.

Now two turnings of the seasons later, I am no closer to a cure than I was on that first day. Every morning more of my people are dead and there is more smoke from funeral pyres. Soon there will be no one left. Every day I die a little inside. I have tried all of the herbs at my disposal to exact a cure and none have worked.

I thought I had the cure at hand until I realized I created an evil concoction. I no more had the cure than I did before. Although the people became well for a short while, they soon began to vomit and lose their hair. I knew I gave them not help, but another curse.

With this knowledge, I have sealed the jar of poison with bee's wax. I will plant bushes at the opening to the sanctuary and seal it from the view of men. Never again will I see the light of day nor will I eat or drink. The jars stand, filled with the food brought to me by the people. Brought when they lived in the hope, I could help them by finding a cure.

Having failed, I vow I will touch not the food, nor will I drink the cool water that feeds the steam from the underground river in the back cavern. It is time I end my life, as none of my line has ever done before. I need to put an end to this agony.

Tears blurred the markings on the leather. Jaycee's heart felt heavy. *How could you take your own life, Sayo?*

She waited for him to answer, but heard nothing.

"I can't go on with this. I have to get away."

"I know."

The sound of Evan's voice startled her. She turned to assure herself she didn't imagine Evan's voice. "How long have you been standing there?"

"Long enough to know what happened to Sayo's people."

"Why aren't you at the sanctuary?"

"Because I need to be here. I'm sorry, so very sorry."

"Sorry? About what?"

"Not waiting for you this morning. For letting you think I don't care, when I do."

Jaycee could only mouth his name. The words couldn't get past the lump in her throat.

Gently, he helped her to her feet and encircled her in his arms. "Sayo is right. I had no business going to the cave this morning without knowing you were safe."

Jaycee pulled back slightly, to look into Evan's eyes. "What do you mean Sayo's right?"

"He's no longer only speaking to you. He's decided to grace me with the privilege of hearing his voice."

"You? You mean he's...?"

"He's talking to me. Before you freed him, he could only communicate with you. Now he can speak to whomever he wishes. For some unforeseen reason, he wants to talk to me. He doesn't think I love you enough. He's very upset with the fact I didn't wait for you this morning. For that, I am sorry."

Jaycee couldn't keep from smiling at his words and put her hand to his cheek. To her surprise, Evan took her hand in his and pressed it to his lips.

"Let me finish. It's been a long time since I've had to consider anyone or anything other than myself and Round Tree. There hasn't been anything else I cared about. Sure, I had the kids, but they're self-sufficient. Kathryn made sure they kept their distance. The people at the dig only need me for guidance. If I'm not there for some reason, they won't cease working. When Sayo accused me of not caring, I realized how very much I love you."

"Are you sure?"

She wondered if she could trust him. Did he only speak these words because Sayo promised Evan prosperity as long as he loved her?

"I'm positive."

Jaycee looked back at the scrolls and recorder on the table. She felt Evan's hand on her chin turning her face back toward him. "This can wait. Something tells me you haven't had anything to eat today."

"Guilty as charged."

"Let's forget the scrolls and go over to the dining hall for some lunch. I haven't had anything either."

"What about the reporters?"

"What about them?"

"They're right outside the door."

"I know where they are. I saw them when I drove up. We'll handle them together. I'm sure I won't do nearly as good a job as you did this morning, though. Bob tells me you were great. He said you fed them a line of bull and they thought you gave them caviar."

Jaycee began to smile. "I only gave them a taste of what they wanted."

"I'm no good at handling them alone. My temper gets in the way when they ask about things, they have no business knowing."

Jaycee looked at his unruly shock of red hair. "It goes with the territory."

Evan ran his fingers through his hair. "I guess it does."

She wondered what would happen with his temper once he realized Vern and Ellie were due to arrive. She remembered the tension between Vern and Evan just days earlier. Would their arrival change Evan's mind about his feelings?

"There's something I need to tell you. Vern and Ellie are on their way here. So is Henry."

"We'll handle them."

The words came as a surprise.

"They aren't the enemy. They're only concerned about the same thing I am, you."

Jaycee allowed Evan to take her out into the hall. She glanced back into the office where she worked for the past few hours. Evan turned her away from it as he flipped the lock and pulled the door shut behind them.

Protectively, he took her hand and they walked toward the front door.

She blinked at the bright sunlight and inhaled the fresh air deeply to calm her nerves at the sight of the reporters waiting for them.

"Dr. Clark, can you confirm the rumors of what has been going on?"

"Yes, I can. Over the past few days, we've learned a lot more about the people who lived in this area. They practiced human sacrifice and they were highly intelligent. Their priest, a man named Sayo, devised a written language so the story of their existence would not be lost."

"Dr. Grant says you found the writings. Can you tell us what they say?"

"You seem to expect miracles."

Jaycee could hear the irritation in his voice and glanced up at his face. Rather than allow him to flounder, she came to his rescue. "I've begun to piece together the meaning of the markings. When I've deciphered more and finished my notes, anyone will be able to read them. Until I'm finished, we will have only bits and pieces of what they contain. It would not be fair to disclose passages taken out of context."

"What about the voices and vision you've been experiencing?"

Evan squeezed Jaycee's hand reassuringly. "They're all part of it. The voice belongs to Sayo and the visions are of the life these people led. I realize it sounds farfetched, but Sayo's spirit feels the time is right for these revelations to come to light."

Both Jaycee and Evan answered several more questions before he held up his hand. "We will be arranging a meeting with the people from the state tomorrow morning. Once we've conferred with them, we will hold an official press conference at two. Until then, please excuse us. Both Dr. Grant and I need to get something to eat. We'll answer all of your questions tomorrow and allow you to see some of the artifacts at the same time."

Jaycee gratefully allowed Evan to lead her away from the group of reporters.

"I can see what Bob meant. You're good. I especially liked your line about taking things out of context. If they knew what you've already translated, they'd be shocked."

"I'm sure they would. I'm a bit shocked myself."

"Let's put it aside for a while and get something to eat."

Jaycee agreed and turned to follow him to the dining hall. The sound of someone calling her name caused her to turn back. Across the parking lot, she saw Ellie running toward her.

"I can't believe the number of reporters around here," Ellie said, her breath coming in gasps.

"It's a bit overwhelming, isn't it? What you have to understand is we've uncovered the find of the modern age."

"You certainly have," Vern said, when he joined them. "I'm afraid I owe both of you an apology. I didn't believe any of this would happen. I thought it was nothing more than sheer nonsense. For the first time, I'm pleased to be proven wrong."

"Apology accepted," Evan agreed, holding out his hand.

Jaycee wondered how long this truce would last. Evan and Vern would certainly never be the best of friends. For that matter, she wondered about Evan's sudden attentiveness. *Will everything blow up in my face, once I finish transcribing the writings, once I no longer held the key to Round Tree's past,* she wondered.

"Have you two had anything to eat?" Evan asked, breaking into Jaycee's thoughts.

"Peanuts on the plane," Ellie replied, her comment breaking the tension Jaycee could feel building within her.

"Jaycee and I are on our way to the dining hall for lunch. Won't you join us?"

"Are you sure it will be all right?" Ellie asked.

Evan's smile was reassuring. "Of course, it is. There's plenty of food."

"Who backs this project?" Vern asked, once they sat their full plates on a table and began to eat.

"We started out with five backers, Bob and me, along with three others. We each invested twenty thousand dollars. Of course, over the past five years Bob and I have bought the others out."

"It sounds like this is a financial drain on you."

~ * ~

From the tone of Jaycee's voice and the look on her face, Evan knew the idea shocked her as much as when he learned of her inheritance. He meant to tell her of it earlier, but the topic never seemed to come up in conversation. Now he knew he needed to explain the facts and go into further detail later, when they were alone.

"I wouldn't say it's been a drain. I have an initial investment of about sixty thousand, but like Bob, I used an inheritance to finance it. Up until this year, we've had state funding to pay salaries for both Bob and me as well as take care of running expenses. Bob and I take care of maintenance of the building as well as the insurance, since we originally financed their construction. With the state monies gone, Bob and I went out on the lecture circuit. We raised enough to keep us going for another couple of years without personal outlay."

"I'm surprised at Matelin's involvement. With him being an accountant, he must have known he wouldn't receive any monetary gain from this."

"He's not just an accountant. He studied under me in Utah. He told me he carried a double major because he wanted to be an archaeologist. He knew it would be tough to pay the bills until he became well known. Up until last year, he ran a small accounting firm out of his home in the winter. You know, doing taxes for people. Last year, we both had to go on the road, so it cut into his income. With what we raised, I decided to increase his salary to compensate his loss."

Vern sat, as though contemplating Evan's words. "What kind of monetary gain do you expect from this find?"

"Probably none. All we want is the backing from the state so we can continue to pursue this."

Evan watched Vern's brow knot and a look of contemplation wash over his face. At the same time, he couldn't miss the look of shock in Jaycee's eyes. He wished they were alone and he could explain away all of her questions.

Without giving anyone else a chance to speak, Vern continued. "I'm sure you're not going to agree with what I have to say, but hear me out. I think you ought to consider legal representation."

Vern's suggestion surprised Evan. They consulted a lawyer years ago when they first started and again when they bought out the other three partners. They certainly hadn't considered one necessary since. "Legal representation? What do you mean?"

"You don't want this project to be exploited. If the wrong people got a foothold, they could make a killing and you would never see a penny of the money. I know you've got the university behind you and the state will be on the bandwagon soon, but there are legal ramifications you don't understand."

"So, what are you suggesting?"

"Let me represent you and Bob?"

Evan's memory of the angry words he'd exchanged with Vern over the weekend returned to his mind. "I should have known. Now who's exploiting me? We can hardly keep Round Tree going and maintain a decent standard of living. How can you even begin to think we could afford to pay your fee?"

"Call it a donation. I can write it off on my taxes."

Vern's statement caused Evan to smile. "There seems to be a lot of that going on around here lately." He winked broadly at Jaycee.

His comment brought blank stares from Vern and Ellie, but Jaycee began to laugh. He was sure she remembered her comment about her donation being a bribe to Uncle Sam.

"I'm serious, Evan," Vern finally continued. "I want to represent Round Tree. You can call it a donation, an old debt to Jaycee for introducing me to Ellie, or an apology for the way I acted last weekend. It would be very easy for the wrong people to come in here. They could take advantage of you and Jaycee."

Evan liked the way Vern linked his name with Jaycee's, he only hoped she agreed with her friend. "I'm not certain I see what you're getting at."

"I don't mean this the way it sounds, but you don't know the kind of people who will be interested in the monetary aspect of this discovery. The networks will be all over Jaycee for the rights to the story of her connection to Sayo, to say nothing of the groups who will want to show the artifacts and have you lecture. For a while, the two of you will be instant celebrities. It will be to your advantage to refer these people to me. I'll be able to sort through the riff-raff and get you the best deal possible. It's what I do. Let me do it for you."

"What about your existing practice?"

"This will fit in. I have several associates. One more client will just mean shifting some of the load to the younger staff who are hungry for the work."

Vern turned to Jaycee and Evan paid little attention to their conversation. He had his own thoughts to consider. He could hardly believe Vern's about face.

"Are you with us, Evan?" Jaycee asked.

"I'm sorry. I guess I was somewhere else. Were you talking to me?"

"It wasn't important. I figured you were off somewhere in never-never land. I'm beginning to recognize the look. We didn't lose you to Sayo, did we?"

Evan laughed. "In a way. I was thinking about what Vern said. He's right. We do need legal representation. I feel guilty about it being gratis, but I do accept the offer. In time, we'll find a way to compensate you."

"Where can I find Jocelyn Grant?" Henry's voice boomed from the direction of the front door.

Evan looked up, but considering the position of their table, couldn't see the face behind the voice.

"What's Henry doing here?" Ellie gasped.

"I meant to tell you. He called right after you did and wanted to come down. I couldn't stop him."

"He's the last person any of us needs to see," Vern said, through clenched teeth.

"Another member of your not-so-well-liked club?" Evan asked, somehow enjoying the uneasiness in Vern's voice.

"You might say that. He kicked me out of Havelin the first semester of my junior year for streaking at a football game, me, with my 4.0 grade point average. I didn't have any trouble getting into another school, though. As a matter of fact, they even laughed about it. In a way, it was the best thing to happen to me. I got into a better school and made some great contacts. It only made seeing Ellie a little more difficult."

Evan could feel himself warming toward Vern. Seeing him in this light made the man seem more normal, almost human.

"I'm over here, Henry," Jaycee announced, getting to her feet.

"Good God, Jocelyn, you look like hell," Henry greeted her when he came to their table.

"You look wonderful too, Henry."

Evan silently applauded her for the barb he heard in her voice.

"I didn't mean it the way it sounded. You look exhausted."

"She is," Evan said, before Jaycee and Henry could come to further verbal blows.

"Dr. Clark, it is good to see you."

The way he spoke the words, made it sound as though he hadn't seen anyone other than Jaycee at the table.

"There's no need for formality, Henry. Call me Evan. I think you know Vern and Ellie Dresden."

Evan couldn't miss the murderous glance passing between Vern and Henry.

"Unfortunate incident at Havelin, Vern," Henry admitted, as they shook hands. "Things have changed considerably since you were there."

"I certainly hope so," Vern replied, venom dripping from his words. "I don't suppose the withdrawal of my father's money had anything to do with it."

"I must assume you came here to see what's going on with Jaycee."

Evan decided it was time to change the subject. He was beginning to feel like a referee at one of the wrestling matches on television, where everyone fought everyone else.

"Yes, I am. From the way she looks, she could do with three days of sleep."

"It's funny, Henry, you never considered my need for sleep when you wanted me to work all those extra hours."

"You never looked this tired then."

Evan wondered if it was his imagination or if he noticed a note of concern in Henry's voice.

"How's Norm doing with the department?"

"He's coming along."

"Glad to hear it."

Evan cringed at the tension he could feel in the direction the table talk took. "I'm sorry to break this up. Jaycee and I have work to do. I trust you're all registered at local hotels. Jaycee and I would like all of you to be our guests for dinner tonight. We'll meet you at The Digs, at six."

~ * ~

Jaycee looked up at Evan, a bit surprised by his comment. *When did we decide to take everyone out to dinner and of all restaurants, why The Digs? From what I've heard, it's the most expensive restaurant in town.*

Evan held out his hand to her and she allowed him to help her get up.

Jaycee waited until they were outside to say anything more. "Thanks for the reprieve."

"I thought you needed it."

"When did *we* decide to take everyone out?"

"We didn't. I have a feeling Vern and Ellie wouldn't agree to come if I were the only host. I think we have something very special to celebrate."

Jaycee smiled. She liked it when he talked in terms of we, even if he was only talking about the discovery of the writings. While her mind wandered, Evan squeezed her hand and led her around to the back parking lot. "Where are we going?"

"To where my Jeep is parked."

"I must be dense. Why go to your Jeep, when we have work to do? If you remember, you just told everyone we had to get back to it. What about the scrolls? This certainly isn't the way to the lab."

She noticed the mischievous twinkle in Evan's eyes.

"It's not. We aren't going to the lab. You couldn't work on the scrolls this afternoon if you wanted to."

"You aren't making any sense. Why not?"

"Because I locked the door."

"Then open it with your key."

"The lab is Bob's domain. He has the only key."

Jaycee felt as though she just walked in on the middle of a

complicated movie and couldn't grasp the plot. "Since you admit we have work to do, are we going out to the sanctuary?"

Evan's smile became broader, giving her no hint as to what thoughts were formulating in his mind. He made no further comment until they were in the Jeep and driving away from the dig. To her surprise, they turned toward town instead of the site.

"Going to the cave isn't quite what I had in mind."

"I don't understand you at all, Evan Clark."

"You will. We're going back to my place."

"Your place? What kind of work can we do there?"

"The kind we should have been doing ever since you got back. We can work on our relationship. I can work on showing you how much I love you."

Jaycee's heart leaped for joy. When Evan said those words earlier, she thought he said them only to appease her. Now they sounded full of sincerity. "Do you mean it?"

"I've never meant anything more."

Jaycee's mind spun. Evan just told her he loved her and meant it. Taking her back to his apartment to work on their relationship could only mean he wanted to make love to her again. Would it be with the curious urgency of last week or the gentle loving she experienced yesterday at the sanctuary? Her questions ceased when he pulled up in front of his apartment.

Once inside, he took her in his arms and kissed her tenderly. She expected him to work at removing her clothing, but he didn't. His unwillingness to undress her was confusing.

Leaning back in his arms, she began to unbutton his shirt, to run her hands over the mat of hair on his chest. To her surprise, Evan took her hands in his and put them to his lips, then led her into the bedroom. From the nightstand, he took a small box.

"I want you to marry me, Jaycee."

"When?"

"How about Saturday. As far as I'm concerned, we're already married, but you deserve more than an ancient ceremony presided over by Sayo."

Jaycee gasped when he opened the box to reveal a pear-shaped diamond resting in a nest of black velvet.

"When did you have time to buy this?"

"Friday night, after I listened to the tape. I planned to give it to you as soon as you got back from New York. After everything that happened, I thought I'd have to return it."

"I would never allow you to do anything so silly, Evan. It's beautiful."

"Can I assume your answer is yes?"

"Yes, yes, yes, yes, is that enough?"

"It's a start. I'll never get tired of hearing you say it, though."

"Aren't you going to use a condom?"

"I didn't use one yesterday."

"What if I get pregnant?"

"It would be wonderful. You see I know the joy of hearing the words that so changed Sayo's life. I know what it's like to have a woman say she's going to have your child. I want to hear you say those words to me."

A warm glow crept through her body. She wanted nothing more than to give Evan a child, but she couldn't help voicing her concerns. "What about Brandon and Sandy?"

"They'll be happy for us."

"I hope so."

Before Jaycee could say more, Evan covered her mouth with his and began to prepare her for his lovemaking.

When they climaxed, Jaycee laid contentedly in Evan's arms, the ring on her finger reflecting the mid-afternoon sunlight. It was Evan who broke the magic by speaking. "I hate to be the one to break this up, but if we're going to have a wedding on Saturday, we have a lot of planning to do. I assume you want Ellie to be your matron of honor, and of course, you want Henry to give you away."

Jaycee giggled. No matter how many verbal battles she and Henry participated in, she knew he, above everyone else, had the right to give her away. Since her dad died, he became her surrogate father. His appearance here today confirmed his concern for her.

"You know what they say about assumptions, but this time you are right, even about Henry. Do you really think we can pull this off?"

"We can do anything. Let's get dressed and call the minister before you change your mind."

Epilogue

Jaycee awoke in the hours before predawn. The twins her body housed moved to a more comfortable position. The clock on the bedside table read two forty-five. Beside her, Evan's even breathing told her he slept, oblivious to her wakeful state.

Quietly, she got out of bed and made her way to the bathroom. Once she finished, she went into the living room to sit in the recliner. As soon as she switched on the light, she focused on the statue of Noya on the end table and the golden deer on the floor. Knowing sleep would be a stranger, she allowed her mind to wander.

Five months ago, she and Evan left for Peru. She purposely refrained from telling him about her pregnancy, for fear he would cancel the trip.

Just after Christmas, the doctor she was seeing from the small Peruvian town close to the dig, confirmed their suspicions that she carried not one baby, but two. At Evan's insistence, they returned to the house they purchased at Round Tree and began looking for a second home, closer to Havelin.

You cannot sleep, Little One, Sayo said.

His voice startled her. Since the wedding, he'd spoken to her only twice.

Not tonight, Sayo. These babies are restless.

They want to be born and know the security of your arms.

Why have you come to me tonight? I thought you left me months ago.

Although I kept my presence a silent one, I never left you. Through your mind, I have learned of many things, including your God. I can only pray I will know him in my next life.

Your next life?

Yes. I feel it is almost time for me to begin again, with no memory of what I once endured. I have come to bid you farewell.

I will miss you.

I cannot allow you to grieve over my loss. The children you carry within your womb, as well as the man who loves you, will consume your mind. I will become nothing more than a pleasant memory.

Do you know who you will be?

Her question met with silence and she knew Sayo no longer hovered close to her. A tear of loss escaped the corner of her eye, just as the first pain of labor passed through her body. Awkwardly, she got up from the chair to go and wake Evan. As she did, a trickle of water ran down the inside of her thigh. Jaycee no more than touched her bare feet on the cool tile of the bathroom floor when her waters broke.

"Evan," she called.

It seemed as though he had no time to get from the bedroom to the bathroom, yet he stood by her side, taking her in his arms.

"What's wrong?" he asked, before his eyes focused on the puddle of water at her feet.

"I think we need to get to the hospital."

She was surprised not to hear the panic that gripped her mind in her voice.

"When did your labor start?"

"Just now. Right after Sayo told me he was embarking on a new life."

Another pain cut through her body and Evan supported her.

"Let's get you into a dry gown," he said, guiding her toward the bedroom.

"My suitcase, and the birthing tapes. Don't forget them."

"I'm way ahead of you. Somehow, I anticipated this and put everything in the car last night."

By the time they arrived at the hospital, Jaycee's pains finally became regular. Within an hour, the doctor coached her to push.

Beside her, Evan whispered words of encouragement, including coaching her to breathe properly.

"One more push and the first one will be here," the doctor said.

In the mirror, positioned over the bed, Jaycee watched as a dark head of hair emerged, followed by the body of a perfect baby boy. With no letup in the pain, another head became visible several minutes later. This one looked lighter and a bit smaller.

"A boy and a girl," the doctor declared, triumphantly.

"You did a great job, Jaycee."

Both babies were laid on Jaycee's stomach. She stroked the soft skin of their faces while Evan cut the cords.

"Do you have names?" the doctor asked, as she delivered the afterbirth.

Jaycee watched as two nurses bathed the crying infants. When at last she held both tiny bundles in her arms, she looked into their eyes. "David Sayo," she said, mesmerized by Sayo's dark and haunting eyes, staring back at her from the child's face. Turning toward her daughter, she continued, "Christine Noya."

"Does he remind you of his namesake?" Evan asked.

Jaycee nodded. "I think I understand what he meant earlier. As for our daughter, she is the picture of her father and older sister, right down to the red hair. It's as though I had nothing to do with the birth of either of these children."

"I wouldn't say that. David seems to have your even temper, which is more than I can say for Christine. I do hope her personality doesn't go along with her hair color. Let's hope we can teach her to keep it in check and not let her get in trouble the way her old man did in New York."

Jaycee smiled and raised her lips to find Evans. As she did, she saw his hands reach out to touch the babies. Tiny fingers wrapped around his larger ones, closing the circle of love.

~ * ~

Contentedly, David looked up at her and she wondered if she only imagined Sayo's soft Tiny fingers wrapped around Evan's larger ones, closing the circle of love.

Would she ever know if this little boy, who so closely resembled the vision of Sayo that she vividly remembered, had been reincarnated from the priest who changed all of their lives forever?

Coming October 1, 2022
by the Author
at
Rogue Phoenix Press

Redemption in a New World
The New World Book Six

Chapter One

Clint Anders rode slowly back to the ranch. The other hands left ahead of him, but he needed time to think. Try as he might, he couldn't remember how he came to be sent to Henderson Ranch. It didn't matter how he happened to be sent there. What mattered most was that he was sent there.

His first memory was of living in the dormitory with his friends, Parker, Roger and Jake. Together they'd learned how to be ranch hands and to live on the meager meals, if you could call them that, served by the Hendersons. At the age of six they'd been sent to work with the older boys on the ranch. Even so, they didn't know much about those who were older or younger than themselves.

His mind returned to the day Jake died. The day before, they'd been tending the cattle in the south pasture when they realized one of the prize steers was nowhere in sight. It was Jake who said he wanted to find the missing steer before he rode off, leaving Clint and the others to tend the herd.

Whether it was coincidence or planned, Henderson came out to where they were working. When he inquired about where Jake was, they told him about the missing steer and how Jake went out to find him. As soon as they finished telling Henderson about Jake, their friend reappeared leading the wayward steer by a rope.

"Where the hell have you been?" Henderson shouted as soon as Jake was in sight.

"There was a missing steer. I went out and found him. He…"

"It doesn't matter where he was. It's not your job to leave your duties. Come with me."

In his mind's eye, he could still see Henderson grabbing the reigns of Jake's horse and taking off at a fast gallop. Clint swallowed down the lump in his throat. That had been the last time he ever saw his friend alive.

The next evening when they returned from the range, Henderson brought Clint and his friends to 'the box' and told them to dig a grave for Jake. None of them dared to ask what happened. They knew that fifteen hours in 'the box' had killed their friend and life for any of them would ever be the same again.

Three years later, he was horrified when he, along with his friends were sold to Senor Alfanso to be used as slave labor on his ranch. As the memory flashed in his mind, the brand on his upper left arm throbbed. It never bothered him unless he was remembering what his life was like before he was rescued and taken to the Alien Complex in Mexico City.

Their rescue and the Alien Complex had been like a dream come true. He'd been given a complete mental and physical examination in the hopes of finding any traces of his birth family. All during the search, he held out hope while enjoying the healthy meals and the education he'd been denied as a child.

He was surprised when Peter came to them in Mexico City and asked if they would be willing to return to Henderson Ranch, only now it was being called Resurrection Ranch. Clint knew Peter had been sold to Senior Alfanso but their paths hardly ever crossed. Like when they were growing up, they weren't encouraged to have communication with the men who worked in groups other than their own. Clint rode mostly with Roger and Parker as well as two of the older hands working on the ranch.

Shaking his head to rid himself of the memories he didn't want to relive, he thought about everything that happened to him since he arrived on Resurrection Ranch. At first, he was reluctant to return to the place that held so many horrors for him. The dormitory had been bulldozed and a new structure was in the process of being built. They only landmark her remembered was the main house. Even that looked different, boasting a fresh coat of paint changing it from dingy grey to sparkling white with black shutters and trim. Somehow, he knew this was where he belonged. More than anything else he wanted to make a difference for not only himself but also for all of the others who had survived this hell hole.

The main buildings of the ranch came into view dissolving the memories of the past. Here was the future, only now he and his friends were down to two from four. Jake had been spared the horrors of becoming Alfanso's slave by dying in 'the box'. Roger had recently been killed by Jake's father as he looked for justice for his son in the worst way possible.

The healing period was beginning, at least that's what Jerilyn, the counselor on the ranch, kept telling them. He wanted to believe her but he was waiting for the next shoe to fall, so to say. Which one of the survivors would be the next to lose his life because of Henderson and the hell he'd put them through as children?

"Hey, Clint, what took you so long?" Parker asked, as Clint prepared to take care of his horse before washing up for the evening meal.

"I had some thinking to do. Needed to be alone for a while."

"If it was Roger you were thinking about, you have to put that behind you. I've been talking to Pastor Joel and he tells me the One God know the number of days we are allotted when we are born. I find that hard to believe, but it does make sense. If that wasn't the case, why would you and I have survived everything we did? I need to know more about the One God as well as all the other stuff we've been studying."

Clint nodded his approval of what Parker was saying. On the day Roger was murdered, he vowed to make Resurrection Ranch a memorial to Roger, Jake and all the other children who lost their lives at the hands of the Hendersons.

Awake in a New World
The New World Book One

Caroline Lewis feels life isn't worth living when she loses her husband to Covid-19 while on a business trip to China. In order to avoid the coming pandemic, she opts to have her body frozen to be awakened in 2070. In 2120, archaeologists exploring the ruins of Los Angeles find Caroline's perfectly preserved body. As she is brought to life, fifty years later than expected, she is forced to learn to live in a world unlike the one she remembers from 2020. Aaron Phillips knows Caroline is special when he hires her as a research volunteer at the library. He hopes she feels the same way about him.

Unwanted in a New World
The New World Book Two

Orphaned at birth, Christopher is sent to a ranch for unwanted children. When he ages out, he is embraced by a militant group of skinheads who are unaware of his Native American heritage. A protest at an Alien Complex outside of Denver opens a new path for his life. While he is receiving his education, his new friends and mentors are working behind the scene to find his birth family.

Melian has come to the complex from the Alien base under the Antarctic ice cap. She takes an immediate interest in Christopher, who now wants to be called Chris, and looks forward to see what their future holds.

Alone in a New World
The New World Book Three

As a child of four, Marco is all alone in the world. With only his mother in his life, her death prompts the authorities to send him to Henderson Ranch for boys. At the age of eighteen, he is sold into slavery to a ranch in Mexico. Two years later, he is recued and reunited with his childhood friend, Christopher. At his friend's insistence he modernizes his name to Mark and embarks on a journey that will bring him full circle back to Henderson Ranch, now called Resurrection Ranch. On his journey, Mark finds previously unknown family and love with one of the alien nurses, Kara, all of whom are willing to journey with him into the future at Resurrection Ranch.

Lost and Found in a New World
The New World Book Four

Peter was kidnapped by his father and sold to Henderson Ranch. There he worked without an education, until his eighteenth birthday when he was sold as a slave to a ranch in Mexico. Once he was rescued, he reunited with some of the others he'd known at Henderson Ranch as well as the mother he'd never forgotten. Helping his friends, Chris and Mark, he becomes involved in the rebuilding of the ranch where they grew up, renaming it Resurrection Ranch, where others like themselves, can work and be given the education they were deprived as children. Before leaving for the ranch, he meets Jerilyn, a therapist who will be transferring to Resurrection Ranch. Almost instantly, he knows she is someone he wants in his life.

Reserruction in a New World
The New World Book Five

When Mark found not only his paternal grandmother but also his step-mother and half siblings, he is amazed when they decide to relocate to Resurrection Ranch to work with those dedicated to bringing their vision to fruition. Chris and Peter's families are also involved in the rebuilding what they hope could be one of the top ranches and educational facilities in the country. They are aided by several aliens who have come to add their expertise to the project. All is well until someone tries to sabotage everything they have dreamed of and built.

The Return of the Ancients
The Aliens Book One

Nina is devastated when she realizes she must leave Plantas along with the man who is to become her mate, Ragnar, and her best friend, Tarena. When Nina arrives on Earth in Peru at the Nazca plains, she is greeted by a young archaeology student, Rand Jacobson. Even though she is attracted to Rand, she is still grieving the loss of Ragnar.

Ragnar is surprised when, after being greeted as a god on the planet Seros, the military opens fire on his family. After being taken prisoner, he is treated like a lab rat until a scientist, Geni, comes to his rescue. At her estate, he learns the physicians who work with her have saved the lives of his family and friends.

My Uncle the King
The Aliens Book Two

When three contingencies took off from their dying planet, Plantas, only two arrived at their destination unharmed. When the lost contingency is hit with a meteor storm, only one ship survives and makes it to their destination of Nalo. Over the generations, the descendants of the original refugees become the ruling class of their adopted planet. Even the rebel group, the Pure Of Nalo, are unable to unseat the monarchy. When relations with Earth are established, it is Prince Nicos who leaves Nalo to find love on an alien planet and bring back new ideas as well as his Earthly family to save the throne and the people of Nalo.

You Again

While attending college at the University of Wisconsin in the 1960s, Carole Martinson fell in love and eloped with Phillip Vanderlin. When his parents realized she was a farmer's daughter and below them socially, they insisted they divorce.

Fast forward to 2019 and Carole is invited to a wedding cruise financed by her granddaughter's fiancé's grandfather. With no knowledge about the groom's family, Carole flies to Florida for the cruise she and her second husband never got to take. Upon her arrival, she immediately recognizes Phillip.

Phillip never forgot his first love. He is thrilled when he realizes the grandmother is the girl he was forced to leave behind so many years ago.

About the Author

Sherry Derr-Wille began her writing career in her sophomore English class in high school. Challenged to get an A on the first test, she won the right to sit in the back of the room and write for a year. At the end of the year no one told her to stop the assignment, so she didn't. At her 40th class reunion, she realized she was the only one who enjoyed the assignment. It was too late because by that time she'd signed seventeen contracts for her work.

Wife to her high school sweetheart of over fifty years, she is the mother of three, grandmother of nine and great-grandmother of six. She is retired and lives in a mid-sized town close to the Illinois border in Southern Wisconsin. Her mantra is READ LOCAL AND BE TRANSPORTED TO ANOTHER WORLD.